chemistry lessons

meredith goldstein

HOUGHTON MIFFLIN HARCOURT
Boston New York

hmhco.com

The text was set in Minion Pro.

Library of Congress Cataloging-in-Publication Data
Names: Goldstein, Meredith, author.
Title: Chemistry lessons / Meredith Goldstein.
Description: Boston ; New York : Houghton Mifflin Harcourt, [2018] | Summary: High school senior Maya, soon to be an MIT student, continues her deceased mother's work on pheromones and attraction, using a stranger, a platonic friend, and her ex-boyfriend as subjects.
Identifiers: LCCN 2017038374| ISBN 9781328764645 (hardback) | ISBN 9781328476722 (ebook)
Subjects: | CYAC: Love—Fiction. | Dating (Social customs)—Fiction. | Friendship—Fiction. | Chemistry—Fiction. | Fathers and daughters—Fiction. | Single-parent families—Fiction. | Cambridge (Mass.)—Fiction.
Classification: LCC PZ7.1.G65212 Che 2018 | DDC [Fic]—dc23
LC record available at https://lccn.loc.gov/2017038374

Printed in the United States of America
DOC 10 9 8 7 6 5 4 3 2 1
4500708952

For Leslie Goldstein
and her piano students

chemistry lessons

1

My phone lit up with a message from Yael.

We're bailing early. Whiff walk, it said, a group text to Kyle and me.

I checked the time. It wasn't even five o'clock.

I work until six today, I wrote back, then put the phone face-down on silent, so she wouldn't be able to fun-bully me into dodging my one responsibility.

I was only a part-time intern in one of the biology labs at the Massachusetts Institute of Technology—hired by my mom's longtime research partner, Dr. Araghi, to transcribe his notes—but I wanted to behave like a professional. I'd be starting at MIT as a freshman in the fall and wanted to prove that I wasn't just my mother's kid, and that I was serious about being there.

Sometimes, though, it was difficult to keep my focus.

Mainly because of Kyle and Yael.

"Maya!" Yael snapped. I whipped around to find her standing behind my workbench with Kyle at her side. Her spiral curls were pulled straight into a tight bun. A few ringlets had escaped and bounced against her freckled-covered forehead as she spoke.

"Don't ignore me, girl. Get your stuff."

"I said I work until six," I said.

"No one cares what you do," Yael said. "You're just an *intern*."

I scowled.

"You'll make up the time," Kyle said. "Besides, Dr. Araghi left early to give some lecture. It's, like, eighty degrees outside. *Everyone* is packing up early."

I walked to the window near our benches, which were clustered in the back corner of the Araghi lab, on the third floor of MIT's Building 68b, a tall, gray structure mostly populated by bio researchers in and out of lab coats.

It had been rainy and overcast for days around Boston, but it finally looked like summer. I spotted two blond girls walking across the quad in shorts and flip-flops, their ponytails moving like synchronized swimmers.

"Okay, just give me ten minutes to pack up my stuff," I said, surrendering.

"Three minutes," Yael said. "I'll give you three."

I placed Dr. Araghi's tiny antiquated tape recorder in my drawer, grabbed my backpack, and followed Kyle and Yael through the maze of workbenches and out into the busy hallway. Once we were down the stairs and on the quad, and Kyle pulled off his hoodie in the heat, I noticed his new T-shirt, which said I LOVE MIT, but instead of the word LOVE—or a heart—there was a picture of a beaver. Kyle couldn't get over the fact that MIT's mascot was a beaver. Much of his wardrobe paid homage to the animal, and it had little to do with school spirit.

"You 'beaver' MIT?" I asked Kyle as he led us off campus.

"I *do* beaver MIT," Kyle responded. "I also beaver chicken skewers. Let's eat after this. I'm starving."

We passed the massive Koch Center for research, slowing down to see the latest fluorescent, bio-themed artwork in the building's lobby, then sped up to get to our real destination, farther down Main Street.

"Come with me, and you'll be, in a world of pure imagination," Kyle crooned off-key as we walked down the road.

"It's from the original *Willy Wonka* movie," I explained to Yael, who eyed Kyle with confusion as he walked backwards with his long arms stretched out, beckoning. Sometimes American cultural references went over Yael's head. I'd learned that not every famous movie was big where she was from in Israel.

"I know the song," she said, grinning. "I just can't believe he's so bad at singing."

At that, Kyle raised the volume of his voice and lifted his middle finger in our direction. Yael was quick to lift hers right back.

I've lived in Cambridge since I was born, so I know every small square and street corner in the city, but I give Kyle and Yael credit for discovering the magic cloud of chocolate on Main Street. On the second day of my internship in the lab, Kyle approached my workspace — which was right behind his — dropped his head to his shoulder as if he were sizing me up, and then asked whether I wanted to join him and Yael on their "whiff walk."

"Really?" Yael said from across the room, before I could answer. "We don't even know her."

"Yes, really," Kyle said. "She's whiff-worthy; I know it. Let's initiate her."

"Initiate me with what?" I asked. "What's a whiff walk?"

Yael released a loud exhale but seemed to be giving in.

They let me follow them out of the lab that day, down to an industrial section of Main Street in Cambridge where, out of nowhere, an entire block of the street smelled like chocolate gas.

"It's a mystery," Kyle had said, his nose twitching. "It always smells like chocolate on this one block. We're obsessed with it."

"I think it's just Cambridge Foods," I explained after an inhale, pointing to the unmarked white brick building in front of us. "It's a candy factory. I went to middle school with someone whose dad worked here."

Kyle and Yael stood silent and stunned, like I'd just solved a great scientific riddle.

"They make the insides of candy bars here," I continued. "Like the nougat you'd get in, like, a Three Musketeers. This part of Cambridge used to be a candy district. You've seen the old Necco building, right? I think they made the wafers there."

Kyle grabbed my shoulders, startling me with the physical contact.

"Why is this not a big deal to you?" he barked, his voice dropping half an octave. His dark brown eyes, which matched his thick short hair, got wide as he raised his brows. "You say, 'They make the insides of candy bars here,' like that's not the best thing ever. Yael and I had joked that Willy Wonka must live here, but now it's, like, true."

He paused and looked up, his eyes glazing over like he was dreaming.

"I mean, they make *nougat*. Right up there." Kyle pointed at one of the building's only windows. He said the word *nougat* like it meant solid gold.

"I guess I've just taken it for granted, you know?" I said. "I'm from Cambridge, so I've passed this building for years. You stop noticing things when you've lived somewhere forever. It is pretty cool, I guess."

"I think I've never had Three Musketeers," Yael said before taking a deep inhale and nodding with approval. "It's not popular in Israel. Also, American chocolate is terrible."

"You've never had a Three Musketeers?" Kyle asked, horrified. "We must remedy this situation. To the 7-Eleven!"

From that day on, I was a regular on their whiff walks, and happily stood outside the building with them, inhaling as Kyle made up stories about what went on inside. Kyle's fantasy was that Willy Wonka outgrew his main production facility and opened a satellite office in Cambridge, Massachusetts, naming it the generic Cambridge Foods to make it less conspicuous to the locals. His theory was supported by the fact that we never saw humans enter or exit the building.

"They live inside, so there's never reason to leave," Kyle told us. "Willy Wonka, who must be very old now, with the Oompas and Charlie. Charlie's basically just a businessman now, and he never married. It's quite sad, actually. He sits up there alone, pondering the metaphor that is the Everlasting Gobstopper . . ."

Sometimes during our trips, Yael allowed Kyle to lift her onto his shoulders so she could attempt to see into one of the few windows on the top of the factory building, to confirm his tale. At five foot one, she was too short to see inside, even with Kyle as a six-foot booster, but they continued to try, hoping for a glimpse of anything magical. I wouldn't let him try to boost me because I didn't want to fall and break my legs.

"Here," Kyle said, now standing in front of a section of white brick at the Cambridge Foods facility. "Stand right here. This is the smell pocket tonight. Right here. It'll hit you in the face."

I stood directly in front of Kyle, close enough that the heels of my sneakers touched the front of his. Yael backed up to me and stepped on my toes, a few of her curls hitting my chin as she tilted her head toward the vents that pushed the scent out of the factory building.

"Now," Kyle said. "Breathe in. We're right in the middle of it."

I heard their chests expand in front and in back of me.

"It's perfect," I whispered as the scent of nougat consumed us.

○ ○ ○

We ate dinner after that, stopping for skewers at the restaurant near campus with the periodic table menu (Hb for hamburger, Qs for quesadilla). Then I texted my boyfriend, Whit, to see if he wanted to stop by my place. It was only eight.

Already here. Waiting on you, he texted back within seconds. I responded with the emoji of the applauding hands. He sent back a thumbs-up.

After almost sprinting the walk home, which took me past the noisy restaurants and graffitied rock clubs of Central Square, and into the crowded residential neighborhoods between MIT and Harvard, I was back at my house on Gardenwood Lane, a short street lined with busy triple-deckers, small houses occupied by university professors, and some concrete apartment buildings designed for transient grad students who never seemed to take the trash out on the right night.

My house was the small yellow one with the red door. In front of it was Whit, who sat on my front steps twirling his phone between his hands, his elbows resting on his knees.

"Heeey!" I shouted when he came into view. My voice was too loud, my tone too eager.

Ever since we decided we'd have sex in four weeks—once Whit moved into off-campus housing, where he'd have his own room—it was all that was on my mind. It was like I was fighting a biological imperative if I wasn't touching him.

"Hey," Whit responded, looking up.

"I didn't know that we were hanging out tonight," I said.

"I needed to see you," he said, his voice soft. My stomach flipped.

I closed the gap between us and placed my hands on his shoulders as I leaned in for a kiss, but before I could attach my face to his, he pulled me down so I was sitting next to him. The ivy that blanketed the front steps of my house tickled my calves.

Whit shifted so that we faced each other and then did the thing where he bumped the tip of my nose with his.

"How was lab?" he asked.

"Great," I answered, hoping that my breath didn't smell too much like chicken skewers. "I'm getting faster at transcribing notes, and this morning, Dr. Araghi introduced me to a woman who studies tumorigenicity in zebrafish. She's doing a fellowship at MIT this year. She said she'll let me sit in on some lectures this fall, even though I'll only be a freshman."

"Hmm. Zebrafish," Whit said as he brushed a chunk of my frizzy brown waves out of my face. "You look pretty."

"So do you," I said, placing a hand on his chest, unable to stop myself from imagining what was going to happen in less than a month. I'd already picked out what I'd wear—a purple silk nightgown I'd bought at the Galleria. Bryan, my best friend and adviser on all important matters, said it looked like the pajamas that Rizzo wears in *Grease*. I assumed that was a good thing.

"Do you want to watch a movie?" I asked Whit, our noses connecting again. "It's early. We could probably fit in *two* movies tonight if we start now."

I was speaking in code. *Watching movies* meant privacy in the dark.

Whit took a deep breath and tilted his head forward so that our foreheads touched. I took in his blue eyes and thick red hair, the genetic combination that made him such an unusual Punnett square.

"I will always love you, Maya," he said in a whisper. *"Always."*

"So dramatic," I teased, closing my eyes, preparing for the night's first kiss.

He pulled his head back and grabbed my hands, squeezing them.

"You need to listen," he said, his tone dark, the way it gets when he reads lines. "I need to talk to you."

His eyes were glassy, and I noticed then that his hair was a mess, much of it pushed to one side on the top, like he'd been stepped on.

"Whit, what's wrong?" I asked.

"I've met someone else," he said, his eyes on my neck.

"Someone else for what?" I asked, lowering my head to try to find him.

It probably took me three full seconds to register what he had said.

I had experienced this delayed reaction before, when my mom died. I now believe that this is just how humans accept unexpected traumatic news — one word at a time, in slow motion. It's this never-ending moment — the exact millisecond a person registers the meaning of those basic words strung together, like when my dad said, "Maya, Mom isn't going to make it."

"Make what?" I had asked just as stupidly back then, my knees locking as I realized that what my mom wasn't going to make was the rest of her life.

Now with Whit, whose gaze had dropped so low he was looking at my sneakers, I whispered the words out loud for my own benefit. "I. Have. Met. Someone. Else."

As a sentence it sounded silly, like trite soap opera dialogue that Whit would ridicule if he heard it on TV. "Lazy lines," he'd say. "No one actually says, 'I've met someone else.'"

I tried to come up with an alternative meaning to the sentence. Maybe he'd met someone else to write with. Like a writing partner. Most people in Hollywood had writing partners, he'd told me. That was what he wanted to do after college — move to the West Coast and write independent films.

"You don't mean another girl to date," I said, grabbing some ivy at my feet and pulling it from its root. My dad had tried to tame the plant, but it had taken over the front of our house, growing at twice its usual speed, like it knew my mother was no longer watching.

Whit glanced up, his expression flat, and ran his hands through his hair. "Yes, another girl to date."

He looked up at the house then and flinched as he noticed my dad walking by the living room window.

"We need to break up," Whit said, now looking at everything but me. "I mean, it's not what I want to do, but there's someone else, and I think I owe it to myself — and to you — to figure out what it all means. You know I love you. But part of loving you is being honest with you."

The last line sounded practiced, each word too rehearsed.

"You're kidding, right?" I asked. My words echoed in my ears. My chest was tight. "We made it through your first year of college. That was supposed to be the hardest part — you in college and me still in high school. But we did it. And I'm going to lose my virginity to you in less than four weeks."

Whit looked around, upset by my volume, probably worried that my dad would hear us through the open window.

"No," I said, anger taking over. "Don't you worry about who's listening. We've been waiting for this. You said we should hold off until you were out of the dorm and in your apartment. That's so soon. You said you were counting down the days."

He hesitated for what felt like an hour and then opened his mouth to speak.

"Wait," I interrupted, before he could respond. "How long?"

"How long what?" Whit asked, having the nerve to look irritated.

"You said you met someone else, so when? How long has this *someone else* been around? We've been planning for July tenth in your apartment for two months now. When you have your own room. When your roommates are away for the weekend. At what point did you meet *someone else?*"

Whit rubbed the back of his neck the way my dad does when he pays bills.

"Technically, I've known her all year, in my program, just as a friend. Nothing's happened; she knows I've had a girlfriend who's still in high school. But over the year, we grew closer, and I tried to set boundaries, but . . . you can't force them. We're both in these summer classes now, and we'll be together all the time. It's just harder to ignore."

I shivered, not knowing whether it was because the temperature was dropping with the sun or because I was so upset that I was experiencing some sort of arrhythmia.

Two girls who looked a few years younger than us walked past the house, singing a song I recognized from the radio. Something about the heart wanting what it wants.

"Have you had sex with her?" I asked loud enough for the girls to hear. I needed some witnesses to prove this was happening. The girls stopped walking and singing and turned to stare at Whit, waiting for an answer, pleased to be part of the drama.

"Jeez, Maya. No," he said. "I just told you—nothing's happened."

"Nothing's happened!" Whit shouted again in the direction of the girls, one of whom yelled back, "Whatever, man," before they continued on their path.

I thought of the past few weeks with Whit and whether I had missed any signs. It seemed impossible that I wouldn't see this coming.

"We love each other," I whispered, more to myself. "There's been no evidence to suggest that anything has changed."

"Evidence," Whit repeated, shaking his head. "That's part of the issue, Maya. I think on some level I'm finally admitting to myself that you and I are just too different. You breezed through calculus, even though you were the youngest person in the class. You know the exact percent chance I'll have kids with red hair. You care about metastatic tumors and . . . zebrafish, or whatever. And I love that about you. You're brilliant, Maya. But I have to admit that being with Andrea — this other person — it's just . . . easy. It's been kind of nice to hang out with someone who gets what I do. She and I can talk about screenplays for hours. I mean, don't you want to be with someone who gets what you do? Someone more like you?"

"No," I said, my voice strong again. "I just want you."

"You haven't even started college, Maya. You don't know what you want."

My head snapped back. He'd never been so dismissive.

I sat still and silent then and focused on the pace of my breathing while Whit explained that he had fallen for a film student named Andrea Berger. Like him, she was going to be a sophomore at Boston University. They had signed up for the same summer-session writing classes, and he was helping her make a short film. He was excited about it.

"You should go," I told him once he stopped talking, my voice flat, my legs too gelatinous to stand.

"Are you sure?" he asked. "We can talk some more if you want. I know there's a lot to say."

"No, there's not."

He nodded and rose, towering above me as I wrapped my fingers around the rusty metal railing of the stairs for support.

He didn't try to help me up.

2

I phoned Bryan from the top of the steps.

"You've reached the Mother of Dragons," Bryan said.

"He broke up with me."

"Hmm?" Bryan was only half listening. I could hear *Hamilton* on in the background. "Hold on; let me turn the volume down. What did you say?"

"He broke up with me," I repeated.

"Who broke up with you?"

"Whit," I snapped. "Who else could break up with me?"

"Right. Good point," he said, now focused on my trembling voice. "Wow. Okay. Tell me where you are right now. Just stay on the phone. I'll come to you."

"I'm home on the front steps. He just left."

I didn't realize I was crying until I had to wipe my eyes because I couldn't see.

"He's a clever little coward," Bryan muttered as I heard him shuffle around his room, probably gathering a bag for the night. "Of course he'd do this right before you took off for Plymouth for a long weekend. He knew you'd disappear and be someone else's problem for the next few days."

His assessment stung, but I was used to Bryan's lack of filter. It's why I trusted him so much.

"Bryan," I said, but nothing else came out. The ivy covering the house looked sinister all of a sudden, like it might be the result of a fairy-tale curse. Before it could trap me, I turned around and went inside. My breaths felt shallow and strained, my legs heavy.

"What's happening now?" Bryan asked.

"Now I'm inside. I just closed the front door."

"Good," he said. "Just hold on, Maya."

I nodded, even though he couldn't see me. Then I slowly climbed the stairs and found my dad in his room packing a suitcase for our long weekend with Aunt Cindy and Pam.

I forced back new tears and tried to compose myself. My phone was still in my hand at my side; I didn't even know whether Bryan was still on the line.

"Cindy says bring a swimsuit," my dad said without looking up when he noticed me in the door frame. "Do you and Whit need dinner? We have coupons for Thai."

"Whit's not here."

"Oh, I thought I heard him outside," Dad said.

"He left."

"That was a quick visit."

I told him then, my tongue feeling too big for my mouth as I said the words.

His head shot up.

"What do you mean he met someone else?" my dad squeaked.

He froze in the center of the bedroom he used to share with my mom, mirroring my pose as his arms fell to his sides. He held a pair of boxer-briefs and a toothbrush in his left hand.

The stunned look on his face was some validation. At least he hadn't seen it coming either.

"Sweetie, I'm sorry," he said after I explained. "Maybe he just needs some space."

"Space with Andrea Berger," I snapped.

My dad flinched.

Before he could respond, the front door banged open below us and Bryan charged through. He lived two houses away and had his own set of keys.

"Okay," Bryan said, after discovering us standing frozen like mannequins next to my dad's king-size bed, which was only ever messy on one side.

Bryan surveyed the room, preparing to triage.

"Kirk," he said to my dad, whose eyes were as glassy as mine, "why don't you go downstairs and make us some of that special grape fizzy water. Get that SodaStream going. You can finish packing later."

My dad nodded but didn't move. Bryan walked to him, took the underwear and toothbrush out of his hand, and patted him on the shoulder, prompting him to march like a robot out the door.

"Bryan!" I snapped as I caught my best friend running his thumb over the waistband of my dad's boxer-briefs.

"Sorry," he whispered. "For the record, I always imagined that he wore boxer-briefs, but gray, not black."

"Bryan," I said, exhaling as my voice broke, "how is this happening right now?"

He shook his head, dropped the underwear and toothbrush into my dad's suitcase, and crossed the room so he could put his arm around my shoulders. "It just is. Come on. Let's talk it through."

Bryan slept at my house a few times a week, so he didn't have to bring a toothbrush when he stayed over. He was the youngest of five — a surprise to his then-forty-something Catholic parents who thought they were done having kids after his sister arrived ten years earlier. He was like an only child when we met, a kid living alone with two adults who had little interest in playing with toys and going to his school concerts. By the end of middle school, Bryan was sleeping at my house every weekend. His parents sometimes sent him over with baked goods, their small acknowledgment that he was being raised part-time in our home.

We went into my room, and I shuddered, noticing that Whit was all over it. The framed prom picture that sat on my desk, the copy of the Oliver Sacks book that he'd borrowed from my mom's bookshelf and left on the small white nightstand. On top of the wicker hamper in the corner was the T-shirt he bought me for Valentine's Day that said YOU ARE HERE next to an illustration of the Milky Way. I imagined that if you shined a black light in the room, you'd see Whit's fingerprints on everything.

My first instinct was to google Andrea Berger, but Bryan wouldn't let me and pulled my phone from my hand. "No phone tonight," he said. "The internet is not your friend right now."

Once we were both tucked under my light purple comforter, though, he agreed to find some pictures of her and describe her to me so that my imagination wouldn't make it worse than it was.

"She's attractive, I guess," Bryan said, his phone glowing in the dark as I lay next to him in my oversize MIT pajamas. "You know, she kind of looks like one of the people from *Pretty Little Liars.* The one with the lighter brown hair."

"What does that mean? Like someone from the show *Pretty Little Liars*?"

"Yeah."

"The show is called '*Pretty*' *Little Liars*, Bryan. Those actresses are *pretty.* That's the point. Is she that attractive? Like, *television* attractive?" I asked, betrayed by the desperation in my voice. I wanted to put myself on mute.

Bryan waved his hand to dismiss my concern. "No, not TV

attractive. I guess she's not a pretty little liar; she's more like an average-looking little liar. She looks more like — actually, she looks a lot like Genevieve Moran," he said, referring to our class's girls' soccer captain, whom I'd tutored in math.

"She has red hair?" I said, thinking of Genevieve's pretty auburn mane, which was just a few shades darker than Whit's.

"Almost a ginger. More like a brownish red. She looks like she could model a fall coat."

"What else?" I asked.

"Well," Bryan said, hesitating as he considered what details to share, "according to one social media account — that you are not allowed to check — she likes hiking and the band M83. It also looks like she had a boyfriend up until a few weeks ago. Before then, it's all shots of her and some guy — and then he just disappears."

"Are there pictures of her and Whit?"

"Not yet," Bryan said, his voice soft. He stroked my head, which was tucked into a pillow next to his chest.

Speechless, I nodded.

"I was going to have sex with him in four weeks, Bryan." My voice was so hoarse.

"Don't make it about that," Bryan said. "This whole 'losing my virginity' thing is a heteronormative concept anyway. You're too smart to buy into it."

I turned onto my stomach. "My point is that we were together. There were no plans to not be together."

"I know," Bryan said.

The room felt too hot, but I didn't want to get out from under the covers. I felt safe there.

"Bryan," I whispered, "were you ever this upset about Matt? I don't remember you ever being like this after you broke up. Or did I miss it?"

"Ending it with Matt — that was up to me. It was different."

"Oh."

I had no memory of falling asleep, but when I woke up in the middle of the night to go to the bathroom, it was still dark, all the bedding was on the floor, and my head was resting against a wet spot made by snot and tears on Bryan's T-shirt.

"There are no M83 songs on this playlist," Bryan said the next morning as he handed me my phone. We stood in the driveway, where my dad was stuffing our suitcases into the back of the green Subaru.

Bryan loaded my phone with new playlists every few weeks because he said it was his responsibility to make sure I had some pop culture in my life to keep me well-rounded. He was thoughtful about the music, carefully curating the collections of songs to match themes, such as "Women of the '90s," or "Songs with Boys' Names in Them," or, after I told him about my plans for sex with Whit, "Summer Awakening," which featured various songs meant to put me in the mood.

"This mix is very different," Bryan explained as I gazed at the phone in my palm. Bryan pushed his pale brown hair to the side and tucked it behind his ear. Now that it was getting longer, he did that about twenty times a day.

"Maya," Bryan said, trying to keep my focus as I got myself into the passenger's seat and shut the door. He knelt so that his face was level with mine through the open window.

"This playlist is the mix that will pull you out of this mess. Because you are bigger than this breakup. You are bigger than Whit Akin. The songs are in order, so do not hit shuffle or it loses its meaning. You have to go from one to two hundred, one song at a time. And when you're done, the grieving is over. It's a deadline."

"Okay," I said.

Two hundred songs. I wondered how he had found time to put it together.

"You fell asleep at eleven, but I was up until one," he said, answering my unspoken question.

I smiled, exhausted by the effort.

"What are you going to do while I'm gone?" I asked.

"I have lines to memorize. Not as many as I'd like, but enough to keep me busy.

"Take care of her, Kirk," Bryan added, glancing over at my dad in the driver's seat.

"Sure thing, B," Dad said.

As we backed out of the driveway and began the hour-plus drive to Aunt Cindy's house, I connected the phone to the car adapter.

"Do you mind if we play Bryan's mix?"

"I'd never say no to a Bryan soundtrack," my dad answered with a stiff voice, looking a little scared of me.

The first track was a Justin Timberlake song I'd never heard before: "Drink You Away." My dad tapped his thumb on the steering wheel to the beat.

I thought of drinking then, of the wine that Whit once stole from his parents' liquor cabinet so we could share it on one of our first real dates. We had carried it in water bottles to the lawn in front of the Cambridge Public Library, where he surprised me with a picnic dinner. It felt like something that might happen to a girl on television.

My dad's thumb-drumming got louder as the song hit a climax.

I felt my stomach burn as Justin whined the same lyric over and over, on top of a rhythmic guitar. "*Tell me, baby, don't they make a medicine for heartbreak?*"

They should, I thought.

I put the track on repeat and closed my eyes.

3

Pam, my aunt Cindy's partner of more than twenty years, was outside with one of the dogs when we pulled up to their house, a four-bedroom colonial not far from the Plymouth town center. Pam called it Very Old Manor because when they bought the place ten years ago, their next-door neighbor told them a million times that even though it was "very old"—built in 1880—it wasn't technically a historic property like *her* home, which was built in the 1700s and had one of those gold plaques confirming its age over the door. "Your house is just *very old*," the neighbor kept repeating, as if "very old," as opposed to "historic," meant that Cindy and Pam had basically moved into a Chipotle.

"If it was built after 1799, you might as well be living in a goddamned strip mall," Pam often said of the neighborhood, which prided itself on its colonial everything.

Pam had a Boston accent so thick it always sounded like she was angry about something. The constant swearing didn't help; most adjectives were preceded by a "fahckin" or a "gawhddamned," even when she was content. Her sound was so authentically local that she'd once been drafted for a Boston crime movie.

The story—told too frequently—was that Pam had been ordering coffee at a Starbucks in Quincy when a movie producer, who was in line behind her, overheard her accent, pulled her aside, and asked her to come to the local set. She wound up being paid eight hundred dollars to spend an entire day in a tight red dress repeating the line

"He's at Williams Tavern." Everyone in our family had at least two copies of the DVD.

I could see Pam's blond bangs obstructing her eyes as she bent over and rubbed the tummy of the dog, trying to snap it out of its funk. Poor Johnny, a retrieverish-looking mutt, was so old that he no longer barked and ran toward guests. He just wanted to sleep and be left alone.

"Wake up!" Pam yelled as my dad turned off the car, her volume prompting the dog to pull itself to its feet. "Say hi, Johnny! Say hi to Cousin Maya!"

My aunts named their two now-thirteen-year-old rescue dogs after their first crushes, Johnny Gill and Ralph Tresvant from New Edition, a boy band from Boston that was famous in the 1980s. When my aunts first started dating, they discovered that they'd both been obsessed with New Edition when they were young, so it became a running theme in their relationship. The group's hit "Can You Stand the Rain" was Cindy and Pam's wedding song. I barely remember the event, but I was told it happened not long after gay marriage became legal in Massachusetts, and there's a picture of me as a toddler in a flower crown holding a sign that says LEGALLY WED hanging in their living room.

Cindy and Pam adopted the dogs a few years after the wedding. The story was that Johnny and Ralph adored each other as puppies, but that their relationship went sour when they hit canine puberty and it became clear that both animals were alphas. After several weeks of fights that led to a scratched cornea and a ruined love seat, Aunt Cindy and Pam admitted that their pets could no longer be in the same room. They couldn't even look at each other through windows or doorways. Just the sight of the other dog caused each to leap into battle for a turf war.

My mom begged the women to give one of the dogs to another loving home, but Cindy and Pam couldn't bear the thought of letting either one go. So for more than a decade, my aunts' lives have been a choreographed dance around the house, punctuated by announcements of each dog's whereabouts.

"Ralph coming up!" Cindy will shout from the living room, to which Pam will respond, "Wait one sec... Johnny secured!" That means that Johnny is in the bathroom with the door shut and Ralph can roam free. Once Ralph has made rounds and has been locked in the bedroom, Pam will yell, "Johnny coming down!" so that Johnny can have free rein of the house for a few hours.

The dogs haven't seen each other in almost eight years, but they occasionally bark at nothing, haunted by each other's scents.

"Where are Cindy and Ralph?" I yelled to Pam. My dad was already making his way inside, his telescope case hanging off his back.

"Inside, marinating steaks for later," Pam said as Johnny climbed my calves. "We're going to fix that broken heart with food, sweetie." I flashed her a look of panic as I caught my breath.

"Your dad called last night," she explained. "We know about the breakup, honey."

"Okay," I said, staring at the lawn, feeling almost relieved, like I'd been given permission to be lifeless for the rest of the trip.

Pam shot me a sympathetic smile and motioned for me to join her inside. She cracked the front door before we entered and yelled, "Johnny coming in!" Ralph began to squeal as Cindy hurried him downstairs.

"I'm not surprised by any of this. He's what, nineteen, babe?"

Cindy called everyone babe. Pam, the dogs, my dad, me—we

were all "babe." It became a very long "baaaabe" whenever she was drinking.

I'd made it through the steak dinner, staying silent as my dad updated Cindy and Pam on all his latest outdoor activities—the hiking, the rock climbing, and all the recreational athletic clubs that would keep him busy during summer vacation from teaching middle school science.

The three of them let me be, allowing me to remain a passive, morose dinner guest, until my dad excused himself from dessert to stargaze. That's when Cindy poured me a full glass of sweet wine and urged me onto the patio.

While I sipped, the alcohol hitting my brain faster than I thought it would, Cindy polished off the last of a bottle of her favorite, Maker's Mark. My mom never drank much, but Aunt Cindy believed in indulgences. Her backyard was evidence of that. Every time we visited the aunts in Plymouth, we noticed a new addition to their back deck. The setup now included a jacuzzi, a space for grilling, and a multilevel garden behind it that was labeled so carefully you'd think my neuroscientist aunt was a botanist.

I leaned back on the wicker chaise lounge by their new fire pit, enthralled by the stars. Cambridge had so much light pollution that I often forgot that the sky could be this bright on its own. No wonder my dad sometimes drove down here to escape with his telescope.

I tried to block out Cindy's voice while I enjoyed the view. The minute we were outside, she had started pontificating about the breakup, as if I'd asked her to explain it to me. I didn't want to hear her thoughts about how Whit was only nineteen and how we were going to break up someday anyway.

What she said made sense—logically, at least—but the point was that we were supposed to be in love now.

"Honestly, where could it go?" she asked. "You're teenagers. It had to end at some point. But the timing and the reasons—he just pulled that rug right out from under you, babe. It's *how* he did it—that's what's heartbreaking. You don't do that to your first love. You wouldn't be this upset if you'd seen it coming."

"I guess."

I leaned over to grab from the bowl of wasabi peas on the table in front of us.

"I just wish there was a way I could remind him of how he used to feel," I said. "I remember how it was when we met. He would wait for me after class. He used to watch me do homework. I understand that crushes on other people happen when you're in a long relationship. I'm sure you've had feelings for other women while you've been with Pam, right? But you wouldn't end your relationship because of some temporary crush."

"I've had crushes on women *and* men while I've been with Pam," Cindy said, letting out a sharp laugh. "But I dated a lot of people before Pam, babe. I met her when I was in my thirties—when I was very much ready to have a partner. It was much easier to ignore the crushes.

"Whit should have told you how he was feeling. Men do this. They don't talk. They process internally, on their own, and then it's too late to work through it. He had probably broken up with you in his mind months ago."

I winced. "Cindy, we were *really serious* a month ago. We were planning a big night for when he moved into his apartment. We were supposed to . . ." I trailed off.

"Oh, babe," Cindy said as my eyes got cloudy with tears, "I didn't mean to suggest that he didn't love you then, okay? I just meant that he might have known it wasn't forever. He might have been realizing that you were too young to make big promises."

I fought the urge to scream at her and decided in that moment that maybe people who have been dumped should be quarantined for several weeks before they're allowed to see friends and relatives —because everything Cindy said to make me feel better was making me feel worse, and I knew it wasn't her fault.

I shifted to my side so I could get a better look at my aunt, who looked royal in the center of her peach papasan. Her eyes were now on the backyard, focused on the shadow of my dad, who had set up his telescope about a half acre out on a small hill in their massive backyard.

"I wish your mother were here right now," Cindy said, giving a sad smile to the small dark blob on the grass that was my father. "Obviously, I always wish your mother were here. But you should have a mother around for your first breakup. Especially *your* mother, of all mothers. She'd break this all down for you. She'd make this her work."

"Yeah," I said, pleased to have another reason to wallow. Not only had I been dumped; my mother was dead.

"Although I'm not sure Mom would have really understood what I'm going through," I told Cindy. "According to her, Dad was her first love. As soon as they met, they were basically married. She never had a first big breakup. She just had one perfect relationship, so I doubt she'd really get what this is like."

Cindy sat up and leaned forward on the papasan, forcing it to tip in my direction.

"But let's be honest: this is what your mom was doing before she died, right? Trying to make love last? Sometimes I just want to steal all of her research from you and continue it myself. Or turn it over to a pharmaceutical company. But I fear it'd wind up in the wrong hands."

I sat up straight and leaned forward, mirroring Cindy's pose. "What research? What are you talking about?"

My mom's specialty had been epigenetics, which is basically the study of modified gene expression. She and Dr. Araghi researched how people can pass down a disease or a trait even if it's not part of their DNA sequence. Like when someone gets cancer from smoking and passes that cancer down to their kids.

"When Mom died, she was starting something with epigenetics and diabetes, right? What did any of her work have to do with 'making love last'?" I asked with air quotes.

"I'm not talking about her primary work, Maya. I'm talking about the research she was doing . . . independently," Cindy said, putting her own air quotes around the word *independently.* "You know . . . her experiments . . . on relationships. The work she was doing with *pheromones* — and attraction."

She whispered the word *pheromones* like she was saying something dirty. A wasabi pea that missed my mouth fell from my lap onto the ground. I reached for it, not wanting to spoil her perfect patio.

"No," Cindy said. "Let Johnny or Ralph get it tomorrow. It'll scare the hell out of them, teach them not to eat everything we drop."

"Cindy," I said, confused, "I don't know what you're talking about. Mom never studied pheromones — "

"I'm talking about her *private* research," Cindy said, cutting me off. "The work she left to you. I assume she talked to you about that project, or that you read it on your own by now. She willed it to you, after all."

I lowered my head and put my hands in my sweatshirt pockets as I felt the night breeze roll over the patio. My mother's will had been specific; I was to be the guardian of all her unpublished research, which was basically a bunch of notebooks, files, and memory sticks now stored in boxes in the attic. Dr. Araghi was to keep everything she worked on in the lab, but her ideas and plans for future research were supposed to stay with me.

The will had caused some awkwardness in the lab after she died. Dr. Araghi didn't object to my taking possession of my mom's unpublished work, but one of my mom's PhD students, Ann Markley, had asked for copies of everything. Ann had become my mom's unofficial protégé during her years at MIT and claimed she was entitled to all my mom's recent notes and ideas because she helped develop them.

My dad and I were conflicted and considered lending Ann the boxes so she could scan what she wanted, but her aggressive insistence on having them — and my mom's specific instructions that all the work be kept under my "guard" — made us reconsider.

It also wasn't as though the will predated Ann. My mom had rewritten it when she got her cancer diagnosis, just in case.

My dad was the one who made the decision.

"I know that Ann and your mother were close — I believe that. But I don't know what Ann would do with the research on her own," he'd said. "I don't know that your mom would want Ann pursuing any of those ideas without her."

Dad, who's usually so passive and polite, was stern with Ann and told her that if my mom had wanted her to have the notes, she would have given them to her.

The decision severed whatever superficial relationship we might have had with Ann without my mother. After years of Ann visiting our house, if only to spend time with my mom in her office, she was now out of our lives. She and I ignored each other when we crossed paths during my internship hours in Building 68b. We behaved like strangers.

As for the boxes of research, I hadn't seen them since we'd lugged them up to the attic after the funeral.

"I haven't read Mom's research yet," I admitted to Cindy. "I meant to at some point," I continued, floundering, "but things got so busy after she died. We only got around to donating her old clothes last month. I feel like we can only do one sad thing at a time, you know?"

Cindy narrowed her eyes at me, her expression telling me that a good grieving daughter would have already pored over her late mother's journals.

"Don't look at me like that," I said, defending myself. "I want to give her work the attention it deserves. Shouldn't I wait to go through it until I have a better understanding of the science? I know more about epigenetics than your average incoming MIT freshman, but it's not like I can really decode her theories just yet. I have the rest of my life to read her research."

"Maya," Cindy said, sounding too sober, "your mother wrote a will that explicitly stated that only you can have her research, and you don't even look at it? Weren't you desperate to know what was in those books?"

I shrugged. The truth was that as much as I was fascinated with my mother's work while she was alive, I was afraid to look at it now that she was gone. She wasn't there to talk to me about her ideas, and the idea of decoding her notes on my own seemed sad and most likely impossible—at this stage in my education, at least.

"Babe," Cindy said with a sagging smile, "when you get home, make those notebooks your first priority, okay? You should know what your mother was dreaming up after-hours in that lab. Those notebooks were her passion. Her legacy. I know how much you miss her, Maya. I can't imagine how you get through it all without her. I'm pretty sure that spending time with her research—maybe it's a way to keep her around."

I felt a tug in my gut, a mix of alcohol and shame. People said this kind of thing a lot—proclamations like "You must be heartbroken about your mother" or "I know you must think about her all the time."

I did think about her a lot right after she died, and it had been difficult to get through the day without falling into a spiral of deep grief. My mom and I had a unique relationship in that we really liked each other as friends. While all the other girls at my school started lying to their parents about their weekend plans and secret social media accounts, my mom and I were taking road trips and watching the same television shows.

A month before she died, when she was exhausted from the chemo, we stayed indoors for an entire weekend and binge-watched the first two seasons of *Game of Thrones*. Bryan came over for the marathon, and we just sat there for two days, eating takeout and sleeping in front of the television while my dad graded tests.

"I should not be letting you watch this," my mom had said during a particularly violent episode, her eyes fixed on the decapitation happening in front of us on the massive high-def screen my dad had picked up to entertain her during treatment.

"Whatever. This happens at school all the time," Bryan had said. "You can run all the anti-bullying campaigns you want, but come prom season, there's always a beheading or two."

After she died, I was in a fog, home every night with Bryan. We watched more seasons of *Game of Thrones* with my dad in a state of intense grief, eating meals that we had put together from the strange things they put in condolence baskets. Stale lemon squares and bruised apples. Port wine cheese and not-yet-ripe bananas. I couldn't really get my head around what had happened, because it was too big.

Then, days later, when I returned to school, I felt an unfamiliar calmness, like I was floating. Everyone was nice to me. Teachers had always been okay with me because they knew I was a good student, but this was different. They treated me like I was one of them, like I should have access to their lounge and special bathroom. My English teacher, Mrs. Mikowicz, whose default mood was furious, took me aside and told me about her late mother and rambled on, in tears, about how other countries are more generous with bereavement time. It was as if this woman, who seemed to despise everyone in school, was suddenly on my side.

I was no longer intimidated by the lacrosse girls, who seemed to be multiplying, taking up more and more of the hallways with their short kilts. I told Bryan at the time that the worst thing that could happen to me had already happened. It was an unanticipated side effect of loss; I felt untouchable.

Then I met Whit. That floating feeling was probably why I connected with him in the first place.

Four months after my mom died, Bryan took me to one of his cast parties. He'd starred in *Guys and Dolls,* the spring musical, and Whit, a senior, was the show's student director.

He wore glasses with thick dark frames and had symmetrical patches of light freckles on either side of his nose. He held a Coke, which showed some confidence, because most of the kids were drinking beer procured by someone's older brother just to prove that they could. I'd never spoken to Whit, but he was someone I stared at in the hallways and whenever I tagged along with Bryan's theater friends.

In that bulletproof state of mind, not caring about the fact that we didn't know each other and that I was a junior and he was a senior, I walked straight up to him and introduced myself.

"Do you know how that happened to you?" I asked, tipsy from one beer.

"How what happened to me?" he answered, grinning.

He indulged me, listening with amusement as I explained all the ways his hair could be so orange while his eyes were so blue. He was riveted, and, for once, I felt as magnetic as Bryan.

From then on, I lived a different life. In place of late-night talks in the kitchen with my mom, I had freedom and a boyfriend. It wasn't that I didn't think of my mom or miss her — I did all the time — it just felt like she didn't have a place in this new world. I couldn't explain this to Cindy without it sounding awful, so I didn't try.

"Babe," Cindy said, her eyes almost closed, "look at that research. I think it'll be of interest to you, especially now. It was all about relationships — why people drift apart, and how science might be able to keep them together. It was almost like she'd come up with the cure for the common breakup. She was onto something big."

"Cure for the common breakup?" I asked, stunned by the description, but Cindy was already on her feet, clearing our glasses from the table and staggering into the kitchen.

Why people drift apart. How science might be able to keep them together. I repeated Cindy's words in my head as I forced myself up to get ready for bed.

For the first time, I was desperate to see my mother's research. I decided that as soon as I had a few hours alone in the house — without my dad around to question my motives — I'd go to the attic.

Because if anyone could fix a breakup with science, it was my mother.

4

I hear that women are still underrepresented in science, but sometimes I find that hard to believe when I think about where I come from. Every woman on my mom's side of the family is some kind of scientist, and they're almost all a big deal in their fields. My mother went to Johns Hopkins and then MIT, where she became a world-renowned geneticist. Aunt Cindy studied neuroscience at Stanford and wrote two books about memory. My cousin Sheila was chosen for some special research fellowship with the Environmental Protection Agency. Technically, my grandmother didn't work, but she was supposedly a gifted chef, and my mom always said that there was science in that, too.

My mom made the personnel decisions in her lab, so it had always been a kingdom of women when I was growing up. Women clicking their flats down linoleum hallways as I spun around in the chair next to Mom's desk. Women's hair ties kept in a jar at the reception desk for anyone who needed one in a pinch.

Most of the researchers came from faraway cities and countries. I remember tagging along with my mom when I was small, fascinated by the tall women in lab coats who spoke with German, Korean, Indian, and South African accents.

The Leschinsky lab was now the Araghi lab, but my mom's former mentor, Dr. Araghi — who postponed his retirement to run her lab for at least a few more years after she died — had honored her decisions when it came to personnel. There were probably about thirty people in the space, and fewer than ten were men. That included Kyle, who didn't really count; he was only there to do full-time lab tech work while on academic leave.

I'd never talked to Kyle about his academic circumstances, but Yael explained that he was almost kicked out of school when he began failing classes at the start of his junior year. His adviser convinced administrators to let him do full-time lab tech work while taking a year to regroup. Kyle was already young for his class because he'd skipped a year in middle school, and everybody agreed he could use the extra time.

Best-case scenario, MIT would let him start again in September. Worst-case scenario — well, we didn't talk about it.

I could tell Kyle liked having me around the lab, because I was another person who was technically a temp and too young to be there.

Yael, who at twenty-three was trudging along with her PhD, had taken Kyle under her wing probably because she liked being the boss, and because he was the only one in the lab young enough to follow her around. Once I turned them into a trio, she tried to mentor me, too, often barking practical advice in her thick Israeli accent.

"You should get your physical education requirement out of the way freshman year!" "Enroll in the minimum meal plan!"

I didn't mind the directives or her big personality; my friendship with Bryan trained me to listen.

That said, I had no interest in seeing her or Kyle, for that matter, when I returned to work the Monday after my trip to Cindy and Pam's. I arrived at the lab early, hoping to beat them in and get out early, but Yael was already there when I arrived.

You okay? she texted after I sprinted by her lab bench, avoiding eye contact.

Whit and I broke up, I responded, keeping my back to her. *I don't want to talk about it. I just need to zone out for the day.*

Sure, she wrote back, after a longer pause than usual. *Whatever you need.*

Thank goodness — no follow-up questions or advice. What I needed was to get through five more hours of transcription so I could beat my dad home and get up to the attic. I wanted to be able to go through my mom's research without him asking any questions.

I powered through one of Dr. Araghi's tapes but paid little attention. Usually I stopped to google all the terms I didn't know — listening to his dictation was like taking a free master class — but I couldn't be bothered. I skipped lunch.

At four, satisfied with my moderate productivity, I gathered my things in my backpack and shuffled toward the door, but Kyle stood in the way of the exit. He wore his gray hoodie, because it was always twenty degrees colder in the lab than it was outside. His dark hair was spiky from a recent cut, the shorter length making his bushy eyebrows look bigger.

"Hey," he said when I stopped short in front of him.

"Hey," I said, looking down, waiting for him to get out of my way. "I have to go."

"Yael told me what's up — you know, about the breakup."

Kyle leaned against the door frame, bending a few inches so we were face-to-face. "Look, Maya, it's going to be okay," he said, those eyebrows raised with concern. "I know you're upset. But . . . you know you're not supposed to wind up with your high school boyfriend."

I felt the Hulk-like transformation begin, where I went from normal person to furious and rejected. I wanted to shout, "You don't know what I'm supposed to do!" Instead, I nodded and barreled past him, my arm smacking his as I made it out into the hallway.

"Maya," I heard him call after me, but I kept moving. Our friendship felt too new for conflict.

I'd had acquaintances in high school, people I knew through Bryan, but Kyle and Yael felt like the first friends I'd made without help. They made me feel like I could survive college on my own, and I wasn't ready to show them anything but kindness.

I ran down the steps of Building 68b in seconds, feeling safe when I made it onto the quad. But then I sprang back, crashing into Kyle, who'd grabbed the loop on my backpack.

"I don't want to talk about it," I said, struggling to get away like a turtle on its back. "Let me go."

"Maya," he said, out of breath, turning me around and taking my shoulders.

We locked eyes and he gave me a sad stare, then pulled me close and hugged me. I was stiff, my arms at my sides.

"I'm so sorry," he said into my hair, and then I sagged into him, forgiving him before I could think about it. "That was a stupid thing to say. If you want to marry your high school boyfriend, you can. I just . . . I'm sorry. Sometimes I say dumb things."

"It's okay," I told him, leaning into the hug. "I just didn't see it coming."

"Yeah, I get it," he said. "For now, just keep breathing."

I went straight for the attic stairs as soon as I got home, and once I made it past the top step, I remembered how creepy it was. The dusty floor was littered with old furniture covered in white sheets. An antique bronze mirror shocked me with my own reflection, making me gasp like I was in a horror film. I tiptoed past the family artifacts, which included a pair of ice skates I'd begged for when I was twelve and then used only twice.

I found the boxes of research where we had left them, in the attic's back corner. There were three of them, half-opened and unlabeled.

If my mom had a system of organization for her notes, my dad and I had destroyed it. Days after the funeral, when we responded to Dr. Araghi's request for us to come to MIT and collect my mom's belongings, we tore through her drawers and shelves, dumping all the notebooks into U-Haul boxes, my dad packing the papers so fast you would have thought we were trying to outrun the police.

Now I wished we had taken our time and been more thoughtful about the process. The boxes were overstuffed with a mess of unlabeled binders and mismatching paperwork. One box seemed to be all spiral notebooks with my mom's loopy handwriting on the covers. They said vague things like *Notes 2* or *Work/December.*

Frustrated, I dumped that box over, the notebooks falling to the dark floor, the number of them making me feel like I'd never be able to make sense of any of my mother's old work.

But that's when I saw it — the One Direction binder.

We'd bought it together at Target, long before my mom got her cancer diagnosis, when life was simple and we did things like run errands for five hours. We were in the office-supplies aisle because she said she needed a new binder for lesson plans.

I grabbed the One Direction binder as a joke; it was dusty in the bargain bin, outdated enough that there were still five members of the group on the cover. They all wore suits with blazers, except for Harry Styles, who had on a leather jacket over a shirt unbuttoned to his stomach.

I expected my mom to laugh at the binder or give me an eye roll, but she grabbed it out of my hands and walked to the cash register while telling me, "At least I know I won't ever lose this one or mix it up with someone else's."

"Wait, Mom . . ." I said, following her down the aisle. "I was *kidding.*"

From then on, she carried it with her to the lab every day. I never thought much about what was in it; I figured she used it for to-do lists and lesson plans like she said she would. If someone asked her about it in front of me, she'd say, "Oh, you mean this One Direction fan item? My daughter picked it out for me!"

"As a joke!" I'd yell.

But the binder rarely left her side. She always kept track of it, like it held something essential.

I grabbed it now and opened the Velcro flap. My breath quickened.

Inside were papers bound with tiny familiar paper clips. My mom had paper clips in all colors and used them for all occasions — to affix notes to my lunch, for makeshift bookmarks in the Ursula K. Le Guin novels she kept by the bed, and to separate the pages of notes in her research. The fluorescent pink, purple, and yellow plastic tips made a rainbow in the binder.

I flipped to a random pink paper clip. It was attached to pages that didn't seem to be lesson plans, but rather charts with dates and numbers. Maybe temperatures and dosages of something.

Nov. 9/98 degrees/.05; Nov. 10/99 degrees/.05.

It was from an experiment of some kind, but I couldn't figure out the specifics.

Sheet after sheet, more dates and temperatures.

I was relieved to see that after the first twenty pages or so, there were papers with words on them. Maybe some explanation of what it all meant.

February 7. Temperature has leveled off at 99 at a dose of 1.5 mg. This dose appears to be almost ideal, based on K's response and the lack of side effects. No dizziness. If my temperature remains stable, will continue with these conditions.

It was the pronoun that surprised me: *my* temperature.

Whatever experiment my mom was keeping track of in the One Direction binder, she seemed to be doing it on herself.

I looked at the next page, even more confused by the notes under February 8. The tone was clinical, but she seemed to be writing about sex. She used words like *intercourse* and *libido.* Then, in another paragraph, I saw my dad's name. *Kirk initiated . . .*

"What the hell?" I whispered, and quickly flipped to the next page.

I couldn't decipher the specifics of the project, but it seemed as though my mom was consuming something — ingesting some sort of chemical at a dose of 1.5 mg — that was meant to alter something related to sex or attraction.

I remembered Cindy's words. *But let's be honest: this is what your mom was doing before she died, right? Trying to make love last?*

My instinct was to slam the binder closed — the way one would slam a door if they'd walked in on their parents having sex. I felt nauseated, and I wondered what my mother was thinking when she left this research to me. But I also wanted to know what it was all about.

I forced myself to turn the page again, which was when I found handwriting that wasn't my mother's — notes on top of my mother's, with observations and additional questions. It looked so familiar.

I couldn't place it at first, but then I remembered where I had seen it before. The squareness of the all-uppercase letters, and the way some words were underlined.

"*You,*" I said aloud as soon as I recognized the script.

I left the other notebooks and papers on the floor and ran downstairs with the One Direction binder in my hands. I needed to take it to the one person who could explain it.

5

Ann Markley still worked in Building 68b — she was supposed to be finishing her PhD and writing her dissertation, like many of the other students in the lab — but once Dr. Araghi had taken over the lab under his own name, she'd moved herself from the main workspace to a windowless room in the back of the building. It had once been a storage space for equipment, but she'd managed to turn it into a lair for herself, maybe so people would forget she was there.

The rumor in the lab, according to Yael, was that Ann hadn't made much progress with her work since my mom died. Her mood had gone from intense to morose. Yael had once heard Ann on a phone call admitting to someone that she wasn't sure if she wanted to finish it at all.

Yael didn't like Ann, and wasn't quiet about it.

"She's a year older than I am, and she acts like she's some tenured professor, like she's the assistant in charge here," Yael had told me. "But she's not the boss of anyone! In fact, she's barely doing what she's supposed to be doing!"

I understood Yael's frustration, but it made my chest ache to know that Ann was floundering. Even though her bristling personality had always scared me, my mom had adored her and said she was one of her brightest researchers. Mom *had* treated her like an assistant. I didn't like the idea of Ann going from star student to someone who'd give up on her degree altogether.

I'd never done more than hurry past Ann's office when I was near the back of the lab, but now that I was here, standing in the doorway, I felt claustrophobic on her behalf, seeing the small desk and chair pushed against the blank gray wall.

I'd waited until after six, when there were fewer people around, and I found her on a small step stool, tending to the one item that gave the room any character: my mom's old aquarium. It was perched on a bookshelf that had no books on it. The aquarium was the only thing in the room that made it clear someone worked there.

Ann wore black jeans and a charcoal long-sleeved T-shirt with the sleeves rolled up. Her pixie-cut hair was so bleach-blond that it was basically white. Since my mom's death, she'd added eyebrow piercings and a gold ear cuff to the package. She was like a full-size, angry Tinkerbell, her thick dark eyeliner looking like a kind of war paint on her tiny pale lids.

At my light knock on the door frame, she gave me a quick surprised glance and then looked down, pulling her hand from the tank and toweling it off before returning to her desk.

"Come in," she said.

"Thanks," I told her, then shuffled toward the fish tank, curious to see whether any of my mom's fish were still alive. My eyes followed a bright pink fish that swam behind a school of dot-size babies. "So cute," I said, instantly regretting that I said the word *cute* in front of Ann Markley.

Just then, the mother fish opened her mouth and swallowed at least six of her babies whole.

"Oh, my god, she's eating them," I said, turning to Ann.

Of course Ann Markley's fish ate its children.

"Look closer," Ann responded, looking up from her computer. "Watch the mother. Watch what she does."

I tucked my hair behind my ears for a clearer view and watched the fish continue their circular journey. The mother angelfish hurried behind her cloud of children and swallowed some of them again in a gulp. "She just did it again! She's devouring them."

But as soon as the words were out of my mouth, the big angelfish spit her babies back out into the water. She wasn't eating them; it looked like she was moving them from one end of the fish tank to the other. She was trying to keep them together in a pack. Whenever three or four tiny fish attempted to defect from the school, she swallowed them and then let go, keeping everyone close.

"She's just telling them where to go," I whispered. "She's . . . herding them."

"She doesn't want them to lose their way," Ann said. "It's biological instinct. I've had six angelfish, and they all do this."

I took a seat in the small wooden chair across from Ann's desk. "Maybe you should have been a marine biologist."

Her response was a cold look, even though I hadn't meant it as an insult. She leaned back, sizing me up in silence.

Eager to end the staring contest, I blinked and reached down to the tattered navy backpack between my feet and removed the One Direction binder. It looked even more ridiculous in this office than it had in the attic. Under the florescent lights, Harry Styles's chest was white. His facial expression looked so goofy that I wanted to put my hand over his face.

Ann's reaction to the binder — the recognition in her wide eyes — told me everything. For a second, I thought she might grab it from me. She took a short, loud breath and then asked softly, "Do you know what that is?"

"It's One Direction," I said, the words out of my mouth before I could filter them. She scowled.

"I mean, yes," I said, attempting a quick recovery. "I know what this — this binder — is. I mean, I think I do. I've read some of what's inside."

Ann took a sip from the can of cream soda that was on her desk.

"Did your mother tell you what's in that binder, or did you read it on your own?"

"She didn't tell me — I mean, not technically. My aunt Cindy told me about it, and then I found it. You know my mom wanted me to have her research. She didn't tell me anything, but with the way she wrote her will, she meant for me to know."

We watched each other in silence then, my proclamation more confrontational than I intended it to be. Ann's threatening glare and her twitching silver eyebrow ring made me want to sprint from the room, but I took a deep breath and fused my feet to the floor, not wanting to back down.

"Cindy told me that Mom was studying relationships." My voice shook. "I found the binder, and it seems, based on what I've read, that you were involved with the research. I saw your notes, in your handwriting."

"Yes, I was involved," Ann said. "I was always involved in her work."

It was clear what was implicit in her comment — that I didn't deserve the research and that I should have handed it over to begin with.

"Was Dr. Araghi working on this project too?"

"Of course not," Ann snapped. "It was your mother's work, your mother's lab. Also, he'd never go off the books for something like this."

"Look," I said, "I know you hate me because of what happened, but Mom was really specific about the research going to me. My dad and I were just following orders, and it was a really hard time for us. It was too much to figure out at once."

Ann nodded and softened her shoulders.

I thought she might say, "Of course I don't hate you," or "I totally understand," but she didn't. Her face remained blank. Her eyebrow ring twitched.

"So what do you want?" she asked, placing her elbows on her short desk. "You didn't come to make small talk — I know you've been working for Dr. Araghi for days now, and you haven't come to say hello. You must want something."

Had she wanted me to come say hello? I couldn't imagine that she had.

"I don't want to cause any problems for you," I told her. "I'm just interested in what you and my mom were doing, and I'd like to know more about what's in this binder. I think my mom left the research to me because she wanted me to know what she was up to. I haven't told anyone about this, by the way. Aunt Cindy said this was private research, and I want you to know that I don't intend to share this with anyone."

Ann took another sip of her drink. With the cream soda can in her hand, she looked younger. She *was* young. But like Yael said, Ann did act like she was older than everyone. It was intimidating. Ann cleared her throat but didn't say anything. My instinct was to beg.

"Can you at least tell me what she hoped to get out of whatever project she was doing with my dad? That's the one I care about."

Ann stood up and walked back to the fish tank, staring at it, deep in thought. After a long pause, she spoke.

"Your mother and I had long been interested in a Swiss study — and some similar research projects — that look closely at pheromones and mate choice.

"In the simplest terms," she continued in a voice that suggested she was dumbing it down for someone with a high school diploma, "decades ago, a scientist gave T-shirts worn by men to a group of female subjects. Each woman was instructed to smell all the dirty shirts and then identify the one that smelled the best to her — without seeing the men. The science here is that each woman picked the shirt worn by the man whose immune system complemented hers — or, more accurately, the man whose immune system most opposed her own. It was as if without seeing or knowing these men, the women were programmed to consider genetic information in their mate choice.

"Your mom used to do this thing where she'd ask me to theorize based on other studies; 'ideas from ideas,' she'd say. We'd read something and then she'd tell me to brainstorm all that could be done with it. Then sometimes we'd try to think up our own experiment.

"I was shocked she was interested in this one; even I dismissed the study as useless when I read it. There are so many reasons to choose a partner, so who cares how someone's T-shirt smells? But your mom loved the idea that perhaps attraction could be revived or sustained — so we started the project."

"And what, specifically, was the project?"

Ann looked around the office, like she was making sure we were alone. She walked to the door and closed it.

"I said to your mother," she continued in a whisper, "'What if people could give off the pheromones that complement their romantic partners?' If we could figure out how to manipulate pheromones to express the right traits, perhaps we could prolong attraction in couples who have lost it. Like, what if we could all wear the perfect T-shirt for our partners, all the time?"

I considered this. "So you wanted to make, like . . . Viagra for couples," I said.

"No, a drug like Viagra helps erectile dysfunction," she said, losing patience. "Our work would boost attraction between two people."

She walked back to her desk and sat again.

"I have to tell you," Ann continued, "your mom jumped on this one. She went all in. We had started some preliminary tests, off the books, that were rather successful. It's a wild theory, but your mother liked wild."

I'd never heard my mother described as "wild." I'd heard her called driven, ambitious, focused. My dad called her obsessive-compulsive because of how she organized the house, each glass in the cabinet a perfect half-inch from the next.

My mom was a creative scientist, but not the kind who'd do anything off the books or focus on questionable studies.

Except that she was, apparently.

"So," I said, trying to make sense of Ann's explanation, "you wanted people to be able to change their smell so that their partners were more attracted to them?"

"Pheromones aren't really the same thing as smell. They're chemicals released by the body—it's not like perfume," Ann said, as if the unspoken end of her sentence was "you idiot." I took a deep breath and remembered that, compared to her, I was an idiot. I was the science and math star at my high school and had aced all related advanced-placement tests, but talking to Ann was a reminder that I was about to start MIT, where I'd be a tiny smart fish in a big pond of geniuses.

Ann took a deep, frustrated breath as she chose her words to help me understand.

"See," she continued, leaning back in her chair, "her particular goal with the experiment was to save relationships. Your mother wanted to alter the way people's pheromones expressed themselves to revive waning attraction. People fall in love for all the right reasons, but then, over the years, the love dies because the physical attraction fades. Couples get bored. They fall for others. She believed that many midlife divorces could be avoided if we could just get a second wind of desire. She believed there were pharmaceutical applications for this work."

"Pharmaceutical?"

"Well, yes. You mentioned Viagra, a pill that helps with function and libido. Why shouldn't there be a prescription to boost physical chemistry for couples?"

It took me a few full beats to consider why my mom wanted to do this work. I could tell by looking at those charts in the binder that my mom had been doing her secret research on herself and my dad. That didn't make sense to me, because my parents were pretty much all over each other up until she died. They were always madly in love. Goofy about each other. It was their thing.

But now I wondered if Ann knew things about my parents' marriage that I didn't. Something must have inspired the work — because why else do it and test it on my father?

"And you kept this project from Dr. Araghi? I thought they were best friends — that my mom told him everything."

It was a safer question to ask. I wasn't sure whether I was ready to hear anything that would spoil the narrative of my parents' perfect relationship.

"Of course," Ann said. "Not that we had to lie. It was your mother's lab; Dr. Araghi was already in emeritus status, just working out of her space, giving talks and teaching classes. He only came back to run the lab after your mom died so people like me could stay put for a few more years. I imagine he'll wrap up that work soon too. I'm sure he'll announce a real retirement next year."

I frowned, thinking that Dr. Araghi's shuttering of the lab would be the real end of my mom's presence on campus.

"Maya," Ann said, leaning in. Her voice was soft, almost kind, for a moment. "What is it you really want to know? We paused these experiments after your mother's diagnosis. And when her will was so specific about all her research going to you, I had to make peace with it. I figured it was her way of telling me to let go. Otherwise, she would have left it to me."

I felt a jolt in the pit of my stomach thinking about how we shut Ann out of her own work by keeping it for ourselves.

"I guess I just wanted to know what it was — and whether it worked," I said.

Ann managed a sly smile.

"Well, we believed that it worked. There was more testing to do. We wanted to try more subjects, with different variables. But yes, I believe that it was working. We certainly saw results."

"Was she having trouble with my dad?" I blurted out, my voice cracking as it tripped over the last two words.

Ann looked troubled as she considered her answer.

I waved my hands in front of her. "Never mind. I don't want to know. Don't say anything."

We watched each other in silence after that, and I could tell that she was ready for me to leave. She glanced at the laptop on her desk, a not-so-subtle hint that she had work to do.

There was little to lose, so I sat up straight and attempted to channel the professional, clinical tone that my mother used when she spoke to colleagues.

"I'd like to continue this project," I said.

It came out strange and too formal.

Ann's face was blank as she took the last sip of her cream soda and threw the can in the recycling bin, which I now noticed was full of empty cans of the same brand. Her eye contact was so direct I felt scolded, even though she hadn't said anything.

"My mom left this research to me," I said, knowing Ann was going to dismiss me in seconds. "She wanted me to see it, and she knew I'd see *your* handwriting. Don't you think there's a reason she did that? Don't you think she wanted us to continue her work? Maybe even together?"

It was manipulative; who knows what my mom would have wanted? Still, it was my best shot.

"You think that's true, Maya? You think that if your mother were alive, she would want you to do this kind of research?"

Ann leaned back in her chair and crossed her arms in front of her chest.

"Yes. I do," I answered.

It was a half-truth, but I said it with confidence. My mother wanted me to be a passionate researcher; that much I knew.

"It takes materials—equipment. With your mother around, that was easy. It was her lab, her budget. But now I'm just writing, and I'm barely doing that. If Dr. Araghi—if anyone, for that matter—saw me messing around, they'd have questions. They'd figure it out."

"He wouldn't see you. We could meet off-hours. No one would know."

I began to beg some more.

"I wouldn't tell anyone—not Dr. Araghi, not my dad. I just feel like I'm supposed to do something with this research. I know that sounds crazy, but I'm sure of it."

I dared to look up and was shocked to see that Ann's eyes were red. She wasn't quite crying, but she was on the verge. Yael and Kyle wouldn't believe me if I told them. Yael didn't think Ann was capable of human emotions, and Kyle was frightened to death of her.

"I miss her a lot, you know," Ann said after a blink.

She opened her desk drawer and pulled out a tissue. Then she blew her nose so loud I wanted to laugh, but I was too afraid to move.

"My parents didn't want this for me, you know. They've never understood what I do, why I'm not out there focused on starting a family. It's like, for every award I've won, every accolade I've received, they've just been more confused. My mom actually said to me, when I got into the program, 'Maybe you'll meet someone nice.' That's her one concern — marrying me off. As if that worked out well for my sister. Two kids. No support from her ex.

"Working with your mother, it wasn't just the research that inspired me; it was how she did it. She lived her work. She was the person I wanted to become. And she never had to choose. She had a family and the lab and it seemed effortless. Everything she did was a passion."

Ann blew her nose again, and then I found myself fighting tears too, mostly because I was relieved that she had felt so strongly about my mother. It had been disheartening last year to watch Ann at the funeral, to see how she declined to speak when everyone got up to say nice things, and how she walked through the room like a stranger, her facial expressions suggesting that she was actually bored.

The day my dad and I stopped by the lab to tell her my mom had died, she was so void of expression that we started to wonder whether we had overestimated their personal relationship. It made me angry back then, mainly because I knew how much my mom had cared about Ann. Always worrying about her. Always wishing she'd make more friends. Now it was clear that Ann had probably just been in shock when my mom died. I guess we were too.

Ann now looked at the binder on her desk like it was a long-lost love letter.

"Why don't you borrow it?" I said. "Just look it over, maybe think about what we could do with it, how we could continue that experiment."

She took the binder into her lap and ran her hands across the cover. Suddenly I felt like I was intruding on her and my mom just by being there.

I got up and moved toward the door, hoping that nostalgia and curiosity would take over and that Ann would just say yes. Before I disappeared back into the lab, I looked back at her and said, "I think it's cool that you and Mom did this. I really do think that she left it all to me because she knew I'd bring it to you. Imagine what she'd say if she knew we were working together."

"You're about to start school, Maya," Ann said, her thumb over the face of Harry Styles. "You're . . . what are you, seventeen?"

"Eighteen." I was lying by only a few months. "It's only June. I'm on campus every day anyway now, and I have almost three months off before school. We could just pick up where Mom left off, and I won't tell anyone. Not a soul."

She was gripping the binder, her knuckles white. I wanted to believe that was a good sign.

"Maya, what is it you want from this? I just don't understand why you'd want to continue this experiment, to keep secrets from Dr. Araghi or your dad. What's in it for you?"

"I just want to fulfill my mother's destiny," I lied.

At least it felt like a lie.

Ann shot me the dirty look she gave me on the first day of my internship, when I came into the lab with an open bottle of soda in my hand, forgetting that drinks were prohibited around equipment.

I bit my lip, closed my eyes, and made a quick decision to try some honesty. I had nothing to lose.

"Also, my boyfriend broke up with me, and I want to get him back. I want to do the experiment on him."

It came out in a rush. I hadn't realized how juvenile it would sound until the words echoed in her small workspace. My instinct was to run out of Building 68b in shame, but I kept my feet fused to the floor, looking down, waiting for her to react.

"Here I was wondering how you intended to continue the research. But it seems you have a subject in mind."

I looked up to find her showing a small smile again.

Before I could decide whether it was an encouraging grin, she opened another desk drawer and placed the binder inside. The smile was gone, her game face back up. "Go home, Maya. We'll talk more next week."

"You'll think about it?"

"I will think about it," she said, sounding a little surprised by her own words.

"That binder," I said as I watched it disappear, "it's the story of her life."

I don't know why I said it. It was a One Direction joke, something Bryan would laugh at. "The Story of My Life" was a One Direction song my mom actually liked. It was on the radio probably every fifteen minutes during one of the last years of her life, and when it came on while we were in the car, we sang together in harmony.

But of course Ann Markley wouldn't get it. She probably didn't even listen to music. She stared at me, confused, as I muttered, "Forget it. Just think about it," and then ran out of the building, feeling two percent more alive than I had when I walked in.

6

I followed Bryan up the stairs of a historic brownstone on one of the grandest, most cobblestone-packed streets on Beacon Hill. There were balloons out front attached to a glittery handmade sign that said WELCOME, JUNIOR BARDERS!

"They need to change that name," Bryan said. "When I'm older and famous and give them money, I'm going to demand that they get rid of 'Junior.' It's so patronizing."

Bryan had been a member of the Junior Barders company since our freshman year. Despite the name of the organization, which Bryan said sounded like an offshoot of the Girl Scouts, the Junior Barders was an exclusive program for young actors run by the group that produced the professional Shakespeare plays performed on Boston Common every summer. Each spring, after the company chose actors for its main production, the director went on to cast area teens in parallel roles. The young performers trained alongside their adult counterparts and shadowed rehearsals. Then, during the course of the run, the teen actors did three performances of their own, on the big stage, with all its professional bells and whistles. On the teens' off nights, when the adults performed, the Junior Barders manned the T-shirt booths and worked as ushers.

The program was super competitive and had a national reputation. Kids traveled from all over New England to audition. Bryan, who had leads in every single one of our high school productions from the time he was a freshman, didn't even get a speaking role during his first year as a Barder but was content to stand there as a friend of Tybalt's in *Romeo and Juliet.*

This summer's production was *All's Well That Ends Well,* a fitting title for the end of Bryan's run with the Junior Barders, now that he was just a few months away from starting college at Syracuse University.

There had been only a few rehearsals, but Bryan was already sour on the production. He assumed he'd have the lead, but he'd been passed over as Count Bertram and cast as Parolles, who, while still an instrumental character, was not the star of the show.

The only consolation was that Bertram would be played by Asher Forman, a Boston native who was sort of a minor celebrity. Most adults had never heard of him, but Asher made YouTube videos that got millions of views. He was a big name among most girls at my high school.

Asher, who was twenty, had been hired to play Bertram in both the adult and teen casts. Bryan said the Shakespeare producers figured he'd draw a younger audience to the productions, and maybe some new donors. Most of the teens were excited to work with him, except for Bryan, who could see Asher Forman only as the guy who stole his part.

"We're supposed to learn from him, like *he's* the expert," Bryan whispered as we made our way into the Junior Barders' welcoming party. "Meanwhile, I'm pretty sure I have more stage experience than he does. He did one play on the North Shore when he was a kid, and now he sings bad covers on the internet. I can act circles around him. I can sing circles around him. It's bullshit."

I wasn't someone who followed YouTube stars and Tumblr-boys, and they all seemed to blend into one nondescript, blurry face on the internet, but I spotted Asher within seconds. He stood across the room, looking bored and staring at the wall, which was covered in a purple and green textured paper that, knowing the neighborhood, was probably three generations old.

Asher had floppy blondish hair and big eyes. It was his tan skin, though, that made him look famous. It was smooth and clean, like he'd never had a blemish in his life.

"Look at him, mouth breathing over there," Bryan mumbled.

We watched as Asher removed his phone from his pocket and took a selfie in front of the nearby bookshelf.

"He's the worst," Bryan whispered to me, his eyes fixed on the young man who stole the role of Bertram.

"You're crazy," I responded. "And jealous. You should be nice. He'll be a good contact for you. Maybe you can make videos together. Maybe he can help you become the next YouTube phenomenon."

Bryan rolled his eyes.

I had planned to spend the night at home, watching television and feeling sorry for myself, but Bryan said I needed to get out of the house and be around people. I'm sure he was concerned that I would spend the whole night stalking Andrea Berger's social media accounts or fighting the temptation to reach out to Whit; I was concerned that would happen too, so I tagged along.

It was strange because, before all of this, I never thought of myself as a boyfriend person. I'd never had trouble being alone, and being best friends with Bryan meant that I had a ton of acquaintances who were happy to invite me to parties or attend my bat mitzvah.

But ever since Whit had come into my life, he'd been my closest companion who wasn't Bryan. He was still the person I wanted to call, and now my hands twitched, wanting to reach out. Without him, I felt lost and like I couldn't sit still.

Over the past week, during my few off-hours at home between work, whiff walks, and sleep, I either played a chess app with Kyle, who was doing his best to keep me busy, or looked up the scientist who performed the original T-shirt study that inspired Ann and my mother's research. I hadn't heard a word from Ann since our meeting, but I wanted to be prepared.

Hours before the Junior Barders party, I was googling every paper I could find about pheromones. Then I got sucked into a study about a protein in the urine of mice that makes the animals attracted to one another. The scientist who did the study named the mouse protein darcin—after Mr. Darcy in *Pride and Prejudice*. I liked that.

When Bryan called to find out how I planned to spend my evening, I answered too honestly.

"Did you know that there's something in mice urine that makes them want to have sex with each other?" I said, and heard Bryan sigh on the other end of the line.

"No, listen," I continued, forgetting that without any knowledge of my mom's research, he would be baffled by my interest. "There's this protein. And it's not just something that makes the mice want to have sex. The smell of the urine provokes a memory of attraction. The mice become aroused based on the *memory*."

"Okay, Maya. I'm not even going to address this—because I can't," Bryan said. "But it confirms my theory that you need to come out with me tonight. I'm taking you to a party. Clearly you need a change of scenery. Somewhere where people aren't talking about rodent urine."

I had been Bryan's plus-one at many Junior Barder events over the years, but this was my first time at the kickoff party, where teen cast members mingled with their adult counterparts, and everyone received their scripts and rehearsal schedules. Bryan assured me that some people would bring friends and parents, but once we entered the party, hosted by one of the organization's super-rich donors, it was clear that I was the only non-actor in the pack. There were no friends, boyfriends, or parents, just the actors from both the teen and adult casts mingling around tables of appetizers, talking about their shared roles.

"Everyone here is in the play," I said, hiding behind Bryan's back as he poured himself a paper cup full of lemonade at the beverage table. "No one brought guests. I should go home."

"It's fine," Bryan responded. "Just relax and eat the appetizers."

"Bryan Russo."

We both whipped around at the familiar voice. It was a blond girl I recognized from some of Bryan's other productions. She had played Tatiana in *A Midsummer Night's Dream* and one of the royal characters in last year's debacle that was *Coriolanus,* a play that should not be performed by teenagers.

"Hello, my treat," Bryan said, kissing her cheek.

"I can't believe Luke Dorian is here," she said, leaning in to gossip straight into Bryan's ear. "He apparently blew his audition, but he's helping backstage."

She glanced over at me, staring at me, really, making a point to check out my simple blue T-shirt, jeans, and brown sneakers.

"Maya, right?"

"Yeah. You were Tatiana, right? Two years ago?"

She beamed. "Yes, thank you," she said, responding as if I had complimented her. "I'm Kimberly Katz." She emphasized the *z* like it was an extra syllable. "You used to date Whit Akin, right? I remember that. So sorry to hear about the breakup."

I flinched and placed my hand on the nearby wall to stop myself from falling.

"How do you know about that? How do you know Whit?" I barely got the words out.

Bryan placed his arm around me like he knew I might drop. "We've all done theater stuff together," he said. "You know, small world."

"His dad and my dad also play tennis," Kimberly Katz added. "Whit and his parents were over last weekend. You know, everybody's home for the summer. Anyway, he told me."

I nodded, and Bryan held me tighter.

"I'm sorry. I shouldn't have said anything," Kimberly Katz said, placing her hands on her cheeks. "I wasn't even thinking. How insensitive."

"No, it's okay," I said, shrugging. "I'm totally fine with it. I mean, I don't know what he's told you, but . . . I think that right now we're just figuring some stuff out, and we're both in weird places, and, you know, I think that once I start school—"

Bryan dug a nail into my shoulder to shut me up.

"Everybody's fine here," Bryan said. "Maya, why don't you grab a snack while Kimberly and I find our Senior Barders? The sooner we do some mingling with the grownups, the sooner we can leave." He squeezed my arm for reassurance.

"Sure," I said, still winded from the news that Whit was alive and well and eating at the home of Kimberly Katz.

Bryan mouthed *sorry* over his shoulder before disappearing with Kimberly Katz to the other side of the party.

I froze for a moment, not sure where to place myself among the guests who had started to pair off after finding their actor counterparts. I moved closer to the food table, a plastic white one that looked out of place in a living room full of antique everything. There were plenty of trays of carrots and zucchini sticks, but I went straight to the end of the table, where I found what I needed, the plate of the mini cheesecakes.

"I envy you," said a voice from behind.

I turned to see those big brown eyes and dirty-blond hair that was styled in a wave that stood inches above his head. It wasn't Whit's rare Punnett square, but it was still a striking combo.

"I'm celiac," Asher Forman said. "I can't remember the last time I had cheesecake."

I took a deep breath, inhaling him. I was distracted by smells now, anticipating the project I hoped would soon begin if Ann got on board.

Asher didn't smell at all like Whit. He was a combination of soap, tobacco, and mint.

"Are you a Junior Barder?" I asked, pretending not to know who he was. Bryan would want me to put him in his place.

"Sort of," he said, popping a small carrot into his mouth. "I'm in both casts. Asher Forman." He held out his hand, and I shook it.

"Oh, right. Bertram. The YouTube star."

"Indeed," he said, reaching to the table for a celery stick.

Asher was in a casual outfit—a T-shirt, jacket, and jeans like Bryan and most of the guys in the cast—but there was something about the fit of his clothes, the way they hung on his frame, that suggested they were expensive. His face shape reminded me of a Lego man, his jaw comic-book square.

"Are you in the crew?" he asked just before reaching out for the table again, this time grabbing for a piece of smoked salmon, which he popped into his mouth.

"No. I'm Maya Leschinsky. My best friend is in the cast. He's Parolles."

"Good for him," Asher said, scratching that jawline like he knew he should draw attention to it. I wanted to scratch it too, and then reached for my own, on instinct.

"He wanted your part," I said for no good reason. "It's his last summer before college, and he thought he'd get the lead."

"Well, he's got a great part, too. I mean, as great as it can be." Asher's voice was husky and dry. "It'd be an understatement to say this is not my favorite Shakespeare play."

I tried to conceal my shock that he'd read more than one Shakespeare play. I was sort of surprised he'd bothered to read the one play he was in.

Based on what Bryan had shown me, most of Asher's YouTube videos featured him in a dimly lit room, maybe a suburban garage, holding a guitar and singing covers of pop songs. His gimmick was that he recorded only songs made by women, which he seemed to think was deep. He didn't strike me as the kind of guy who'd sit around contemplating *King Lear.*

"I don't know much about this play at all," I admitted. "Is it a comedy or a tragedy?"

"I don't even know. That's the problem with this one. It's not sad, and it's definitely not funny. The ending makes you feel unsettled, which I hate," Asher said. "Do you smoke?"

"Smoke? Like, cigarettes? No." As if I smoked anything else.

"Want to come outside while I smoke?"

I was startled by his request for my company—and that he was so open about having a cigarette. Bryan said serious performers had to be careful with their vocal cords.

I looked over Asher's shoulder and spotted Bryan and Kimberly Katz at the other end of the party with their adult counterparts, all four of them gesticulating wildly, almost poking one another as they spoke.

"Sure," I said, then followed Asher Forman out the front door and into the street. He crossed the empty road and walked past some trees into a small park.

I always felt like a tourist when I was in Boston, especially in this kind of neighborhood, with its cobblestone side streets and old brownstones. My entire life was over the river in Cambridge, where university buildings were lined up next to tech companies that inhabited pristine glass offices around MIT. It looked like a city of the future over there.

But when I traveled over the Charles River, I was reminded of what Boston was known for, what it looked like on postcards, the old churches and historic cemeteries that seemed frozen in time. We visited these places on school field trips, as if they were a world away.

This particular street was field-trip-worthy, for sure, the buildings so preserved it looked like Paul Revere could trot by wearing a tricorn hat at any moment. The only anachronisms were a nearby streetlight and Asher, who checked his phone and then pulled a box of American Spirits from his jacket pocket.

As he lit a cigarette with a tiny yellow lighter, I wrapped my arms around my chest to stay warm. It felt like summer most days now, but the nights still required layers. I hadn't thought to bring a sweater, because we'd left so early. I shifted on my feet, cold enough to wish I were inside, and maybe a little nervous to be alone with Asher Forman.

He'd asked me to come on this walk, but he was silent now, just smoking, as if I weren't even there.

"So how did you get involved with the Boston Shakespeare Project?" I asked, trying to fill the silence.

He exhaled a cloud. His free hand rested in the pocket of his jeans.

"I guess they called my agent. I've got a big YouTube following, like massive. And I'm from Boston. So they asked me to take the role, and because I'm pretty young, they thought it'd be cool for me to work with the kids, too."

"I'm sure the Junior Barders love it. Some of them are probably big fans."

Asher inhaled again and was silent, like he hadn't heard me.

"So you're in high school?" he finally responded.

"I start MIT in the fall."

He looked up then, like he was just noticing me. "That's impressive. You must be really smart."

"Smart at science. I come from a family of scientists, actually. My mom taught at MIT. My dad teaches middle school science."

"You've seen my videos?" he continued without a pause, like he wasn't changing the subject back to himself. "Is that why you're here?"

I wished Bryan were with me to hear it — the narcissism.

I paused, not sure how to answer. For Bryan's sake, I had to be nice. Also, there was a small part of me that had been curious to meet a YouTube star. I decided to be honest, partly because I wanted to keep talking so that I didn't have to go back inside and stand by myself in the corner of the party.

"I have seen your videos, but that's not why I'm here. My boyfriend broke up with me a week ago, and I've been kind of a mess, so Bryan just wanted me to be around people. I think he wants to keep me distracted."

"And are you distracted?" Asher took a drag from the cigarette again. I rubbed my forearms because it felt like it had gone from cold to freezing, and he quickly shrugged out of his jacket. "Take this," he said. "Please."

Without a thought, I put it on. I was so cold. "Thanks. And yeah, I guess I'm distracted. For now. Until I get home, and then it will be terrible again. Nights are the worst."

"See, I always hated the mornings," Asher said, dropping the cigarette butt into the otherwise pristine grass and stepping on it with one of his suede sneakers. "In the morning you wake up and you're like, 'Oh, shit, she's still gone.' It's like you wake up, you're happy for one full second, and then you remember reality. Breakups are killers, man."

My eyes filled with tears at his description. It was becoming so instinctive, this constant tidal wave of grief that passed over me whenever someone made me remember what I'd lost.

"Sorry. I can't help myself," I said. "My eyes just do this now."

I smiled through the tears, almost amused by how quickly I had unraveled. Without thinking, I dragged the sleeve of Asher's coat across my nose.

"Oh, god," I said as we both stared at the jacket. A thick, shiny stripe of snot made a line across the black fabric of his dark coat. "That's so gross. I'm so, so sorry. I'll wash it and bring it back to you. Oh, god . . . I feel so bad. I'm so embarrassed."

Asher Forman let out a loud laugh. "Don't worry about it. Take it home with you. Don't even think about it. That was awesome."

He looked across the street at the brownstone, where, based on the movement of the silhouettes in the windows, the party was still going strong. "I think we have to go back in there."

"You do, at least. You're sort of the star of the show," I said.

He grimaced.

"What's the matter—you don't like parties? I'd think in your business, you'd have to be used to attention."

He smiled, both hands now in his pockets.

"It's not that. I mean, this isn't exactly what I thought I'd be doing this summer. I thought I'd have something big. A TV pilot or something. I had, like, forty auditions in L.A. a few months ago — and then nothing. And now I'm back living with my parents for three months and doing Shakespeare with high-schoolers."

"And adults," I offered. "This company is really good. Bryan says a lot of people go on to big things after the Boston Shakespeare Project. There are, like, Broadway people in these productions."

"I don't know; maybe. My agent said it'll look good on my résumé. He said I have to diversify my work."

"I'm sure that's true," I said, my tone more patronizing than I wanted it to be.

"Sure," Asher said as he started to walk. "Come on. Back inside."

I followed him across the street and back into the brownstone.

Asher walked straight to the woman hosting the party and gave her a smile I now knew was disingenuous. I stood by the snack table and watched him circle the party, shaking hands and having short conversations with other cast members.

He left about ten minutes later. On his way out the door, I ran to him and tapped him on the shoulder. "I'll clean your jacket and give it to Bryan for you," I told him.

"Don't even think about it," he said and winked, then trotted out the door like he had somewhere to be.

It was hot inside the party now. Too many bodies in one place. Bryan, whose face was red, came over and grabbed my hand. "What was that? Did I see Asher Forman wink at you? Explain." He tugged on the sleeve of the jacket. "What is this?"

"I was outside with him. I was cold, so he gave me his jacket. Then

I wiped my snot on it, so he probably didn't want it back," I said, holding up my arm, the sleeve shimmering under the party lights.

"He gave you his jacket?"

"Check out this landing strip of mucus. I was mortified."

Bryan looked at me like he'd never seen me before, then shook his head.

"Let's get out of here. It smells like Shakespeare's armpit."

We googled pictures of Asher Forman on the Red Line home and watched a YouTube video that featured him singing a cover of a Sia song. *"I'm gonna swing from the chandelier,"* Asher wailed. It had more than a million views. Then we watched one of him covering Ariana Grande. *"Something 'bout you makes me feel like a dangerous woman,"* he sang.

"Like, why?" Bryan said, shaking his head.

"I think he's trying to make a statement," I said with a shrug.

Once I got home, I grabbed my phone to call Whit to tell him what happened, then felt a wave of nausea as I remembered that I couldn't. It was so odd, the idea that something cool had happened to me and Whit just wouldn't know about it.

It had become the best part of good experiences, having someone like Whit to tell about it, and hearing him react like I was the most interesting person on the planet. The only other person who'd ever been that interested in what I did was my mom, and that didn't count. But now Whit was with Andrea Berger, not having any idea that I had talked to a YouTube star and was now wearing his coat.

But I would remember all of this — every detail. If I could get him to change his mind, I would tell him everything he missed.

7

It was still as bright as morning when I arrived at Ann's office on the following Monday afternoon. My brain felt foggy. The June run of the longest days of the year had begun, which only made it harder to sleep. I tried to get to bed early all weekend, allowing myself to listen to a few songs on Bryan's playlist each night (I was on track forty, Beyoncé's "If I Were a Boy," which I found myself putting on repeat). After music, I'd toss and turn for a few hours until my eyes popped open with the sun, feeling a hollowness in my chest as I counted the hours until I could get to the lab to be around people, specifically Kyle, who was now distracting me by sending links to *Star Wars* fan fiction, some of which was really good.

Ann had sent me an email earlier in the day asking me to drop by, which I assumed meant she'd made a decision about our secret project. Based on how she carried herself when I entered her office, I figured she was about to say no.

After all, what I was proposing was reckless and irresponsible. It was one thing for her to do covert research as an assistant to my mother, who had three degrees and was an expert in her field, but it was another thing to run it with me, a not-quite-eighteen-year-old who hadn't even started her undergraduate education.

I walked into her small office and stood in front of her desk, waiting for her rejection.

"Maya," Ann started, pulling the binder from her desk drawer.

She held it vertically and upside down so that Harry Styles was looking right at me, his grin taunting and cruel. "Take a seat."

Yael was right; Ann had no authority in this lab — she was just like any other PhD student — but she behaved as though she were a tenured professor. She wanted to be intimating, and it worked. I was already feeling the heat of embarrassment creep up my neck, and, for a moment, I wished I'd never asked her about the binder in the first place.

"If we do this," Ann said, "I need to be able to trust that you won't tell anyone. I expect detailed notes. I expect complete transparency."

My head snapped up. "You're saying yes?"

She leaned back in her chair, her lips pursing as she tried to suppress a smile.

"I'm saying yes for now . . . But if Dr. Araghi finds out we're doing this, we're in big trouble — like kicked-out-level trouble — so there are rules," she said.

"First rule," Ann continued, "we work quickly, and finish the project before the end of the summer. That's the only way we won't get caught. In June and July, the lab is short-staffed, with fewer people around to notice missing resources. But come late August, everybody's back and paying attention. I want this done by then."

I nodded. I liked the idea of fast.

"Rule Two: No telling anyone. Not even your lab friends. And definitely not your dad."

"Of course," I said.

"And Rule Three: At any point, depending on how you respond to the project," Ann said, her voice stern, "I reserve the right to shut it down."

"Of course," I whispered. "I understand — "

She cut me off.

"When I say *respond,* I'm talking about your physical response to the reagents. This experiment involves taking something—a serum—to mask the expression of your pheromones. Your mother developed a formula for this, and I worked with her to come up with an ideal dosage, which proved to be safe, but we never tested it on anyone but her. If you suffer any negative side effects, we'll end the work. Already, I fear putting you at risk, but . . ."

"If it was safe for my mother, it'll be safe on me," I assured her before she could talk herself out of it. "You'll never find another subject who's as close to my mother as me, right?"

"Every subject is unique," Ann said. "But this project requires only a very small dose of the serum that builds up over days. We should know early on whether there's an allergy or any adverse side effects—hopefully long before there's a real problem. Your mother's body temperature did go up throughout the experiment. That's something we'll have to monitor."

I nodded. The emptiness in my stomach was replaced by a buzzing that happened whenever I got excited about an experiment. Beyond trying to get Whit back, I was finally going to be doing something hands-on instead of just transcribing someone else's notes.

Ann opened the One Direction binder to a page marked with dates, temperatures, and numbers, and began to explain what it all meant. I was pleased at how much I understood; paying attention to my mother had taught me a shorthand for research talk.

Ann and my mom had already figured out the most complicated part of the project, developing the serum that altered the appearance of pheromones and HLAs, or human leukocyte antigens, which are what regulate our immune systems.

When Ann explained how the sublingual process would work, I cut her off.

"I know this part."

"You do?"

"Yes, *sublingual* means under the tongue. The serum is absorbed by the tissues under the tongue, through the bloodstream. Smart that you and my mom used this method; it was probably the easiest way to get it into her system."

Ann nodded, looking more uncomfortable than impressed with my knowledge.

Then she had questions for me. My mother had one obvious subject: my dad. Whit, my desired subject, was an ex, meaning he wasn't around anymore.

"Your mother lived with your father. Saw him every day. Your subject is not with you. How did you plan on using him for this project?" Ann asked.

"I could take the serum until it enters my system and then make a plan to see Whit. Wouldn't we be able to gauge its effect by how he responds to me then? I could tell him I need to see him and spend time with him. Then we could see how he responds to me."

"Maya, there needs to be some method here," Ann said, sounding a bit like my mom. "How would we know whether it was the serum working or if he just missed you? Your ex-boyfriend isn't the best control subject at the moment."

I frowned. He was the whole reason I wanted to do this.

"Wouldn't you have had the same issue with Mom and Dad? How did she know whether my dad was responding to the serum or whether he was just attracted to her on specific days because of his mood—or what she was wearing? I don't want to do this if I can't do it with Whit, Ann."

"I understand," Ann said, opening a can of cream soda. I hadn't even seen where the can came from. It was like she pulled it out of thin air.

"Don't get upset; Whit is still in the mix here. But I thought we could try something different, something your mom and I hoped to address in our next phase of research. I'd like to broaden the experiment and test it with more than one subject. Three subjects; three types of relationships. A friend, a stranger, and eventually, to finish the project, your ex. These would be short-term tests, the results qualitative but informative based on what we already know from your mother."

"*Three* subjects? I'd just hoped for the one . . ."

"It would give us more data, which makes it better for me. Also, your mother's research indicates that she saw a response within two weeks of use of the serum. That gives us exactly enough time to get through three experiments by the end of the summer. All you have to do is choose them and get DNA samples to make the serum."

Ann looked down at her laptop.

"It's late June already. We'd should start now," she said. "So . . . am I calling your bluff, or are you in?"

My mind went to the sweatshirt balled up in the corner of my room with Whit's hair all over it. He'd worn it through the winter, whenever my dad was being cheap about the heat.

Those strands of hair were the key to this.

I'd already mapped out a fantasy scenario where we'd set a date to catch up, and I'd smell just right. We'd be like the darcin mice, recalling the memories of attraction and falling in love all over again. We'd go back to his new apartment, and that'd be our new beginning.

But two other subjects. A friend? A stranger? No one crossed my mind.

"Please think of someone you're around frequently for the first test. Someone with whom you share a specific, platonic routine."

"Routine," I whispered.

A vision of the chess app flashed in my mind. "Kyle," I said.

He was a guy who liked me as a friend and saw me in the lab almost every day. He was clear about his intentions or lack thereof. He had spent the previous night sending me pictures of his roommate's bedroom. *I signed a summer sublet with this guy,* Kyle had texted after sending a shot of the roommate's dirty underwear on the floor next to spaghetti stuck to the carpet. *Three whole months with this angel of a human.*

What we'd developed over the past couple of weeks was sort of like my friendship with Bryan, in terms of ease of conversation, but it was new, and maybe less familial.

"Kyle," I repeated. "Kyle works. I don't know about a second subject, though."

"There's time; the first test will take a few weeks, just to set it all up and begin. But for now," Ann continued, "get me samples for subjects one and three as soon as possible. It will take me five days to do the DNA test and to get the reagents we need to make the serum, so we should get going as soon as we can."

"Samples," I said out loud.

"Hair. Saliva. Something I can use with a DNA kit," Ann said casually, as if it would be easy to just stick my hand inside Kyle's mouth.

"Okay. I think I can make it happen."

"Good. And Maya, I know I'm repeating myself, but this is a secret. Just you and me. If anyone knew I was doing this work, especially with you, I'd be kicked out. Already they don't know what to do with me. I'm sure Dr. Araghi probably thinks I'll never finish this PhD. I'm sure he thinks I'm wasting space just by being here."

"I know how to keep a secret," I told her. "Also . . . I don't think Dr. Araghi thinks that."

Ann narrowed her eyes at me.

"I don't blame him," she said, her voice soft. "Sometimes I think I'm wasting space here too."

Before I could come up with something positive to say, she stowed the One Direction binder in her desk and began to pack her bag for the night. I wondered what she'd do then, and what she did every night after she left her office. I imagined her in a small, cell-like apartment, a larger version of her office, eating a frozen vegan dinner with a can of cream soda, alone.

"Ann?"

"Mmm?" she mumbled, looking up, her softer expression making her look like a different person for a second.

"This means a lot to me — more than you know," I said, turning to the door before she could change her mind.

"Me too," I thought I heard her whisper as I shut the door behind me.

8

The unfortunate reality of lab work, based on what I've seen, is that ninety percent of it or more is busywork without results.

In elementary school, you put baking soda into vinegar and it explodes right in front of you, within seconds. Or you put red food coloring in water, stick the stem of a white flower in the mix, and watch the colorless buds turn scarlet over days. Experiments for kids are great that way. They make science look like magic.

But when you get older and you're researching something specific that might involve a small change in temperature or the structure of a protein, you have to be prepared for hours and hours of nothing. Even if you're lucky enough to see big results in your work, they're often anticlimactic and difficult to explain to someone who's not a scientist.

Yael, for instance, is working on a project involving epigenetics and pyelonephritis, which is basically the science of why people have troublesome kidneys. Her greater goal is to figure out why some bodies are prone to urinary tract infections. The work she does now could help women who get chronic UTIs in the future, but on a daily basis, not much happens. Yael has spent most of her time at MIT dropping various chemical reagents onto cells on slides, over and over, like she's stuck on repeat.

My mom used to tell me that being a good researcher meant accepting small victories. Even her epigenetics breakthroughs sometimes seemed underwhelming when you explained them outside the lab. She had developed seeds of possible cures for diseases, but still, just seeds.

I think that's one of the things that surprised me most about my mom and Ann's work: that there was a baking-soda-volcano type of result. A formula dropped under the tongue, and a potential change to the system within weeks. My mom had trained me to believe that it shouldn't be possible.

I gave Ann Whit's sweatshirt and the sample for Kyle, handing over three of his favorite pens in a plastic bag. One was particularly wet when I found it. He'd taken it out of his mouth, left it on his bench, and walked away, almost like he'd wanted me to take it.

It was just a pen, but grabbing it and sealing it in a plastic bag made me think about the ethics of the experiment for the first time.

While it bothered me that my mom had done an experiment on my dad without him knowing, her intentions had been good. She was only trying to improve marriages, and there was something about doing this with a spouse — someone who'd already signed up for a lifetime commitment — that made the work seem less sinister.

But taking Kyle's pen made me feel like I was doing something immoral, especially when I returned to the lab and had to face him for the rest of the day. He wasn't my husband or even my boyfriend. He was a friend I really liked, someone I wanted to talk to all day, which was important and new.

But this was a temporary project, I told myself. Sort of like putting on the perfect perfume and seeing if someone noticed. After we completed the first test, the serum would be out of my system within a matter of days. It probably wouldn't even work on a platonic friend anyway.

I was experimenting with the first two subjects only to appease

Ann, I told myself. The only part of the experiment I cared about was Subject Number Three.

For the rest of the day, after stowing the bag with the pen in it in my backpack, it seemed that Kyle was everywhere, bumping into me as he reached for equipment, offering to grab me lunch, and hovering by my workbench — his long lashes batting , his eyebrows raised — as he told me about his roommate's latest hygienic transgression.

Our lab was a maze of parallel and perpendicular workbenches built so close to one another that there was no room for personal space. The tightness of the layout had annoyed me before — people often bumped my back as they whizzed by while I was transcribing — but now I was thankful for the proximity; at the very least, I could count on Kyle noticing any changes in my pheromones. This sterile, cramped lab provided an almost ideal set of circumstances for the plan.

Ann did her part. Within days, she'd used the pens to do the DNA test. Now we had to make the formula, though, and that required materials. My mom had access to everything in Building 68b, and no one would have ever questioned why she needed specific materials for her work. But Ann, who, despite her air of authority, had gone from a superstar's protégé to an ordinary PhD student — one who was close to a year behind on her dissertation — had access to nothing.

"Basically, this is theft. It's a crime," she said when I met her in the quad that Sunday night.

"First of all, it's not a crime. I mean, not really. We're just using some chemicals. It's not like we're walking away with some thousand-dollar centrifuge," I told her.

"Then why are you wearing that outfit?" she asked. "You going to rob a bank after this?"

I'd dressed in black sweatpants and a long black T-shirt because it seemed appropriate for our night's work. Ann also wore black jeans and a black T-shirt, but that was her daily uniform.

Ann shook her head and brushed past me, opening the door of Building 68b and ushering me inside.

The facility looked sinister at midnight, the almost-full moon casting weird shadows on the walls of the sterile lab building. It didn't help that 68b was so close to MIT's Stata Center. The multicolored Frank Gehry building, one of the more famous structures on campus, looked like a cheery, colorful setting for a Dr. Seuss book by day, but after dark it resembled a horror-film fun house, with crazy angles that made it appear as though the building were collapsing under its own weight.

It seemed unnecessarily dramatic to meet right at midnight, but this was the best time to do work without a major risk of being caught. Ann knew that the basement lab and storage area would be dark and unmanned. She could grab what she needed and make the formula in about two hours, but she needed a lookout.

"What's your story?" Ann asked in front of the lab doors.

"If security shows up, my story is that I lost my wallet. I'll ask the guard to take me up to the third floor to look for it."

"And what if he asks you why you're in the basement?"

"I'll say that I used the bathroom down here on Friday. I'll say I looked for the wallet here first but haven't found anything."

"Good," she said. She paused at the door of the lab like she was afraid to go in, because once she did, she couldn't turn back. I knew that she was desperate to do the project—to get back to the kind of work she was doing with my mom—but that she also knew she shouldn't be doing it with me.

Her desire won out. She swung open the door and shut it behind her. I sank to the floor while Ann got to work making a quick grab for what she needed so we could be out of the building as fast as possible.

For the next hour, every noise sent me into panic mode. At some point, the building's air conditioner turned off, and the sputtering of the vents made my heart skip. Occasionally I'd hear footsteps, and I'd practice my lie — "I lost my wallet," repeated to myself in a confident whisper — but the padding against the lab's linoleum floors always turned out to be Ann's feet. I could hear her moving from one side of the room to the other.

At about two in the morning, at which point I was cross-legged, my head resting against the wall, Ann emerged, the sound of the swinging doors causing me to scramble to a standing position.

"Get in here," she whispered, almost hissing.

For a moment, I assessed what we looked like in the dim hallway. We did look like criminals. All we needed were ski masks for our faces.

She waved her hand, urging me into the lab storage room, which was mostly dark, except for one row of glowing lights.

"Sit," she said, pointing to a stool.

As I tried to get comfortable on the metal seat, Ann paused and asked, "By the way, how did you get out of the house? Where does your dad think you are?"

"He was still at some hiking-club party when I left," I told her. "Don't worry," I added when she looked nervous. "I'm not the kind of kid who sneaks out. Even if he notices I'm missing, he'll assume I'm at Bryan's."

I spotted the One Direction binder on the black workbench counter. It was open to a page I must have skipped when I first found it. I could almost make out a handwritten list of directions and chemicals. As soon as Ann noticed me eyeing it, trying to make sense of the recipe, she flipped to the back page of the book, where there was a yellow folder.

She removed it and slid it in my direction.

"This is for you," Ann said.

I opened it. The first page was a spreadsheet almost identical to the one my mom used to document her work. There were daily instructions and spaces for me to log the date, my temperature, and the dose of serum. It was to build from six to twelve drops in each cycle.

"You'll fill this in every day," Ann said. "Be consistent and accurate. If you don't want to fill it in by hand, make your own spreadsheet on your laptop—just make sure you include all the same information."

I nodded.

"This," she said, pointing to a vial filled with amber liquid resting in a test-tube rack, "this is your first serum. It's Subject Number One."

I stared at it like the image of Kyle's face would somehow appear as a cloud in the formula. Then I grabbed for it, eager to begin the project, but Ann ripped it from my hand.

"Careful," she said, raising her voice. "Maya, listen to my instructions first."

Bringing her voice back to a near whisper, she explained that I would use the eyedropper to place six drops of the liquid under my tongue.

"Let it sit, hold it under your tongue, and then swallow after two minutes. You can breathe through your nose," she said. "Just let it sit under your tongue until I tell you it's time to swallow."

There was something about her instructions, and maybe the fact that it was the middle of the night, that made me feel like Cinderella, like the serum might transform me into someone else right then and there — a better and more appealing version of myself. My black sweatpants would become the kind of colorful fitted dress worn by Kimberly Katz. The rubber tie that held my hair back would become a jewel-encrusted tiara.

Ann was the opposite of a fairy godmother, though; there had yet to be a moment when she didn't look frustrated with me. In the low light, the circles under her eyes were darker, and her skin looked pale.

"Take the first dose now. Six drops," Ann said. "The sooner you start, the sooner we can watch for any problems or allergic reactions."

I unscrewed the top of the bottle and used the dropper in the cap to place the serum under my tongue. I took a breath to say something, but she cut me off.

"Quiet," Ann said, holding up her hand like a stop sign. "If you talk, you might accidentally swallow some of the serum too soon."

She eyed the wall clock. The room was so quiet, I could hear the second hand ticking. "You have until one thirty-six. Hold it under your tongue until then."

The two minutes felt long, especially with her staring at me like I was a lab rat, which I sort of was.

"It tastes good," I said, once she gave me permission to swallow. "Like children's vitamins."

"That's because there's sugar in it," she said.

"Thanks. It's much easier to swallow something that tastes like candy."

"You're welcome, but I didn't add sugar for taste. Sugar helps your body absorb the chemicals. It speeds up cell metabolism."

I ran my tongue over my teeth, imagining what Kyle would say if he knew that the serum based on his DNA tasted like it was cooked up by Willy Wonka.

"Over the next half-hour, we'll check your temperature. Then, after tonight, you're on your own. It will be up to you to fill in all the data, the most important part being your temperature, which will spike but should never go above one hundred degrees, understand? The minute it goes over ninety-nine-point-nine degrees, you call me, and we reassess."

I nodded. I learned from scanning my mother's notes that her temperature had gone up as she used the serum — a tame side effect, but one she wanted to keep in check. The most appropriate dose was effective but kept her body temp at ninety-nine.

"Should we wait for reactions outside, just so we're out of the building?" I asked. "It seems risky to stay any longer than we need to."

"I'd rather stay in here, where there's a first-aid kit," Ann responded. "We'll wait another ten minutes just to make sure you don't go into anaphylactic shock or anything."

"Okay."

Then it was awkward, at least for me. I didn't know how to sit there in silence with Ann just watching me, waiting for a reaction.

"So, how is your work going?" I asked, after clearing my throat. "Are you . . . feeling good about your dissertation?"

"No," Ann said, her voice flat. "It's not as easy to push forward with it now that . . . well, you know, I had a specific mentor, and now I'm a bit adrift. Dr. Araghi is doing his best."

"I'm sorry," I said, as if it were my fault my mom had died.

Her face softened, and she took a deep breath.

"Do you know what you'll want to study at MIT? You'll follow in your mom's footsteps, I assume?"

"Yeah, but I want to take her work with disease a step further. Like, my mom's cancer went metastatic so quickly, and then our options disappeared. I want to look at the role of epigenetics in metastasis—to see if epigenetic markers might determine how a cancer moves. If my mom's cancer hadn't spread, she'd be alive."

Ann moved closer, like we finally had something interesting to talk about, but before she could respond, the door swung open, and she yelled, "Shit!" as I registered why.

A small frame came into the light.

"Maya?" Yael barked.

"Yael. Hi," I said, waving hello like that was normal.

Ann took the small vial of serum from the workbench and hid it in her fist. Yael flipped on a second set of lights so that brightness took over the room.

"Maya, what are you doing here?" she asked, looking at me and then Ann, and then back at me.

"I forgot my wallet, and then I ran into Ann," I said, my voice rigid. "What are *you* doing here? It's so late."

Yael rubbed her eyes; it was clear she'd rolled out of bed for this visit.

"I woke up in a panic that I hadn't closed the freezer. But of course I had. I always do. I'm so OCD these days that I literally had to get out of bed and check—and then, once I got here and made sure everything was locked up, I wanted a Diet Coke, so I came down to the basement to the machine, and then I heard your voice and got freaked out. Maya, why wouldn't you just wait until tomorrow to find your wallet? It's not safe to be walking around campus this late."

My brain wasn't alert enough for follow-up questions.

"I don't know."

She looked at Ann. I silently prayed that she wouldn't ask any more questions.

"You guys should keep the lights on. It's freaky down here."

Ann didn't react.

"Well . . . okay," Yael said. "Good night — I guess."

Ann let out a breath as my friend exited and the door swung closed behind her.

"Shit."

"It's okay," I assured her, even though I wasn't certain it was.

"I hope you're right," Ann said, looking even paler than she had before. "Open your mouth. Let me take your temperature, and then let's get out of here."

It was 98.9. Just right for a first dose.

"Take the bottle with you," Ann said, handing the small vial to me. "Take your temperature again before you go to sleep."

She placed the One Direction binder in her black satchel and then returned the test-tube rack to the shelves of equipment.

"Come on," she said as I followed her out the lab doors. "Don't get abducted on your walk home; that's the last thing I need."

"I won't," I promised.

For a moment, it felt like we should hug goodbye or something, but she about-faced and went for the stairs like I had already left.

I assumed that when I arrived back home, I'd be able to sit in the kitchen with a thermometer, taking my temperature and documenting my initial response in peace, but my dad was home and awake.

I found him on his knees on the living room floor. He was in pajama pants and an old, stained MIT T-shirt, leaning over what appeared to be rock-climbing equipment. This was his life now, one constant string of outdoor activities that required harnesses, vests, and florescent backpacks.

He turned to me, smiling as if he had no idea that I was returning home in the middle of the night, not asking why I was out past two a.m.

"Do you think this is a bent-gate carabiner?" he asked, holding a silver clasp. "They all look the same to me."

"You might be shocked to hear this, Dad, but I don't know much about carabiners," I said, leaning against the staircase.

He smirked. "Fair enough."

He glanced at the clock over the television. "You coming from Bryan's?"

"Yeah," I lied.

I watched my dad move around on all fours, hovering over different pieces of equipment. Nearby, his orange running vest was hanging on a hook between the front door and his bike, which was covered in mud. My mother would never have let him bring that thing into the house.

"Can I ask you something, Dad?"

"Of course," he said, his eyes still on the silver clasps.

"Do you actually like all this outdoor stuff? Like, enough that you really want to do it every day?"

He paused and looked up at me and smiled.

"Maybe? I don't know," he admitted. "But I like that I *can* do it. I like the challenge. And especially with the biking and the rock climbing, it takes so much focus that I can't think about anything else. That's probably why I do it. My mind can't wander off to sad places if I'm hanging off a rock-climbing wall or biking down a trail."

His wide smile suggested he didn't know how depressing that sounded—that he'd just admitted to hanging off rocks so he didn't have to think about my mom.

"Am I leaving you alone too much, babe?" he asked, his smile gone. "I know I'm not home that often, just with all of these activities, and the fact that I'm doing more curriculum work this summer. Maybe I should be around more often before you leave for school. I know with Whit not around . . ."

Sometimes we were awkward like this. I was so close with my mom, and my dad was always there, but without her around, our connection felt different, like we weren't sure of the rules. He asked me for parenting advice, and I had no answers. I didn't know what we were supposed to be doing.

"No, Dad, it's fine. I'm busy with work and Bryan. Really, it's okay. I just wanted to make sure you're having fun."

"Something like fun," he said, his voice weak, his eyes back on the equipment. "Well, get some sleep, my dear."

"Good night, Dad," I said, and ran upstairs to take my temperature one more time in my room, then pass out, knowing that the sooner it was tomorrow, the sooner I could take a second dose.

mom had kept the table clean back in the day, but now it was covered with unopened envelopes and a few candy wrappers.

I leaned toward the mirror to look at myself up close. The curls on top of my head were wet with sweat and pressed against my forehead. My lips looked weirdly full — not enough to suggest a severe allergic reaction, but maybe a minor one. My face was flushed, like I'd been sprinting — or kissing.

After a long, cold shower, I put on a pair of jeans and the T-shirt with ladybugs on the shoulders that Aunt Cindy had given me for Hanukkah last year. Bryan always said it was my least flattering top, and that it made me look like Mrs. Holmes, our art teacher, but I figured that would help me set the tone for the experiment. I would wear something I put on when I didn't care who was looking. I slipped into my favorite brown sneakers, grabbed my backpack, and began the walk to lab.

Kyle had beaten me there, as usual. He arrived at the lab a half-hour early most days, eager to prove that he wanted to be there, that he was ready to be back in class. It was silly, because no one really noticed the extra effort besides Yael and me; Dr. Araghi rolled in around ten.

We had already been on two whiff walks that week. He'd been concerned about my mood post-breakup, and kept asking if I needed more distractions in the form of more chess games or shrimp skewers.

Yael had been just as concerned. One afternoon, she told me the story of her first breakup — how a woman she'd met in undergrad pursued her for months only to dump her for a guy on the rugby team.

The conversation made me feel worse, but I was grateful, mostly because Yael never said anything mean about Whit, unlike Bryan, who had taken to calling him names. His breakup soundtrack had entered an angry place, with Kelly Clarkson yelling more than she sang.

With Yael, there were no deadlines or eye rolls whenever I said nice things about Whit and talked about missing him. She understood that I needed to love him and to be sad.

Kyle stayed silent whenever Whit came up, sometimes shaking his head or apologizing for not being "good at girl talk."

Now, at the lab, I saw him hunched over his workbench, holding a pipette.

I watched him as he worked, really examining him for the first time as a subject. His fitted light gray Beaver Nation T-shirt showed off his tan arms, which were covered in dark hair. For a lab guy, he was athletic, built more like the guys on my high school's soccer team.

"What?" Kyle said, looking up in a flash. "What are you looking at?" He pointed at me with the pipette. "You're making me self-conscious."

"Nothing," I said, feeling myself blush.

"You're weird," he said, his eyes down, back on his work.

I didn't have a plan, other than to be around him and to observe his response to me. I asked Ann if there was anything I should do to speed the process, like ask for a post-breakup hug so we could get close, but she said the more naturally I behaved, the better.

"Just be normal," she'd said in a calm tone I guessed she'd learned from my mother. "Whatever that means for you."

I left him alone until three, when I stopped by, hoping to talk.

Before then, our only interactions were accidental bumps in our small space. I'll admit that this nudge was intentional; I collided into him from behind and leaned in close to get my balance.

"Watch, it Maya!" he said—yelled, actually—after the interaction caused him to drop a piece of equipment that looked like a screwdriver.

"Shit," he muttered, grabbing it from the ground.

"Sorry."

"That's, like — a very expensive homogenizer."

"Did it break?" I asked, panicked.

"Thank god, no," he said, placing it back on his bench.

My face flushed as I sat back down at my desk and put in my earbuds to hear Dr. Araghi's latest tape for transcription. I had already stolen chemicals at midnight on the weekend, and now I was messing with expensive lab tools. *No more intentional bumps,* I promised myself. If I caused Kyle to break something, he'd be too stressed to even notice me.

After a minute, my phone lit up with a message. *Sorry,* it said. It was from Kyle. *I didn't mean to snap at you.*

I almost broke your homogenizer, I wrote back. *You wouldn't have been able to homogenize.*

I saw the dots appear on my phone, but I wrote back before he could finish.

We should take a whiff walk later.

At that, he wrote back quickly, *It's Friday.*

We didn't hang out on Fridays, usually. I don't know what Kyle and Yael did, but my Fridays had been reserved for Whit, up until the breakup.

Yeah, well, I have lots of free time these days, I wrote back, adding the flatlined smile. *I could use the company. Or maybe we could go out and do something distracting.*

Dots bubbled on my phone, and then, finally, *Sure. I'll tell Yael.*

Let's give her a night off, I wrote back before he could approach her. *I could use a night of no girl talk. Don't ever tell her I said that.*

Sure, he said.

Yael walked in then, speaking Hebrew on her cell phone. The conversation sounded heated, but it probably wasn't. Kyle and I often thought Yael was fighting with her family only to find out she was just chatting with them about something innocuous. "Hebrew is bigger than English," she told us. "It's a more passionate language."

I gave Yael a nod and found myself too embarrassed to make eye contact with Kyle, like we shared a secret. In reality, I was the only one with something to hide. It wasn't as though Kyle and I were texting love notes; we'd just made plans on our own. I doubted Yael would even mind.

Almost as if she knew we were waiting for her to disappear, Yael announced at five thirty that she'd be heading out. She had a phone "date" with her girlfriend Amit, who was staying up late for the scheduled call.

"I know there's a light at the end of the tunnel, but it feels like I'll never get to her," Yael confessed before leaving. "Three years feels so much longer than I thought it would."

"Don't think about that now," I said, offering love advice like I had any idea what I was talking about. "Just get to your date."

"Right. Date," Yael said, letting out a sigh before she ran out the door, her bag making clapping sounds as it slapped against her back.

Kyle and I decided that instead of the usual shrimp and chicken skewers, we'd go to the pizza place and bowling alley in Davis Square.

We split a mushroom pie, and once we started eating, it started to feel normal, like we were just hanging out the way we always did. Kyle asked about Bryan's play and whether I had received my dorm assignment for the fall. I told him how I'd requested a single room, and he teased me for being an only child who likes her space.

I got brave and asked about the state of his degree, and whether his adviser thought he had a good shot at trying school again in the fall.

The question made him pause. We'd never talked about it before.

"Do you know what happened? Why I had to take time off?" Kyle asked, his eyes on the pizza.

"Yael told me you were failing some classes. I didn't ask for any information; it's none of my business."

Kyle folded his hands together, his elbows on the table.

"I have a tough time explaining it without it sounding bad."

"You don't have to tell me."

Kyle shook his head. "No, I want to."

I took another slice of pizza, feeling shy as I waited.

"You've always been good at math and science, right?" he asked.

"Yeah," I said. "I'm bad at many other things, but yeah, I'm good with science."

"Well, me too. This kind of work has always come really easily to me. I skipped seventh grade, and then in high school, *everything* was kind of easy. Math, English, soccer — being soccer captain — all easy. I started at MIT, and that was easy too.

"But then, junior year, like halfway into fall semester, things weren't easy. Like, things were *really* not easy . . . I'd never been in an academic situation where I didn't just get it. And in two classes, I was dragging. I couldn't make it easy. And what kills me is that I should have stopped to figure it out before I fell behind and started messing everything up. But instead of admitting that I needed to work at it — to maybe get some help — I kept pretending that I was just going to magically figure it out. I ignored it and went out all the time. There were girls and parties, and it was about everything but sitting down and making sense of it. I think I figured that it would just click after a while, but then I was behind and failing, and it felt like I couldn't dig my way out of it.

"My dad was furious. He called my adviser, the school, everybody. He was looking for anyone to blame, but it was all me."

"Oh," I said, not knowing what else to tell him.

"Anyway, my adviser came up with the idea to take time off. He said that because I skipped a year before getting to college, and that I was starting MIT at sixteen going on seventeen, maybe it was an adjustment thing, or something to do with maturity. I don't know, maybe it was."

"If it helps, you do seem really immature," I said, trying to lighten the mood.

"Thanks," Kyle said, with a laugh. "That makes me feel better."

It was a lot of information, and it felt nice to be trusted with it, but my brain hung onto three words: "There were girls." Kyle looked like he played soccer in high school because he did. I wondered if he would have even noticed me if he'd been at my high school.

"So, like, are you going to be a superstar researcher like your mom? Sorry for your loss, by the way. I've seen her picture in that big frame outside Dr. Araghi's office."

"Thanks. Yeah — she and Dr. Araghi were super close. They were, like, inseparable when she was coming up in his lab. I'm sure that's why he reached out to my dad about me doing the internship this summer. I think he somehow feels responsible for me, like a grandparent . . . And yeah, I want to do my mom's kind of work with disease and epigenetics. I'm sort of obsessed with figuring out why her cancer spread. I think about it a lot, like why the cancer cells in her body did what they did — why they traveled. What causes that? I guess I don't want that to happen to other people."

Kyle's eyes were sad.

"Sorry. Depressing cancer talk."

"No, it's impressive. You're really thoughtful."

I felt heat creep up my neck.

"Come on," Kyle said, downing the rest of his soda. "Let's bowl."

I nodded and glanced at my phone on the table. It was nine thirty, and there was nothing notable about the evening so far, at least in the context of the experiment.

"I forgot that this was going to be candlepin. I'm terrible at this. You New Englanders with your small balls," Kyle said as we approached the lanes. He groaned as he scratched his head.

"Candlepin is the only kind of bowling that counts," I said.

"At home in Maryland, we play with big balls," Kyle said. I rolled my eyes.

It turned out he was terrible at the game, the small balls hitting just one pin or barreling into the gutters after every toss. I was having a good night; three spares in a row.

"How are you so good at this?" he asked.

"It's all in where you look," I said, approaching him with a ball in my hand, realizing that I was in a position to get close. I stood right behind him and placed one hand on his back.

"Don't look at the pins," I said, pointing at the end of the lane in front of him. "Don't look at the ball. Keep your eyes on the spot where you want the ball to land. The brain will correct your arm." I took a step to the right of him and tossed a ball underhand, down the alley. All but one pin fell down.

"Now you," I said after pressing the button to clear the lane.

He shook his head as he took a step forward, winding his arm back like a softball pitcher. He focused, his eyes narrowed.

"Forget the arm," I reminded him. "Just keep your eye on the target."

Kyle relaxed his shoulders, dropped the ball in front of him, and watched as it took down all but two of the pins.

"Whoa," he said, whipping around.

"I know, right? It's all in where you look. My dad taught me that trick."

He hugged me then, just like he had after the breakup.

I noticed our alignment, which was becoming more familiar.

There's a thing that happens when you hug someone over and over. After the fifth or sixth embrace, your bodies just know how to slide together. Bryan is a side hugger; he throws his arm around my shoulders and pulls me in, like we're posing for a picture. At five foot ten, my dad can place his head right on top of mine for a totem-pole hug. With Whit, my head fell right into his neck. He'd wrap one arm around my lower back and place one on the back of my skull, holding me in place.

But Kyle was an inch or so taller than Whit, and his arms were stronger. He squeezed me without thought, my face mushed against his chest so that all I could do was inhale him. When he let go, I staggered back.

I hoped he'd inhaled me, too, but the hug didn't seem to faze him; he just grabbed another ball to continue the game. As we wrapped up, our score tied, I started to worry that I didn't have enough data from the evening. He had hugged me, but he wasn't flirting, just excited about improving his bowling skills. I didn't know what I thought would happen—it's not as though any of my subjects were going to tell me that because of some phantom smell, they suddenly found me irresistible.

"Too late for a whiff walk?" I asked when we threw money on the counter to pay for the lanes. I was desperate to extend the night.

"Are you kidding?" Kyle said. "It's, like, ten thirty. You want to hike back to Main Street?"

"I'm just a little wired for some reason. What if we, like, watched a movie or something?"

"Your dad won't mind if I come over this late?" Kyle asked.

He wasn't even looking at me now. He was checking his phone like he was done with me and wanted to go elsewhere. I felt defeated.

"He'll be psyched I'm not moping. I haven't exactly been the best company since Whit and I broke up."

Kyle shot me a pitying glance. That did it.

"Well, now I have to come over," he said. "But no girl talk."

"No girl talk, I promise."

My dad was upstairs when we got back. I could hear him in the bathroom, probably washing up for bed.

Kyle looked tall in our living room as he eyed the titles on our bookshelf and the pictures of my mom and dad and me on vacations, sometimes with Cindy and Pam.

"You used to have bangs," he said.

"Don't remind me," I said.

He smiled. Then he walked to inspect my dad's bike, which was resting against the wall in the hallway. I shook my head at the mud that had accumulated around it on the floor. We needed to get better about cleaning.

"Nice ride," he said, touching one of the tires.

"And that's not even his best bike. There's a fancier one out back. My dad sort of became an Activities Person after my mom died. Activities all the time. He spends every weekend on a bike trip or hiking in New Hampshire, and the new thing is rock climbing. It's like an addiction. My aunt says it's a grief coping mechanism and that he'll slow down when he's ready. I guess it could be worse."

"Yeah, not bad as far as addictions go."

"I guess," I said.

I took out my phone and texted my dad upstairs. He had the bedroom television on now. I could hear the theme song to *Nova*. *Kyle is here,* I wrote. *Don't do anything embarrassing, please.*

Tell him I said hello and welcome. Unless that's embarrassing, he texted back seconds later.

I sent back a smiley face, feeling guilty for the first message. He wasn't an embarrassing dad; I was just nervous.

"We should watch *Hanna,*" Kyle said. He was sitting on the couch now, his feet up on our coffee table like he had been here a million times.

Kyle had talked about the movie before; it was his favorite. Yael had said she loved it too.

"It's that good?"

"You'd be so into it," he said. "It's about this young girl, and she's genetically modified to be a killer. It's really clever. And very feminist, or so I'm told by Yael."

I found the film, pressed play, and went into the kitchen to get us water. It was now almost eleven; usually I took the serum drops around now. Ann and I never discussed whether delaying the routine would mess with its effects. In a panic, I ran to the refrigerator and dug out the serum bottle from where I had hidden it, in a brown bag behind the condiments. The vial had to remain refrigerated. I counted on the fact that my dad rarely used ketchup.

"I'm pausing it; you can't miss the beginning!" Kyle yelled from the other room as I let the drops soak the space under my tongue. "The beginning scene sets up the whole thing."

I hurried back with the drinks and fell into the couch, taking a moment to notice that Kyle sat in Whit's spot, with the pillow on his lap that Whit usually put under his feet. I sat down next to him, trying not to let it upset me.

The movie was riveting, as Kyle had promised, and more up my alley than anything I'd watched from Whit's list of favorites. It was violent — the genetically modified girl killed a lot of people — but it was mostly about how she related to the regular humans she met on her journey. The way the girl talked, in staccato, monotone sentences, reminded me of Ann.

I was so into the story that I forgot about my own experiment until Kyle turned to me and asked what I thought so far. He looked excited, maybe nervous. The tops of his cheeks showed a blush. It could mean that the serum was having an effect, that he was feeling an attraction, but it could also mean that the room was warm or that the movie was really good.

Ann and I had made a list of some biological and behavioral indicators to consider during our research, but they weren't as obvious as I thought they would be. I ran through them in my head as Kyle yawned.

We were "mirroring," which was what behavioral psychologists would call simple imitation, what people sometimes do when they find each other attractive. Sometimes people laughed the same way, or copied each other's speech patterns, or even sipped a drink at the same time. But to be fair, Kyle and Yael and I had been mirroring one another ever since we had become friends. We had inside jokes and developed the spoken shorthand that close companions often do.

"I am in love with this movie. It's so good," I told him, turning back to the film, my eyes fixed on Cate Blanchett's rubber smile. "I wonder if Bryan has seen it. He wants to *be* Cate Blanchett."

I turned to Kyle to get a response and was surprised to find his face coming at mine, our mouths attaching for a kiss that was surprisingly not awkward, given how we were sitting and the fact that I didn't see it coming. Our lips fused, mouths closed. After a second or two, he pulled back about an inch and waited for a response. All I could think about was the fact that I had just put the drops under my tongue, and how he probably tasted some of the sugary liquid that was now penetrating my bloodstream.

I thought, in those seconds, that I was also a bit like Hanna, the genetically modified girl in the movie, who, based on what I could see out of the corner of my eye, was about to slaughter more innocent people.

I took a breath, my mouth falling open.

My silence must have served as an affirmation, because Kyle went for another kiss, this time with his mouth open. I made a noise, not one of objection but of confusion, because that's what I was — confused and sort of excited and surprised by the fact that I didn't want to stop. Kyle was only the first subject in this experiment. A test run. There was not supposed to be kissing.

He tipped me back so that my head rested against a couch pillow, and then he was half on top of me, one leg on the couch, one on the floor. Every time he pulled back a little to catch a breath or check my expression, I noticed something new, like the tiny hairs that came out of the top of his T-shirt, or the little smile lines, like baby parentheses, next to his mouth. He ran his hand up my neck as he kissed me, and tucked my hair behind my ear. I shivered and found myself placing my hand on the back of his neck, urging him to continue.

After a few minutes or maybe longer, he pulled back and asked, "Are you okay?" — a question I took to mean, "Do I have permission to do more than just kiss you right now?" The pause lasted long enough to remind me of my original mission.

"Kyle," I said in a rough voice as I peered into his dilated eyes, "have you wanted to kiss me before tonight? Or, like, before the past week? Or is it something that you just decided you wanted to do just now?"

He opened his mouth but snapped it shut before speaking. After another second he asked, "Is that a trick question?"

He was propped up on top of me, his hands on the armrest of the couch behind me. I wanted to ask a more specific question, but I was distracted by his muscle control and how his arms framed my face.

Kyle finally answered by leaning in again to give me another kiss. I placed my hand on his cheek and tried to estimate his temperature. He pulled my hand away and kissed me again.

I attempted to make the mental notes — to pay attention to all the observations I knew I'd want to document later. It wasn't just his attraction that was important; it was my response. My sex drive wasn't something I had even considered. But it seemed that it had been affected by the serum, because why else would I be tracing the line of muscle in Kyle's shoulder while I leaned into his hand on my waist?

He shifted so that his knee fell in between my legs. Then I felt a wave of embarrassment — because this was Kyle, and because it had taken me months to get to this physical place with Whit.

"I want you," Kyle whispered, which made me shift my head to the side and sit up.

This wasn't Whit, and it didn't even seem to be Kyle. He looked totally different, like someone who wanted us to be naked, as opposed to the friend who took me on whiff walks and sent me geeky fan fiction.

"What's wrong?" he said, looking panicked as he sat up.

On the screen, the brutal Hanna calculated her next move.

"I'm sorry, Kyle," I said, my eyes on the television so that I didn't have to look at him. "We should stop right here."

"No, I'm sorry. Did I push it? I didn't mean to move so fast. Really, this can be slow." He was sitting up now, looking concerned. "When I said I wanted you, I meant, like, I wanted to keep kissing. Kissing is great."

"No, I mean, *this* isn't right. We shouldn't be doing this. I'm just upset about Whit, and we're both probably confused because we're alone, without Yael. It's so late . . ."

Kyle froze for a moment, then scrambled off the couch, mumbling that he needed to use the bathroom.

"Wait, I'm sorry," I said.

"No, I'm sorry," he said, his back to me as I followed him through the kitchen. He was almost running.

"Don't apologize—you didn't do anything wrong," I said. "It's just that . . . I think we're tired, and I've been so out of it lately . . ."

He went into the bathroom off the hallway but didn't close the door. He turned on the sink faucet and then leaned over to splash some water on his face.

"Are you okay?" I asked from the doorway.

Kyle grabbed a towel from the rack and patted his face, the drops from his neck falling to his T-shirt.

"No, it's fine. I just feel bad. That was just a thoughtless move on my part. I guess I thought you were interested. I don't know what I was thinking. But it's fine, really."

"No, it's me. This is my fault. I'm the thoughtless one," I mumbled, thinking of what got us here. "I'm so sorry. I don't want you to be upset about this. Please don't be upset about this."

"No, it's totally no big deal," he said. "I should go."

He bounded by me. At some point *Hanna* had finished. The credits rolled down the screen as electronic music played in the background. The soundtrack made me panic; I just wanted to press pause on the whole night and stop Kyle from moving.

"This is totally my fault. Please, don't even think about it again," I said, grabbing the remote and shutting off the television.

"Hey," he said, turning toward me. "It's all good. This happens. Get ready — it happens in college all the time. It's no big deal."

His words felt like a punch.

"Okay," I said, not knowing what else to say. He reached out and grabbed my hand, lifting it up so that my palm was out, and then he awkwardly high-fived it. "See you Monday, Maya," he said, then walked to the door, shutting it hard behind him.

Stunned, I walked in slow motion, turning off all the living room lights, and then went upstairs to my bathroom. I was overheated, my hair slick with sweat, my cheeks the color of red wine. My pupils were dilated — big and brown with light brown halos. Curious, I opened the medicine cabinet and grabbed my thermometer. My temperature was exactly one hundred — high but still inside the margin.

I moved to my bedroom and stood in the middle of it, not knowing what to do. "It's no big deal," I said out loud to comfort myself, and then I stretched out on top of the covers. I considered calling Ann, but it was so late.

Feeling frantic, I jumped up and grabbed my laptop from my desk and brought it into bed with me. There were two new messages in my inbox, one from Ann and one from *Akin, Whitman*. My chest, which had finally stopped its thudding, sped up again. It had been so long since I had seen Whit's name in my email. The night after the breakup, Bryan had moved all of Whit's messages into a password-protected folder so that I wouldn't pore over the old notes.

I double-clicked on Whit's new message first. It was a short note.

Just saying hi. Want to make sure you're doing okay. I thought I saw you near the bowling alley tonight but I'm not sure. Hoping you're all right. — W

I threw my hands over my face, exhaling through my palms, and then closed the message, not sure I should answer. I opened the message from Ann instead. She'd sent it an hour ago.

Check in, please was all she had written.

I began typing my report then, the detailed description of Phase One of our experiment. At first I considered skipping the part where Kyle and I hooked up — the idea of confessing it to Ann seemed strange and embarrassing — but the behavior was part of the results. I had to tell all.

I was as clinical as possible, detailing my heart rate and temperature, as well as Kyle's swift reaction after I'd taken my nightly dose of drops.

Subject One, the email began, with the date and time.

I didn't get to sleep until after three, which is when I finished my written narrative of the results and detailed my questions about the evening.

In the subject line of the email, just to get her attention, I wrote in all caps, *SUCCESS.*

10

I'll admit that I hadn't thought about what might happen if the experiment worked, especially on Kyle. Even if there had been no kissing, a temporary attraction might have caused some confusion and awkwardness. It would be worse with a hookup, which I'd called a *brief physical interaction* in my notes to Ann.

What is a "brief physical interaction"? she wrote back.

We kissed, I responded, my face hot as I typed.

Oh?

Yes, I wrote back. *Just kissing. Then I put an end to it. It only lasted a few minutes, I think. He didn't seem to think it was significant.*

Interesting, she emailed back.

As I typed, I wanted to tell her that it *was* significant, at least to me. At what age did making out with a close friend stop being a big deal? Kyle had dismissed it like we'd accidentally bumped elbows in the hallway.

This kind of thing happens all the time in college, he'd said.

I didn't get it. Before Whit, I had only been kissed twice — once when I was fourteen, by a sixteen-year-old named Beckett on a trip to Yellowstone with my parents, and another time before that, by Bryan, when we were thirteen and trying to figure out if we were capable of sticking our tongues in another person's mouth. Those first kisses still felt like big deals. Then there was Whit, who was the first person to kiss me like an adult, like the kissing could lead to something else.

But Kyle was probably right. I did have to get used to the fact that not all kisses would be significant. At my high school, all hookups were important, because no one disappeared. You saw the person the next day, no matter what. But in college, you could probably make out with a person and maybe never see them again.

During my visits to Whit's dorm, I'd seen students bring strangers back to their rooms and then say goodbye forever the next morning. Some of Whit's friends were in real relationships, but many headed out at ten at night with party plans and fake IDs, and returned at one thirty with someone they had never met before.

To Kyle, the kissing was probably a routine mistake between friends. That was probably a good thing, because it meant that we could go back to normal. But when I got to work on Monday, Kyle wasn't even there. According to Tish at the front desk, he'd called in sick early that morning.

I grabbed my phone to text him to see if he needed anything, but then paused, wondering if he'd want to hear from me. Maybe he wasn't as breezy about the night as he'd seemed.

Yael was sitting in front of her laptop, humming softly. I could tell she'd added some new photos of her girlfriend to the small bulletin board behind her bench. They were tacked under a postcard that showed a pretty beach I assumed was in Israel.

"Hey," I said, standing behind her, and then I moved in front of her, waving my hands so she'd take her earbuds out.

"What's up?"

Her voice was flat, like she was annoyed. I wondered if she suspected something was off, but there was no reason she'd know what happened.

"Sorry," she said, her voice warmer. "I just need to send this note to my adviser."

"Kyle's out sick? Is he okay?"

Yael pushed a curl out of her face and shrugged. "I think something's going around. I'm sure he's fine."

I returned to my bench and began transcription, but I had trouble focusing. I spaced out every few minutes, my mind drifting to memories of Friday night, how easy it had been to kiss Kyle and how quickly he left when it was over. I kept having to rewind the tape and listen to Dr. Araghi say the same thing over again.

At about two, Yael's phone buzzed. She looked at it, typed back a message, and yelled over to me, her earbuds still in, "Kyle's fine. He says hi."

I stopped the tape recorder and walked to her desk. She paused whatever she was listening to and looked up at me from behind her laptop.

"Did he say anything else? Does he need anything?"

"Nope. He was just coming down with something. He probably just needs to sleep it off."

It wasn't the answer I wanted, but I knew Yael couldn't tell me what I wanted to hear. She didn't know whether he and I were okay. She couldn't tell me whether his "hi" was a message of obligation.

Yael's facial expression let me know that my level of concern was strange. I was still standing there, in front of her desk, now staring at her phone, hoping it'd buzz again.

"Great," I said, sounding as casual as I could, then shuffled back to my desk. I was so distracted that it took me two more hours to get through another half-hour of tape.

Right before I left for the day, I decided to text him. I felt compelled.

You need anything?

I stared at the word *Read.* Then the dots appeared as Kyle typed something back. It was probably just seconds, but it felt like minutes.

The dots appeared and disappeared, like he kept changing his mind about what to write.

Nope I'm good.

That was the entire response. After all that time.

I wrote back, *Feel better. You better not have given me germs.*

As soon as I pressed SEND, I wanted to punch through the phone screen to pull back that last part. I shouldn't have made a joke about what happened.

He started typing, but then the dots vanished. I waited, staring at the phone, hoping he'd start writing again, but after several minutes, it was clear the conversation was over.

Later, I hoped my dad would be home, just for a distraction, but as I approached our door, he was pulling out of the driveway. He spotted me and rolled down his window.

"Rock climbing again?" I asked, guessing his destination.

"Yeah. Looks like it's going to rain, so I thought it'd be a good night to practice at the gym. I'm hoping it's late enough that there are no birthday parties. Last time I was there, the place was overrun by kids." He shot me a toothy smile. "No offense, kid."

"None taken, senior citizen," I responded.

"Do you want to come? They'll give you an intro class for free."

His offer made it clear I looked lost.

"No, thanks," I said, trying to be normal. "I'm feeling like a TV night. I'll re-watch *Sherlock* or something."

"Okay. But if you change your mind and go out, try to shoot me a text."

"Yes, sir."

I stared up at my house, overwhelmed by the idea of being by myself for the rest of the night. I wished Bryan didn't have so many rehearsals.

My phone buzzed.

Karaoke? it said, with Bryan's name above the message, like he had read my mind, as always.

YES, I wrote back, my body flooding with relief. I made a detour back down the street in the direction of the T, just a little bit ashamed that I was so scared of spending the night alone. I'd never been that kind of person before.

11

I must have been pretty desperate to agree to a night of karaoke with Bryan and his friends. I had nothing against karaoke, but only when doing it with normal people like my mom and dad. It was a different, more terrifying experience to do karaoke with aspiring actors who believed that if they performed a song dramatically enough, they might end the night with a record deal. Whit had warned me about this. "Never do karaoke with theater people. They like it too much."

The Junior Barders were meeting at the all-ages karaoke bar not far from Boston Common. It was weird in there, a place clearly designed for tourists, with big pictures of Boston's skylines and landmarks on the walls. It was freezing and smelled like beer.

I scanned the faces at the tables until I spotted Bryan near the stage, flipping through the songbook. "Hey," I greeted him.

I hadn't told him about what had happened with Kyle. There had been no time, and I wasn't sure whether I should. Bryan couldn't know about the experiment, so I'd only be able to tell him about the kissing, which I wouldn't be able to explain. I felt strange, never having kept anything from my best friend before.

"Hey," he looked up, his voice urgent. "'Kiss' or 'Rolling in the Deep'?"

"What's 'Kiss'?"

His jaw dropped, and then he placed his hand over his heart. "It's Prince, Maya. It's Prince! 'Kiss'!"

"I don't know everything you know. I choose 'Rolling in the Deep.'"

He mumbled something about making me a new playlist as he registered his selection, and then we sat down at a small table next to Kimberly Katz and a girl I didn't recognize. She had the look of a friend, a shy non-actor like me who was just along for the ride.

Before I could introduce myself to her, feeling like we should bond, a voice boomed over the speakers, "Kimberly K. You're up, Kimberly K."

Kimberly jumped from her chair as if she had just been named an Oscar winner and ran to the stage, grabbing the microphone from the DJ.

I leaned into Bryan and whispered, "If she does 'Let It Go'—or anything from *Frozen*—you have to buy me a soda."

Bryan shushed me and glanced over to Kimberly Katz's friend to make sure she hadn't heard me.

"Sorry," I said, meaning it. I disliked Kimberly Katz, but only because she'd seen Whit more recently than I had.

Her choice was not "Let It Go," but Rihanna's "Stay," a song that Bryan had put on many of my playlists. I loved the song and feared Kimberly would ruin it, but she was a pro and had clearly performed this one before. She hit every note and strolled around the stage with the mike like she was performing at a real concert—like she was begging someone to stick around.

It always amazed me how theater people could be like this, forever on, always ready to make use of a spotlight. I supposed scientists could be naturals too. My mom was always thinking about research. So was Ann.

Whit was like that with his writing. Sometimes he'd jot things down in a little notebook he kept in his back pocket. The ultimate flattery was when he scribbled something down after I spoke.

Kimberly took her seat when it was over, still panting from the performance.

"That was amazing," I said, leaning over, surprising myself.

"Oh my god, thank you!" she screamed so loud that all of a sudden I hated her again.

Bryan's name was called next. "You're up, Adele," I said, patting him on the back.

No one dared sing along when Bryan was performing; he was too good. Even through the fuzzy bar mike, which was probably soaked with beer, his voice was flawless and whatever he wanted it to be. He could sound like Frank Sinatra or Justin Bieber when he wanted to, and for Adele, he made his voice husky, allowing it to crack for effect.

"Your friend is kind of a star."

My trance was broken and I turned to my right, where Asher Forman sat in Bryan's chair.

"He's really, really good," I said, unable to stop myself from beaming. "He's always been this good."

Bryan finished to a room full of whistles and applause, and was greeted on the side of the stage by spectators who wanted to compliment him and shake his hand.

"Instant fan club," Asher said.

"I know. He's going to be famous someday."

It was an awkward thing to say to someone who was sort of famous but probably not as famous as he wanted to be.

"Are you singing?" I asked.

"Yeah. With you. We're up soon."

I shook my head. "Very funny."

"No, really. Prepare yourself. Steal someone's drink if you have to. Loosen up your vocal cords; release your inhibitions."

"I don't sing."

"I promise you won't actually have to sing. Just talk."

"Asher F. Do we have an Asher F.?"

The voice boomed through the speakers, and Asher stood, pulling me up from my seat by my white T-shirt sleeve.

I tried to sit back down, and the crowd began to boo. Bryan noticed me from across the room. I mouthed the word *help,* but he shook his head, looking thrilled.

"You won't have to sing, I swear," Asher whispered in my ear, grabbing my hand to pull me onstage. "I promise it'll be painless."

On the karaoke platform, the lights were blinding, and I could barely make out faces in the crowd. The beat started, and I felt my heart sink into my stomach. I had a new appreciation for Bryan's stage presence, because this was frightening.

It took me a few lines to recognize the song. Taylor Swift. Of course he'd want to sing a song by a woman. There were squeals from the crowd when Asher started, his voice too serious as he sang.

His voice wasn't as thick and smooth as Bryan's. Asher had the strained, thin tenor sound of a pop star. But Asher was more limber onstage, his body moving like a guy who was meant to have backup dancers.

I faced him, both enjoying his performance and panicking each time a new line would pop onto the screen, waiting for the moment when Asher would expect me to contribute. But he kept singing on his own, the audience chiming in to help him during the chorus. *"Wee-ee!"* they sang, before adding, *"are never, ever, ever getting back together."*

Then, just when I thought he was going to let me stand up there silent, he leaned in and whispered, "Come alive, my friend. This is you."

The prompt on the karaoke screen said SPOKEN, and then there were scrolling italicized words — words I knew, thanks to the radio and to Bryan, who had put this song on many playlists. It wasn't quite a rap, just Taylor Swift giving an angry speech to an ex.

I said each word into the microphone, not quite hitting any sort of beat. I did manage to say the final phrase, "like, ever," at the right time and with a little bit of character. That much I could do.

The Barders cheered, and I felt my legs get solid as I relaxed. I even sang the final chorus with him, keeping my microphone as far from my mouth as possible.

"See? No real singing," Asher said, and pulled me in for an unexpected hug when the music ended.

"You're a good Taylor," I said.

"So are you," he said, and then let me go and walked toward the bar. Even though he was only twenty, he'd somehow avoided the fuchsia bracelet for patrons under twenty-one. I was still flushed and shaky from being onstage, and hurried back to my seat before any more attention came my way.

Bryan held up his phone. "I filmed that. I filmed it, and I'm going to watch it every day for the rest of my life."

"I thought I was going to pass out."

"You were awful. You sounded like a fucking robot, and I loved it."

The music started up again for Kimberly Katz, who was back onstage looking somber as the music got louder and I recognized the song.

"Oh, no," I said. "Bryan . . ."

"Nope," Bryan answered, shaking his head. "We're not talking about it."

As she started with the first line of "Let It Go," Bryan whispered, "Fine, we can go home and watch something. But I pick the movie."

Just before we made it out the door, I spotted Asher at the bar and smiled. He raised a drink in my direction and winked.

Hours later, after we had finished watching television with my dad, Bryan went to the guest room and fell asleep, and I went back to my room and opened my laptop.

I still hadn't responded to Whit's email—it seemed there wasn't much to say, at least not yet. But tonight he had emailed again. I took a deep breath as I clicked on the new message, which appeared to have been sent at eight.

Hey, maybe you don't want to hear from me, but I am worried and thinking about you. I know tonight was supposed to be our big night, and maybe it's stupid, but I wanted you to know that I hope you're doing okay. I hope we can talk at some point. I would really like to be friends.

Our big night, I said to myself, checking the date on my phone.

"July tenth," I whispered.

Whit had moved into his apartment today. The roommates were gone for the week. I was supposed to sleep over. We were supposed to have sex. We would have been having it right now, maybe. I fell back onto my bed, thinking of how I might respond to the email.

I heard my dad rattling around in the kitchen, but I couldn't talk to him about this. Something told me that if I mentioned that Whit had reached out at all, my dad would be as miserable as I was. When Whit came into our lives, it was like my dad needed him as much as I did. They met on our third or fourth date—it was supposed to be a romantic evening; at least that's what I had planned for. Whit and I hadn't even kissed yet, but I figured that "Let's sit around and watch a movie" was code for that, so I was nervous and excited and couldn't sleep the night before. Whit arrived at the house and I was ready to pounce, but before we could head to the flat screen to settle in, my dad, incapable of reading a room, invited us to go outside to play with the telescope.

"I'd love to," Whit had said before I could decline.

The next thing I knew, we were all in the backyard taking turns with the massive telescope. Whit was into it, or at least pretended to be, as my dad talked about the meteor shower he was able to catch at Aunt Cindy's the week before.

After an hour passed, I accepted that the night had become a family affair. Whit listened to my dad talk about the middle school science curriculum, our family vacations, and a bunch of other topics that no one would possibly want to hear about. All I kept thinking was that Whit was so kind and enthusiastic, and that it was the first time my dad had been engaged in a conversation with a stranger since my mom had died.

I hit reply and typed, *Thanks for thinking of me,* because at least he had.

12

Ann guessed that it would take a few days to get the Kyle serum out of my system. It was a bit of a guessing game.

My mom's notes showed, based on blood tests and other indicators such as temperature, that she was back to her normal numbers after about a week, but Ann and I hypothesized that it took longer for her to clear the serum because she had been absorbing it daily for more than six months.

Her research suggested that, when taken sublingually over time, the mix would build up in the system for a cumulative effect. My work had been short-term, so after forty-eight hours or so, it felt like I was back to normal. I had trouble describing exactly what I meant by "normal," but once the serum was flushed from my system, it felt like the inside of my body had been reset. My sweat felt pure. It was probably all in my head, but I felt like my insides were lighter and cooler. I could prove that last part, at least, as I was back to my usual 98.7 degrees.

Another piece of evidence was that I slept a ton during those first few days off the formula. Almost twelve hours a night, two days in a row. I knew this might happen based on my mom's notes. On Day Four, I felt like myself again and was back to waking up with ease after eight hours.

Ann agreed that my body had probably restored itself, but she demanded a weeklong break before we moved on to Phase Two of the project. She said it would make the experiment more legitimate, and that the extra time could be used to evaluate the research and consider the second subject.

The break gave me too much time to consider my next steps with Whit. It also forced me to think about what my mom had planned to do with her own research long-term. I wondered whether she intended to stay on the serum forever to maintain whatever it was doing for her and my dad.

It was a sad thing to think about — the idea that maybe my parents weren't as happy as I thought, and that my mom believed she needed this kind of science to maintain her marriage.

Standing in front of Building 68b, wishing I didn't have to go inside and focus on transcription, I wondered what it would be like to have to hide in the bathroom every night, dripping a potion under my tongue for the rest of my life to prolong Whit's interest. Maybe my mom could pull that off, but that wasn't possible for me. I wouldn't want it to be. The goal here was to remind Whit of what we had and to get us back to where we were so we could keep going.

Kyle was officially back to work since taking two days off after Reaction One (R1), which is how Ann and I now referred to the hookup in our notes. I liked calling it R1 because it glossed over what had happened — that I had used a serum to hook up with one of the first friends I had made at school.

Those first three days after Kyle had returned to the office, I'd smiled but kept my distance, mainly afraid that my pheromones were still a match and that I would only make our situation worse. We had taken one whiff walk as a threesome, because it was the routine. The night felt normal — like R1 hadn't happened — until Yael went to the bathroom at the restaurant, and Kyle and I just sat at the table silent, keeping our mouths full of shrimp skewers until Yael returned. We didn't even make eye contact.

Now that I was confident that the serum was out of my system, I flashed a friendly smile at Kyle before getting comfortable at my desk. He smiled back and then resumed cleaning test tubes. Yael muttered a quick "Hey," and kept her head buried in her laptop.

"What's up?" I asked both of them, my voice breezy as I tried to read the energy in the room.

"Someone changed the temperature of the incubator last night," Yael answered, her voice intentionally loud enough for neighboring workstations to hear. "And now I am a day behind, and I might as well have not come in over the weekend because I have to prep this nonsense all over again."

I relaxed as Yael continued her monologue about how she came in to find her neatly prepped and marinating materials ruined by a ten-degree temperature alteration. This was the most common fight in the lab; there were dozens of researchers in all stages of their work and degrees, sharing the same sorters, cooler, and storage areas. They were bound to occasionally and unintentionally mess with one another's materials while tending to their own experiments.

Yael's rant was long and laced with harsh words, but I didn't get the sense that the culprit was even around to hear it.

". . . And whoever it was, maybe you should think about how it would feel to come in and find your warm materials nice and cold, because I could arrange for that!" Yael yelled a bit louder, to mark the end of her tirade.

"Hey, we should go get bubble tea tonight," I said, hoping that one more outing with Kyle would mean I could start texting him again. I missed our daily back-and-forth, and all his games and roommate commentary. I waited and watched as he continued his work.

"I can't. I'm going to yoga," Yael said. "But you guys should go."

I turned to Kyle.

"Sounds good to me," I said, hopeful.

"Depends on what I can get done today," he responded without turning around.

"Okay," I responded, smiling like I took his words at face value. "Keep me posted."

Later, Yael broke the silence by closing her laptop and removing a yoga mat from under her desk.

"She's becoming a yoga person," I said, testing Kyle as Yael ran out. "I don't know if we can be friends with her anymore."

The desperation in my voice made me want to hide under my desk.

"I think it's sort of cool," Kyle shot back. "I might go with her next week."

I saw that he was closing his backpack, preparing to leave.

"You're done already?" I said, my voice too high. "Does that mean there's time for bubble tea?"

"I think I'm going to meet up with a friend who's back on campus for the week. We're going to see if we can get last-minute tickets to the game."

"What kind of game?"

"Red Sox," he said, looking at me like I was an alien for not knowing. He'd never mentioned liking baseball before.

He gave me a long look then, his right hand grasping his workbench like it was the edge of a cliff. I scanned my brain trying to think of something to say, anything to change the mood.

"Have fun," was all I could come up with.

He looked away, like he was disappointed.

I should have chased after him and told him I was confused and sorry, and that I wished the kissing during the movie had never happened because I should have never put our friendship at risk. I wanted to ask why he seemed so casual about the whole thing when clearly he wasn't. But instead I just stood there.

Then, all of a sudden, I was desperate to see Whit. I longed to be comforted by him — or to yell at him for setting off this chain of events that had messed up my world.

I grabbed my phone and did what Bryan had forbidden me to do for weeks now. Alone in the lab space, I opened a browser and typed in the name *Andrea Berger.*

All I knew of her face was what Bryan told me — that she looked like Genevieve Moran from our high school. But I needed to know more.

I sat on my stool, settling in for some research. At first, there was little to discover about the woman who had stolen Whit's heart. Most entries for Andrea Berger led me to older people in other parts of the world.

When I narrowed the search by typing *Andrea Berger* and *Boston University,* I saw a few social media accounts and several student newspaper articles about her work in the film department at the school. There were also race times, which I clicked on first. Andrea Berger had run a half-marathon in California in under two hours. I glanced down at my short legs.

My hands shook as I clicked on one of her profiles. The first photo showed her frozen, mid-laugh, as she was being nuzzled by a large black cat.

"Dammit." I shouted the word at the computer screen loud enough that Tish peeked her head in from the front office.

"Everything okay?"

"It's fine," I spat. "I stubbed my toe. It's nothing."

Tish disappeared back to her desk, and I grabbed my elbows to control my panic. Whit had grown up with two cats, but I'd always been allergic. He had made jokes—at least he said they were jokes—that by being with me, he was condemning himself to a life without his version of man's best friend. Andrea Berger, however, was cat-friendly. Her face looked bright and rash-free as the feline covered her face in saliva. I'd be covered in big red hives.

The photo also showed that she had very straight teeth and auburn hair. The picture was mostly of the cat, but I could tell that Andrea Berger was fit, her thin, muscular arms jutting from her tank top.

I toggled back to my search results and saw that about three entries down there was another social media account, so I clicked again.

It was a worst-case scenario. She was a frequent poster, at least once or twice a day, her life spelled out like a diary entry. Everything she had been doing over the last weeks was chronicled in small bites.

Her bio said simply, *We fell in love, alone on a stage.* It was ambiguous, but I jumped to the conclusion that it was a reference to Whit. They took classes together. On stages. Sort of. For a second or two, it felt like someone was standing on my chest.

I threw my arms up to my head, and my elbow knocked a burette that someone had left near my bench, causing it to fall to the floor.

"Dammit," I said again, leaning over to pick it up before someone saw that I had dropped expensive lab equipment.

"Maya!" Tish ran into the room. I must have been louder than I thought. "Sweetheart, are you sure you're all right?"

"Sorry, sorry," I said, clutching the glass measuring tube. "I didn't break anything."

"It's okay if you did. Just be careful, okay?" Tish made her concerned-camp-counselor face and then disappeared to her desk again.

I turned back and tried to steady my breathing. I mumbled

Andrea Berger's bio aloud, like I could decode it. *"We fell in love, alone on a stage."*

"Arcade Fire," a voice said behind me.

I turned around to find Jawad, one of the guys in the lab, standing a few feet behind me.

"What?"

"I've seen them four times."

"What?" My voice was shaky and loud.

"'*We fell in love, alone on a stage.*' Those are Arcade Fire lyrics."

"Are you kidding me?" I asked.

Jawad looked confused.

"No. I'm not."

I tried to decide whether this decoding of Andrea Berger's profile made me feel better or worse. Perhaps the falling-in-love-on-a-stage thing was not about Whit. Maybe she was just a big Arcade Fire fan.

But that was worse.

Arcade Fire, one of Whit's favorite bands, was also an inside joke in our relationship.

One night, not long after Whit and I started dating, he and Bryan were at my house, watching television. Arcade Fire was the musical guest on a late-night show, and after a few minutes of listening to their performance, Bryan proclaimed in his most authoritative voice, "This is horrendous."

"They're fantastic," Whit had said.

"Nope," Bryan replied, shaking his head, "This is nonsense, just like every hipster band you listen to. That one idiot is playing a zither. Look, Maya, that's a zither."

I looked away, trying not to laugh as Whit adjusted his position on the couch and got defensive.

"These people, they make real music, with instruments," Whit said. "All you listen to is . . . people like Justin Timberlake, someone whose music is a direct rip-off of what's come before him.

"I mean, this," Whit continued, pointing to the television, "this is new. This is actually original music."

"You do not say that," Bryan snapped, his eyes serious. "You do not say that about Justin Timberlake." Bryan pointed at the television then, where Arcade Fire's frontman now looked directly into the camera, like he was listening, "This is what is wrong with music nowadays. The singers can't sing. And what was that nonsense you made me listen to the other night?"

"Interpol."

"Whatever. Interpol. Yes. Boring. These bands — it's all a pyramid scheme. You're being manipulated in some sort of alt-rock pyramid scheme invented by guys with beards who believe that they have the right to your time and money even though they're just standing there, mumbling or playing a goddamned zither, without even knowing how to use their voices. Singing counts for something!"

Whit paused, clearly unable to come up with anything to say. Then Bryan started doing an impression of the lead singer that was ridiculous but kind of accurate, and even Whit was laughing as he pelted Bryan in the head with popcorn.

After that, Bryan and I called all of Whit's moody music "zither-rock," and when Whit bought tickets to Arcade Fire's Boston show months later, I whispered "pyramid scheme" in Bryan's ear and he couldn't keep a straight face.

Now Whit was with a girl who referenced Arcade Fire in her social media bio, and the lyrics made reference to falling in love on a stage, which is where she had probably met Whit, on a stage at Boston University, while I had been a clueless high school senior daydreaming about what life would be like with my boyfriend after I finally graduated. I put my head down on my workbench and tried to steady my breathing.

13

Whit had taken me to this theater space before. He liked to have his film-major friends read drafts of his scripts here while he sat in the audience and made notes for himself. The seats were arranged as bleachers, like the kind you'd find in a gymnasium. The sides were covered by black sheets that hung haphazardly to hide props.

Like a zombie unable to control my own path, I had traveled there straight from the lab. Andrea Berger's most recent social media post had read *Black box read-through!!*, so I knew she'd be here.

I don't know why I was so desperate to see her in person. I knew it would make me feel worse, and that it was reckless, but that hadn't stopped me. All I wanted was a glimpse. I tried to talk myself out of going at least three times during the half-hour T ride to the BU campus, but my feet kept moving. Step after step, toward a horrible decision.

For all the signs about campus security, it was easy to enter the building without a student ID, and even easier to make my way into the black-box space without being noticed. The night's rehearsal appeared to be a lights-off affair, so it was easy to shuffle into the space beneath the bleachers without anyone knowing I was there.

The view wasn't great because of the black sheets draped on all sides of me, but there were pockets of light that gave me a sense of what was happening onstage. Two girls read dialogue from pages they held in their hands.

It wasn't until they started speaking that I came to terms with where I was and just how low I had sunk in the past two hours. Kyle had blown me off, and now I was hiding under bleachers at a college I didn't attend so that I could see my competition. Still, I wasn't going anywhere.

I kept as motionless as I could to remain undetected. My breath was shallow, and I crossed my arms so that I wouldn't hit anything and make noise.

The words sounded familiar, I thought. The women onstage took turns reading their lines, but otherwise it was quiet. This wasn't Andrea Berger's script; it was Whit's. I had read these lines before, with Whit, at my house, after he'd written them.

"Okay," a female voice said from offstage.

Then I saw her, Andrea Berger, walking toward the actresses, her feet in flip-flops that made a popping noise as they smacked the ground beneath her.

"Sorry to interrupt again," she said. "I was just thinking, can we try it faster? Almost like you're finishing each other's sentences."

Her voice was thin in a way that made her sound young. Not nasally, but higher than mine. She looked different in person, with new, perfect bangs that were straight and stopped just short of her eyebrows. She was more beautiful than Genevieve Moran, and a lot more stylish. She wore tight jeans and a pale blue tank top. Her arms were half-marathon, I-go-to-the-campus-gym arms.

"I agree," bellowed a voice from above. "Let's pick up the delivery."

I slapped my hand over my mouth. It was Whit's voice coming from the bleachers. He was here—and sitting on top of me.

"I think it needs to be very fast. Like—line, line, line, line," he said while clapping along with each word, giving the actresses a cadence.

The bleachers squeaked and rattled as he descended the steps to the small stage. Then he was in front of me, just there, existing, wearing an outfit I knew—his Cape Cod T-shirt and those dark jeans—looking the same as he always had, but also like some stranger because I hadn't seen him in weeks.

There was a part of me that couldn't believe he was alive and animated. He should have been frozen like Han Solo in *The Empire Strikes Back* since the breakup, stuck in a block of ice waiting to be unthawed for our reconciliation.

As my brain attempted to process all of it—where I was, what was happening, how he looked, and what he was wearing—my body buzzed. It was my cell phone on vibrate in my backpack. It buzzed again and made a soft rattling noise against something in my bag.

I slid my backpack down my arms in a desperate attempt to find and silence the phone before Whit and Andrea Berger noticed the sound. Whit paused and looked behind him, trying to find the source of the noise.

When it buzzed again, I grabbed the bag, lunged through the black sheet, and bolted out the back door, hoping no one saw me. I kept running, just in case someone had followed me, until I found the closest Green Line stop.

I didn't check the phone until I was safely transferred to the Red Line and was crossing the river back to Cambridge. The buzz had come from Bryan.

Wanna hang out? the message said. *I'm done with rehearsal!*

Please, I responded.

Do you have food? he wrote back seconds later.

We can order.

Ok. Will be there in half hour.

Later, I confessed to Bryan what I did, and he scolded me, although he admitted to being impressed with my "sit-com high jinks."

"There's no way they would have seen you with stage lights on," he assured me. "And, for the record, if Whit left you for someone who had used an Arcade Fire lyric as her bio, he's unworthy."

"A lot of people like Arcade Fire," I said, defeated.

"A lot of people are stupid," Bryan responded.

14

If we're going to stay on schedule and finish this by the end of the summer, I need your second sample by the end of the week.

I stared at Ann's text, racking my brain to think of a subject that met our needs for the second phase of the experiment. It needed to be someone I didn't know well, who had no real opinion of me. That was our Phase Two — seeing whether an indifferent acquaintance would be swayed by my pheromones. It needed to be a stranger, but someone I knew I would see for a test of the serum. I also needed their DNA.

I scrolled through the address book in my phone, hoping to spot a name that might be a good fit, as my dad, Yael, and I arrived on Boston Common for Bryan's first performance of *All's Well That Ends Well.* My dad was holding a large bouquet of yellow roses; he always bought flowers for Bryan's opening nights, which only fed Bryan's love for him.

I had invited both Kyle and Yael to the play. They still hadn't met him, and Yael, in particular, was desperate to be introduced to the character at the center of all of my best stories. Kyle had been excited about it too, but that was before the experiment and the aftermath. After we'd all arrived at the lab that morning, he said he'd be skipping the show because he was exhausted.

"But this is our big outing to Boston," Yael whined. "All you have to do is lie down on a blanket and watch."

"Not even a blanket," I chimed in. "We rented fancy reclining chairs right up front. And my dad is bringing thermoses of his special

Prosecco drink. It's like two percent Prosecco and ninety-eight percent grape juice, but still, it's tasty."

I felt a hollowness in my chest as I watched Kyle react, his eyes darting away, his head making a slow, horizontal shake as he turned himself around, back to face his computer.

"You guys go," he said, his back to us. "We'll just do something else next week. You know I have no attention span anyway."

"So disappointing," Yael responded with more volume than necessary. It was the kind of too-loud Yael reaction that ordinarily would have had Kyle and me sharing a stifled laugh, but he'd already plugged his ears with his headphones.

After an almost silent day, Yael and I took the T to the Common and found my dad guarding the reclining lawn chairs in the second row. He looked excited, which made me forget my own misery for the moment. I liked my dad like this, looking genuinely happy, even though he wasn't in motion, on a rock or on a bike. Seeing him at the play reminded me of how he used to be when he was someone who could sit still for more than fifteen minutes.

"Where's Kyle?" my dad asked after noticing that we had arrived one person short.

"Not feeling well," I said.

"I don't believe that," Yael said, dropping her bag next to one of the reclining chairs.

"You don't?" I asked, clearing my throat

"He's been weird and depressed all week," she answered casually. "I assume he's freaking out about his adviser meeting. He told me they'll make a decision soon about whether he can go back to school."

"Oh," I said.

Maybe none of this was about me.

"Kirk? Maya?"

We whipped around when we heard our names. I was about to pepper Yael with questions about Kyle's behavior and his upcoming meeting, but the familiar voice silenced me. I scanned the faces in front of me until I found Whit two rows behind us. I took a step back, tripped on my own backpack, and fell into my dad, who steadied me and left his hands on my shoulders for support.

I should have anticipated that Whit might be there. He'd been a theater person for most of his life, and he was in the audience for Junior Barders events long before I knew him.

Whit was standing with a bottle of iced tea in his hand. Next to him, Andrea Berger smiled too sweetly at me, like I was a kid who'd fallen off her bike.

She looked even prettier than she had in the black-box theater. Her face was dewy, like she was in a makeup commercial. She wore a loose, short sundress and somehow managed to have no mosquito bites on her legs, even though it was July.

"Kirk," Whit said again, cutting through a row of seated spectators to approach my dad, who let go of me to give him a hug. They went big with their embrace, like they were long-lost relatives. It made my chest tight.

"Hey, Maya," Whit said next, his voice soft.

It was Yael's tap on my arm that made me realize I hadn't responded.

"Yeah," I said back.

It wasn't an appropriate answer, but it was all I could manage. I was still focused on Andrea Berger, who now stared at the ground. I wondered if she had to blow-dry her bangs to get them to look like that, or whether she just woke up that way. They were so straight.

We probably stood there in silence for only another few seconds, but it felt longer. The three of us just passed awkward facial expressions back and forth until Yael said, in a command, "We should sit. It's going to start, right?"

"Yes," Whit said, relieved. "Well, it was great to see you guys."

Before I could respond, he was back with Andrea Berger on a blanket.

My dad turned to me, panic in his eyes, as Yael took my hand and pulled me down into my seat. "Just sit and relax," she said.

My dad sat to my left and handed me two silver water bottles filled with his special juice drink. I passed one to Yael.

"You're corrupting a minor," she whispered to him over my lap.

"I'm teaching her that alcohol isn't something you consume in excess for the purposes of getting drunk. This is good wine. Plus, after what just happened, she deserves it."

"Fair enough," she said. "I hope mine is strong."

"I want to disappear," I said in an exhale before taking a sip of the beverage.

"Don't be dramatic," Yael responded.

"Okay, fine, I want to leave."

"Honey, we're here for Bryan," my dad said, leaning over and placing his hand on my head. "I know it's hard, but let's just focus on him. He's going to be looking for us in the audience. This is his night."

I nodded. "You're right."

I heard a few *shhh* noises as a group of Junior Barders took the stage wearing frilly, lace-collared costumes. Asher Forman's dark blue suit was clean and well-tailored, while the other actors, the high-schoolers, looked as though they were in attire they had borrowed from people who were not quite their size.

Asher had one of the first few lines, but as he opened his mouth, his voice was overtaken by someone in the center of the crowd, a girl who screamed, "Marry me, Asher!" Her outburst was followed by more *shhh*-ing and laughter.

He nodded briefly in the direction of the outburst, looking like a real lord with the scarf around his neck, and continued his dialogue with the other actor.

Then it was time for Kimberly Katz. She looked devastated and had lots of lines.

I am undone: there is no living, none,
If Bertram be away. 'Twere all one
That I should love a bright particular star
And think to wed it, he is so above me:
In his bright radiance and collateral light
Must I be comforted, not in his sphere.

I didn't really understand it, but the words *not in his sphere* rang in my ears. Whit was in Andrea Berger's sphere, two rows back.

My dad must have seen my face fall because he handed me a paper towel from his snack bag. I blew my nose louder than I meant to and then whipped around to see whether Whit had noticed. He was obscured by a woman passing through the row to find her seat.

"Save you, fair queen!"

I turned to the stage again when I heard Bryan's voice. His feet were close to the edge, and he was wearing the lightweight tunic he'd tried on for me a week ago. He peered down at me, shifted his eyes to my dad, and then blinked. It was a quick glance, one that would go unnoticed by the audience, but I grinned, knowing that he was now performing for us.

"What is this play about?" Yael whispered, her voice almost soundless for once. "Is this supposed to be funny?"

"I don't know," I whispered back, remembering Asher's description. "That's the problem with this one. It's not a comedy or a tragedy."

The rest of the show had all the staples of an opening-night high school performance, even though the Barders were almost professionals. One actor forgot his lines. There were a few big crashing noises that came from backstage.

Bryan was incredible. He had grown so much as a performer over four years, and when he shared scenes with Asher Forman, who was more skilled than I thought he'd be, I got chills thinking of all that my friend could accomplish when he did this for real.

At some point I looked over to see my dad with tears in his eyes. It was like he was watching his own kid.

I wondered whether Whit wished he was sitting with us. Bryan was our shared person, the friend who brought us together. At the end of the play, when my dad and Yael and I stood up to whistle and applaud, I heard Whit shout "Go, Bryan!" behind us. Maybe he wanted me to hear.

The last I saw of Whit that night was his back. He ran out before the end of the bows, with the entire cast still onstage, his hand in Andrea Berger's. It looked as though they were trying to escape Boston Common before the rest of the crowd. It hurt, because I thought he might try to talk to me one more time. It was also odd because Whit once told me never to leave a show until the curtain call was over. He said it was an insult to the cast.

During the last bow, Bryan blew a kiss toward my dad from the stage, and my dad clapped louder and whistled, always oblivious that Bryan was messing with him.

Then Asher Forman stepped forward and took two deep bows in front of the group. On his way down for a third, he spotted me, held my gaze for a second, and then clownishly crossed his eyes. I screamed like I was at a rock concert.

That's when I realized my second subject was right in front of me.

15

I gasped when I saw the inside of Ann's apartment.

I expected her to live in a dingy grad-student cave, the kind with crumbling walls and uneven floors, but when I arrived at the address, it was the opposite — an airy loft in a modern apartment building near Central Square with a nice elevator and fancy restaurants on the bottom floor.

Her clothes were also a shock. I had never seen Ann in anything but dark denim, black cotton, and leather — what Kyle and Yael called her Dragon Tattoo attire. But tonight she wore gray leggings and a big baby-blue sweatshirt. She looked younger, like someone I'd be friends with.

It would be difficult not to tell Kyle and Yael about this, the fact that I'd seen Ann after-hours, and that she owned an item of clothing that was almost pastel.

"Come in," Ann said, ushering me into the small area by the door where her leather jacket hung on a hook.

"Great building," I said, adding an "Oh, wow!" once I realized that what I thought was a studio was actually the first of three rooms. The place looked like it belonged in a fancy design magazine. "This is gorgeous."

"Thank you," she said softly as she removed a teapot from a burner on her shiny silver stove. "Tea?"

I nodded, still in awe of the place.

"My parents are very wealthy," Ann said without looking up as she went into the kitchen and poured hot water into mugs. "They're not great parents, but they make up for it with money." She paused, her grip tight on the teapot. "You were lucky to have your mother."

I could have followed up with some questions, but I was distracted by the beautiful photography prints on the walls, which reminded me of my mom's taste in art. Our house was filled with abstract photos she found during local studio tours.

I walked past several framed pieces on my way to the big gray couch.

"We'll eat," Ann said, bringing in two plates with grilled-cheese sandwiches on them. "I've been living on grilled cheese these days," she said. "I hope you're not lactose intolerant."

"I eat everything," I said. "Also, good news: I have a perfect subject for Phase Two."

"Maya," Ann said, leaning back into the couch with the small plate in her lap, "are you sure you want to continue?"

She said this in the most maternal voice I'd ever heard her use. In the lab, she was as she'd always been, cold and robotic, like we barely knew each other. But when she opened the door to her apartment, it was as if she'd transformed into someone else.

"I have some concerns about how this is working out for you," she said. "I want you to talk about what happened with Kyle before we move on. It seems worth discussing."

I didn't want to talk about that. Fearing that she was about to tell me she wanted to stop the experiment, I tried to distract her.

"I got my dorm assignment — my first choice. Simmons Hall."

The letter had come that week; not only had I been given my first choice, but I'd snagged a single. Simmons Hall was one of MIT's stranger buildings. Some people said it resembled a sea sponge, but to me, it looked like it was made of children's building blocks. I'd wanted to live there ever since I'd seen it when I was a kid.

My dad and I had celebrated the dorm news by going to Target and buying a bunch of dorm things — crates for storage, a mostly purple quilt that reminded me of my duvet cover at home, and a beanbag that my dad claimed would be "very cool" for company.

"Maya," she said, ignoring my news, "I asked you if you thought it was appropriate to continue the experiment, and I'm going to ask again. We've talked about what happened, sort of. We talked about it clinically. But we didn't talk about the aftermath."

"I logged in all my temperatures after the serum. I wrote up all the physical changes."

"Yes, but I'm speaking of your qualitative observations days after the experiment. I have to ask — how is Kyle? I saw you guys in lab today. You weren't interacting like you used to."

The truth was that Kyle was fine; he just didn't want to deal with me. The awkwardness had improved in the two weeks since our evening together, but only enough to make us functional. We'd managed to bond over Ann when she dashed through the lab wearing thick, dark pants and her leather jacket on an eighty-degree day.

"How is she not sweating?" I had whispered before turning back to my work.

"Vampires don't sweat," Kyle responded, and we grinned at each other like we used to.

I had reveled in the normalcy of the moment, but the status quo had not been fully restored. On the one night we'd taken a whiff walk, he rushed through the experience, claiming he was starving and that we needed to hurry up and get to dinner. The normal parts of dinner weren't really normal. At the skewers place, he barely ate. Yael seemed oblivious and filled the gaps in the conversation with talk about an ex-girlfriend who'd recently posted old pictures of one of their trips to a beach in Tel Aviv to her Facebook profile.

"Who does this?" Yael had asked us. "Why would you post a picture of your ex-girlfriend from six years ago on your Facebook page?"

"You're still Facebook friends with your ex?" Kyle asked.

"No!" Yael shouted, prompting the table behind them to look our way. "I de-friended her years ago. Her profile is public."

"Why are you looking?" Kyle asked.

"Because she's my ex-girlfriend. You're telling me you don't google your ex-girlfriends? Maya, you're telling me you don't google Whit?"

"We all do things we shouldn't do, but the point is, we shouldn't do them," I muttered.

Yael mumbled what I assumed was a Hebrew swear word and looked down at her plate.

After dinner, Kyle bailed again. "You guys go ahead — I just need to check on something back in the lab," he said, and left us.

"What do you think that was about?" I asked Yael as we watched him run.

"A girl, I think," Yael said, shrugging. "A few days ago, when he told me he had to 'chat with someone from another lab,' it turned out he had hooked up with one of the techs from next door — the one who wears those sleeveless turtlenecks. He admitted it the next day."

"He hooked up with her?" I was surprised by the rage in my voice.

It wasn't just that he had hooked up with Turtleneck Girl, it was that he had told Yael about it and not me. Also, if he was capable of hooking up with other people, then I shouldn't have to be up at night worrying about how we'd ruined our friendship.

"Whatever. He can do whatever he wants," I said before Yael could speak.

I didn't want to explain any of my confusion about Kyle to Ann, who was now waiting for me to make a case to continue. I needed to downplay any negatives.

"The thing is," I started, thinking of a way to sum up the aftermath of the tests so that Ann would allow me to continue the project, "it's awkward because Kyle and I are friends, and then we kissed. But what happened between him and me . . . it's not relevant to our project, and really, that won't be a concern with the next two subjects."

Ann arched one of her brows.

"Maybe I should have picked a different subject," I admitted. "Maybe Kyle and I had become too close. I also should have stopped that kiss. It was just late, and I was confused, I guess."

Ann placed the soda can she'd retrieved from the kitchen on the short bookshelf next to the couch. I noticed that she owned a copy of *The Dispossessed,* which was a staple of my mother's collection.

"Did my mom give you that book?" I asked.

"Which one?" Ann asked.

"*The Dispossessed.* It was one of her favorites. We have two copies at home."

She cleared her throat. "I bought it at a used bookstore after your mom died. I knew she liked it. I haven't read it yet."

"I tried to read it when I was in high school, but I couldn't get through it. It's weird; I sort of don't like reading science fiction. Maybe that's a bad sign. My mom loved it, which I find odd, because most sci-fi doesn't make much sense when you think about the science. I mean, she even loved time-travel books. She loved teleportation books, even though she could tell you why it would never be possible."

"Maya," Ann said, clearing her throat and eyeing the One Direction binder, which sat on the other side of the couch, "you're the one choosing these subjects. We didn't talk about your feelings for them and how this experiment might affect your life."

"I didn't think it would," I admitted. "I mean, my feelings for Kyle are what they've always been. He and Yael are, like, my closest friends now, if you don't count Bryan."

Ann nodded. "I ask this without judgment, Maya, and I'm treating you like a real colleague — like your mother would have treated me — so please don't be offended when I ask, why did you reciprocate with Kyle? Why do you think that happened?"

"I don't know," I said, because really, I didn't. "It's like I said in my notes — I felt physically altered. My temperature was up. I was flushed just like him. It was almost like I was responding to his pheromones too, like my body knew we were suddenly a match. I wish my mom were here, because I'd ask her to get more specific about whether she believed the serum affected the person taking it."

"I wish your mom were here too."

I watched Ann as she pulled a stray thread from her sweatshirt. Her eyes were glassy.

"It must be hard for you without Mom," I said.

It was the same statement that was often directed at me. *Must be hard.* I knew there was no good answer.

Ann smiled.

"She was a good friend and an incredible mentor. She's the reason I chose MIT. Dr. Araghi is trying to work with me, but it's not like it was. I just have to figure out where to go from here. I really thought I'd have a career with your mom."

I placed the grilled-cheese plate on the coffee table and pulled a yellow couch pillow onto my lap.

"I wish I had known her like you did. I mean, we were really close. But I didn't know her like a real friend. I wish I had known the person who did all of this." I pointed to the binder, to the experiment. "She never seemed like someone who would have done secret research. I wish I could have known her as that kind of person."

"You weren't supposed to know her like I knew her," Ann said in the flat tone I was learning not to take too personally. "She was your mother, not your friend or colleague. You knew her as you should. That's how it's supposed to work. Our parents are our parents."

She shook her head before I could respond.

"I'd like you to consider your own mindset as you document your findings, Maya. Spend the weekend writing out some more detailed thoughts about the variables that could have been at play with Subject One before, during, and after the serum. It's relevant, at least to me. I want you to get more specific about what changed that night."

I nodded.

"As for this second subject, I'll need to begin that serum soon. We need to stick to our calendar. Once we hit mid-August, the lab is going to be crowded with the kind of people who notice when something is missing."

"Do we even have to do the second subject?" I tested. "Can't we just move on to Whit?"

Ann stood up and brought our plates to the kitchen. I followed her and stood in the doorway as she washed dishes.

"It seems to me that the second subject is even more important now," she said over the running water. "It turns out you were unclear about the nature of your relationship with your first subject. I think it's important to try this with a stranger, someone with whom you share almost no emotional history."

I nodded, knowing that my desire to skip the second step was about impatience, not science. Whit hadn't checked in since the run-in at Bryan's performance on the Common.

"I have a pretty good Subject Two," I said. "A perfect test case. No emotional bond at all on either side. No potential for weird aftermath. He'll leave town in a few weeks."

"And you have access to this person's DNA?" Ann asked.

I brought out my backpack and removed a plastic bag, which held Asher's jacket.

"It's on his jacket, which was in my bedroom."

Ann's eyebrows arched again.

"It's not like that. This guy has never been in my bedroom. He's a friend of Bryan's who let me borrow his jacket, and I brought it home, but I swear, there's no bond there. I just keep forgetting to return the jacket. The guy is in the play with Bryan this summer. He knows me as Bryan's sidekick."

"Sounds good," Ann said, just before letting out a yawn. "Let me drive you home."

"You have a car?"

"I told you, my parents are well off. I don't use it much, but it's late."

"I'm fine to walk," I said.

"It's after ten. Your mother wouldn't want me to let you wander around Central Square by yourself."

"I'm out this late all the time," I said, groaning like I used to with my mom. Ann was basically the same age as Yael, but she acted so much older. I followed Ann as she slid on sandals and left the apartment with her keys. I was both annoyed and somewhat comforted that I was in the presence of an overprotective-parent type. It had been a while since I'd been policed.

We were mostly silent on the ride back, trading yawns over the voices on public radio. When she pulled up to Gardenwood, I could barely keep my eyes open.

As I fiddled with my keys in front of the house, I could hear her motor running, waiting for me to get safely inside.

This time when I checked my email before bed, there was a third message from Whit, with a new subject line that said *Another super awkward message.*

I let out a laugh and opened it, less scared to read one of his notes now that I'd survived seeing him in person.

Hey, it was nice to see your dad, and Bryan was great, it said. *It was also nice to see your face. Please let me know if we're allowed to get coffee like humans. If it's too much, I understand, but it would be nice to hang out. — W.*

I hit reply.

Soon, I wrote. *I just have to figure out some stuff and then I think I'll be ready.*

He responded within seconds, the new message popping up in bold. *Great. It would mean a lot.*

Okay, I wrote back.

Great, he responded again before I had time to breathe.

I shut the computer down then, forcing myself to quit while I was ahead.

16

The Boston Shakespeare Project had a big private party midway through its summer run. The expensive celebration was called the Midsummer Soiree.

Unlike the group's official fundraising events, where actors were expected to work the room, charming donors, the Soiree was the cast's chance to drink too much and let loose.

The teens in the Junior Barders program had no business being invited to the festivities—if their parents knew what happened at the event, they'd probably sue—but the kids were welcomed every year and managed to keep everyone's misdeeds a secret.

Bryan first brought me to the Midsummer party during his second Junior Barders summer, when he was King Oberon. I was surprised to see that he had not exaggerated the scale of the event; it was, as promised, the most over-the-top fete I'd ever seen.

The hosts of the annual affair were Bradley and Nicholas Epstein, a local couple who gave tons of money to theaters around town. They lived in a colonial historic home off Centre Street in Jamaica Plain, steps from a historic community theater, which was also on their list of beneficiaries.

This year's party was already packed when Bryan and I arrived at seven. We could see bodies through the windows and hear Beyoncé playing from the street. Bryan clapped his hands as we approached the front door. "Look!" he shouted. "It's happening!"

I followed his eyes and spotted the top of a tent that had been set up in the backyard. I couldn't even begin to guess what Bradley and Nicholas had done to the house for the affair this year.

Last summer, they'd decorated all the rooms to resemble different Shakespeare productions. There was a cauldron in the kitchen with catering staffers dressed up like witches for *Macbeth,* and a *Tempest* tent out back that had a wind machine and sprinklers. That last feature became too popular with the drunk guests, and by the end of the night, they had ripped the plastic down and were using it like a Slip 'N Slide.

"Think this party will have a theme?" I asked as we made our way through the door. "How would they decorate the house like *All's Well That Ends Well*?"

"It could be . . . something Parisian. Or Italian."

"I still don't understand the point of this play."

"It's not about the point; it's about the story."

"Nothing really happens."

"You weren't paying attention, then."

I wore a loose sundress, which Bryan said looked like a bag with flowers on it. Maybe so, but that would be better for the experiment.

"Remember, you are the control," I had whispered to myself in the mirror before we left, allowing myself some Vaseline on my lips and one stroke of mascara on each eye, which was all that had been on my face the last two times I'd seen Asher.

Once inside, Bryan slammed the front door harder than he intended to, and then the Epsteins' dog was on us, barking wildly and hopping up on our knees.

"Rita!" a man yelled, running after her. "Rita! No. No, girl."

The fuzzy terrier stopped and barked at me twice, its eyes full of so much rage I retreated until my back was against the door.

"Rita," the man commanded again, causing the dog to spin around to face its master.

They stared at each other then, like they were having some sort of silent conversation. Then Rita ran away, her head down in shame, as if she had been sent to her room.

"Hello, hello, come in," the man said after Rita's departure. "Nick Esptein. I'm so sorry. I don't know what's gotten into her."

"Well, she's a dog," I said.

Nick glared at me for a second, like I had insulted him.

"We slammed the door too hard. I'm sure it upset her," I added.

"Well, she knows better," Nick said.

Bryan stepped in front of me. "I don't know if you remember me —I'm Bryan Russo, one of the Junior Barders, and this is my friend Maya."

"Of course! The fairy king! And now Parolles!" Nick pronounced the character name in a French accent. Or maybe Italian. I couldn't tell. "We're big fans. Welcome, welcome. The other Junior Barders are out back. Ignore the adult debauchery in the living room."

We followed him through the house to get to the backyard, passing the living room, where I could see a pack of adults smoking something in a circle.

I also spotted what appeared to be a new hand-painted antique piano in the corner of the room. The Epsteins kept their place looking like a museum and added to their collection of antique musical objects every year. Bryan tugged on my hand to make sure I was keeping up. Nick stopped when we got to the kitchen, where a man in a tie and sport coat, whom I recognized as Bradley Epstein, inspected a tray of stuffed mushrooms on the counter. Behind them, the actor who played the clown poured whiskey into a tumbler.

"Bryan!"

The piercing voice of Kimberly Katz was unmissable, especially because she was shouting and perhaps already drunk.

She came into the kitchen from a sliding-glass door that opened into the backyard. She wore a sundress similar to mine, but hers fit better because she was taller. Mine went to my ankles, but seeing hers, I realized it was probably supposed to hit midcalf. I tried to correct my posture, suddenly feeling like a toadstool.

"Maya," Kimberly said, reaching her hands to my shoulders and straightening my dress, "you look adorable."

"You guys look like twins," Bryan said, eyeing the red and yellow flowers that covered both our dresses. I glared at him.

"Come outside. There's croquet. And everything's French!" Kimberly grabbed Bryan's hand, and he followed.

"I knew it! Come!" he yelled back to me. I followed until I got to the patio, where I spotted my subject.

Asher sat on the back porch, sipping something clear from a tumbler glass. I sat down next to him and took one of the plastic champagne flutes that were lined up on the table.

"What is this?" I asked, taking a sip. It tasted a little like my dad's spiked grape-juice concoction, but it was pink.

"They're calling it Puck's Potion or something, but I think it's just wine and soda water," he said.

"It tastes like cough syrup, but sort of in a good way," I said.

Only one drink, I told myself. More than that, and I wouldn't be able to concentrate on my reason for being there.

I'd spent days dropping the second serum under my tongue, and I figured that the fate of the second phase of the experiment rested on this night. The party might be my only chance to see Asher, at least offstage. He'd probably pack up and get out of town as soon as he was finished with the last Barders performance, which was only a week away.

"These guys must be so rich. This place is crazy," he said. His eyes were on the pack of Junior Barders who were attempting to start a game of croquet on the lawn.

"Yeah. Everything in the house looks breakable. I can't believe they let people come over and get wasted around their stuff."

"So," Asher said, ignoring my comment and turning his chair toward me, "you're officially a hanger-on, like a Shakespeare groupie? Just coming to all the parties?"

It sounded like an insult, but he was smiling, so I tried to relax.

"Hey, I help Bryan memorize lines every year. That earns me rights to the parties, especially this one."

"Fair enough," Asher said, finishing his drink and reaching for a champagne flute. Suddenly my goal for the night didn't seem so easy. I was supposed to do what I did with Kyle — spend time with this person and decide whether he showed signs of attraction that he hadn't before. But with the alcohol and all the distractions at the party, it would be difficult to tell what was causing his interest or lack thereof. With Kyle, at least, I knew how he usually behaved, which gave me some basis for comparison. Asher seemed like the kind of guy who got bored every few minutes no matter who he was with, so how would I be able to guess?

Asher tapped his foot on the patio like he was nervous. I noticed that his eyes kept finding all the exits — the back gate and then the garage door. He was planning his escape.

"I'm beginning to think you hate parties."

"What gave me away?" he said, smiling before taking a gulp of his drink. "It's too crowded. I hate crowds."

He placed the plastic glass on the table and looked over at me. "How bad would it be if we took a walk?"

"You want to leave? There's free booze here. And probably, like, sixteen rooms full of French food," I said.

"Just a break," he said. "You can blow your nose on my clothes like last time. Any item of clothing you want."

"Hey," I said, grinning. "I didn't blow my nose. I just wiped snot on your jacket, ever so gracefully. You make it sound so intentional. Also, I will get your jacket back to you. I just need to get to the dry cleaners."

"No, I meant it: it's yours now," he said, and stood up from the table. "Come on. Let's go somewhere."

I floated out of my chair, the night now less hopeless. My altered pheromones were at work, and Asher had given us a reason to get close. I'd have to figure out a way for us to stay where it was well lit so I could watch his behavior, specifically his eyes, which, at the moment, weren't dilated.

"Follow me," I said, leading him around the croquet game and through the gate at the back of the yard. "We can head over to the pond."

"Wait," he whispered, and then ran into the kitchen before returning with an uncorked bottle of wine. "Best of both worlds. Let's go."

Jamaica Pond is like an oasis in the city, a gorgeous spot with a walking path and a pretty boathouse. It was a perfect place to get close, except for the fact that the streetlights stop about a quarter of the way around the water, making most of the walk too dark for me to notice much. Sometimes headlights from passing cars illuminated our faces, and I turned to Asher, trying to figure out whether he was reacting to me at all, but he just looked normal, like a human taking in new scenery.

We filled the time with shallow conversation and a few awkward silences. I tried to keep myself parallel to him so we were sharing the same air space.

I could see the silhouette of a fisherman by the water below us. Behind him was a small patch of sand. Asher stopped to watch him.

"Why would someone be fishing this late?" he asked.

"I don't know," I said. "Maybe that's when the fish are out."

"Right on," Asher said.

I didn't know what to say to that, so I just muttered, "Right on."

"I think I dated a girl who lived in Jamaica Plain once," he said. "Her mom used to drive her to my house in, like, middle school."

"Do you keep in touch?"

"Nah. I don't know where she is now. She might have emailed me a few times after one of my first videos came out, but I don't think I ever responded."

"I'm surprised people like her haven't mobbed you after your performances this summer. Live theater makes you so accessible. You must be getting stalked by fans and old acquaintances after shows."

Asher tilted his head, but his hair barely moved.

"I saw my old dentist on opening night. And there were these six girls waiting for me by the stage exit last week. I thought they were going to pounce, I swear. But really, fans just want a quick picture and then they're gone. You have to figure, my most devoted fans are, like, fourteen. I don't think they're allowed to go to Boston Common with their friends after dark. If they come to one of the shows, they're with their parents."

We were about to start our second loop now, past the brown

boathouse and the streetlights all over again. This time, though, I stopped when we got to a flight of stone stairs off the walking path. I knew it led to a secluded patch of grass above the pond. Bryan, my mom, and I had picnicked there once.

"Check this out," I said, holding my dress to make sure I didn't trip over it as I ascended.

"This is so cool," Asher said once we got to the top. He surveyed the open space and the view of the pond from above.

"It looked like the stairs were going nowhere, and then it leads to this, like, secret beautiful patch of grass with, like, pretty flowers. It reminds me of that kids' book."

"*The Secret Garden*?"

"No," Asher said, frustrated. "What's the book where they go through the closet?"

I turned to face him. "The closet?"

"The kids—they go through the closet, and it's, like, this super-beautiful world with talking animals."

"Are you talking about Narnia? *The Lion, the Witch and the Wardrobe*?"

"Totally. Yeah, that's it. Narnia. It's like Narnia up here."

I shrugged and led him to the grass.

"Be careful," I said as I sat down. "People walk their dogs here, and not everyone cleans up after them. Sometimes there's dog poop in Narnia."

He let out a "Ha-ha" and settled across from me. My eyes had barely adjusted to the darkness, but I could swear his were closed. He appeared to be meditating, his legs crossed, his arms resting on his knees. He had been taking sips of the wine straight from the bottle throughout the walk; it didn't seem like he'd had that much, but now I wondered.

"I think I might record a song tonight when I get home. This walk is inspiring."

"I have to ask," I said, working to keep my tone even, "I know you only cover songs by women. Is there a reason? I didn't know if it was a coincidence . . . or whether the songs are in your range . . ."

"It's because of feminism," Asher said, his voice serious.

"Oh." I searched for more words. "I see."

We were quiet then. I didn't know where to go after his last statement.

"I'm going to New York on Monday morning," he said softly, saving us from the silence.

"You're leaving? In the middle of the run?"

"Just for a day. We're dark this Monday, and I'll be back by the next performance. I have an audition — for an off-Broadway play."

"That's really cool," I said, thinking of how great it would be when Bryan gave me this kind of news about himself in the future.

"I don't know," Asher said, looking down while fondling a twig near his feet. "I sort of thought I'd be on television or in movies by now. I really thought I'd be moving to L.A. . . ."

"You're still really young, though," I said.

"Yeah, but think about how many people my age are, like, really famous already."

He scratched the top of his head and then his hair bounced back into place, as if each dirty-blond strand knew exactly where it was supposed to be.

"You get a million fans, and you have this window, right? A window for using it to get to the next thing. And if an off-Broadway play is the next thing, I just feel like I blew it."

I leaned in, forcing him to pay attention. "It's a *play* in *New York*

City," I said. "It's a big deal. I know from Bryan it's a very, very big deal to do that kind of work."

Asher shrugged. "It must be nice to know you're good at something. Like for it to come naturally to you," he said, watching me.

"What are you talking about?"

"You. You're just naturally good at something. You're going to MIT. That means you're awesome at something. I feel like half the time I'm just faking it. I can sing, but the acting stuff isn't easy for me. Memorizing lines was the worst. Really, if I try anything beyond making my videos, I feel like I don't know what I'm doing."

His honesty surprised me, but I was more shocked that he remembered I was going to MIT.

"You don't know that I'm naturally good at science."

"Sure I do, because you can't fake being good at science and math. It's not like you're a shitty singer who can be put through Auto-Tune. You can't fake math."

"You can't fake acting, either; trust me. I've seen a lot of plays, thanks to Bryan. I don't think there's a way to fake that kind of thing. Some people are just forgettable onstage. But you're really good. I saw it myself."

My eyes had adjusted to the darkness enough for me to get some data, so I leaned into Asher and checked his eyes. They looked about the same as they had when I arrived at the party. Maybe slightly dilated? He was sweating—tiny circles of perspiration lined his scalp like raindrops. He surprised me by grabbing my hands and pulling me into his lap. I steadied myself, my hands on his gray V-neck T-shirt.

"You smell good," he said.

I pulled back. "I do? Are you kidding me?"

Asher nodded, now close enough for me to see his lashes flutter.

"Asher," I said, sitting up straight so I could look down at him, "this is a weird question, but what do I smell like? Can you describe it for me?"

"Um . . . I don't know," he said, placing his hands on my waist. "You smell like *girl.* You just smell nice."

I reached back and tightened my ponytail. "Okay . . . thanks."

I sat there frozen, not sure what to do next. My arms were on his shoulders, my head just above his.

"You're a good listener," he said, trying to turn and lower me so that our faces were closer. "Thank you for listening."

"No problem," I said, sinking into his lap, not sure what was supposed to happen next.

I took a deep breath and gave myself a second to enjoy the moment. I was out by Jamaica Pond with a YouTube star and he was holding me, possibly because he was under the influence of alcohol and altered pheromones, but also because we had shared a nice moment and I had made him feel better about his career for a second or two.

I was always good at that with Whit, giving him encouragement when he felt bad about his writing. He always said I was the best audience.

"You're really talented," I said, high on how it felt to make someone feel good again.

He pulled me close and hugged me, and I reciprocated with my arms around him. Then I felt a tickling wetness on my neck.

"Are you licking me?" I asked with a laugh.

"I kissed your neck. With my mouth open," he said, his very white YouTube teeth almost glowing as a car passed by, yards away.

This couldn't happen again. Not kissing, not with Asher.

When this whole project started, Ann implied that our best results would be enlarged pupils, mirroring, and lowered voices. A lot of studies suggested that when men feel attraction, their voices get deeper. I was hoping for that, at best, tonight.

But with two subjects now, it was like I had taken a fast-acting aphrodisiac. It had been nice kissing Kyle — I had to force myself to stop — and now I didn't want to peel myself out of Asher's lap. My heart raced, and I was covered in sweat.

He put one hand on my butt like it was no big deal.

"You've got to be kidding me," I said, shifting away.

"What's wrong?" Asher asked.

"I don't know if I need to be doing this," I responded, more to myself. I had enough data, it seemed.

"I think you should let me kiss you again," he whispered.

"We're outside," I said, pointing to the dim row of car headlights on the road that circled the pond. "And you can go back to that party and hook up with anyone you want."

"I like *you,*" he murmured into my neck.

I just kept letting him do whatever he was doing, which was some sort of neck gnawing that was making me lightheaded.

He stopped for a moment and looked at me. "I haven't talked to anyone like this in a long time. You're really great to talk to."

"Wait," I said, realizing that I was less certain than I needed to be about my results. Maybe he had been seduced by my compliments. "You want to kiss me because of the talking?" I asked, leaning back. "If we had not talked, would you want to kiss me?"

Asher looked baffled. "Yes? I mean, I like talking to you. And kissing you. Wait — what's the right answer here?"

"Just be honest," I said, desperate for clarity. I held the sides of his face with my hands. "Just relax for a second and think. Do you want to make out with me because I told you you're a good actor or because you're randomly attracted to me tonight?"

Asher threw his hands up, shaking me in his lap. "Either one? Both? Why are you being weird?"

I could see panic in his dilated eyes.

"It's okay" I said, trying to keep my tone breezy. "I'm just curious. Did you have any interest in kissing me before tonight?"

Asher dropped his hands to his sides and looked thoughtful. "I thought you were nice when we met. And I felt bad for you when I saw you at the karaoke place looking so miserable."

"But you didn't want to sleep with me then, right?" I said, cutting him off.

"I didn't *not* want to sleep with you. I wasn't thinking about whether I was attracted to you, I guess. I slept with Kimberly Katz that night, after karaoke. That was a big mistake. You have no idea."

"You had sex with Kimberly Katz?" I pushed at his shoulders.

I shouldn't have been shocked, but I was; people had sex so easily.

"Forget I said that," he said, his hands tightening on my hips.

"Fine. But just to be clear, tonight is the first night you've had the desire to kiss me."

"Yes," he said, after a beat. "That's right. Jeez, why all the questions? Am I out of line here? I thought you might be into it. You seemed like a fan, and we've been talking . . ."

"You're not out of line," I said, pulling him in for a hug because I felt so bad. This had to be the most confusing sexual experience he'd ever had.

Asher spoke softly in my ear. He sounded exhausted. "This is confusing. Did you not want me to hit on you?"

"I did," I said, being honest. "It's just complicated."

He pulled back so that we were face-to-face, and then he leaned in. We were kissing then, or at least he was kissing me. I couldn't do much besides keep my mouth open as his tongue began wagging from side to side inside it. Whereas kissing Kyle felt like a shared experience, this kissing was happening to me — or on me.

After another minute, Asher's head fell to my neck and he started licking it again. He maneuvered his hand up the bottom of my dress and kept it on the back of my underwear. I tried not to think about how sweaty I might be after sitting on the grass in the humidity.

I felt his teeth at my collarbone. Not a lick or a kiss or even a bite, but again, a strange gnawing, like he was trying to work his way down an ear of corn.

I was ready to push him away, but he beat me to it and unsuctioned himself. Then he leaned forward so that I was on my back and he was hovering on top of me.

I exhaled, relieved that the neck business had stopped, and perhaps a bit curious to find out what he would try next, but it turned out to be more of the same. He gave me a quick closed-mouth peck and then dropped his mouth to my neck. The gnawing began all over again.

All I could think about was how with Kyle, there was no awkwardness, and how nice his hands had felt when they'd traveled down my arms, and how it felt like whatever we were doing, we were doing together.

Asher, meanwhile, seemed to be having his own experience, with me as a random accessory. The minute he started pulling up my dress, I placed my hands on top of his to stop him.

"I think we should get back to the party," I said. "You know, I'm just dealing with this breakup, and it's probably not a good idea. I'm not making great decisions right now."

"Sometimes the best way to get over someone is to get under someone else," Asher said with pride, as if he had come up with that expression. "No, really," he added. "I didn't get over my last breakup until I had sex with someone else."

"That would work, maybe, if I'd ever had sex," I muttered, before thinking about the reveal.

"You're a virgin?" he asked, popping up to his knees, away from me, like I was carrying a contagion.

"I guess, technically," I said. "Although that's a pretty heteronormative concept, right?"

He looked confused and just stared at me. After a defeated sigh, he took my hand to help me up. It was over.

We were mostly silent on the way back to the party, and when we did talk, his guard was back up. No more discussion about the New York audition or his fears about his career. Instead, he told me a story about how he deals with his fan mail, and about the time his parents caught two thirteen-year-old girls trying to break into their house.

"They lived down the street, and they were probably harmless. Just trying to steal my underwear or something," he said with a smug smile.

"Probably," I agreed, not knowing what else to say.

When we arrived back at the Epsteins' gate, he leaned in for a hug and said he was going straight home. Just before he turned to leave, he grabbed my hand and squeezed it.

"So," he said.

"So," I answered, nodding and smiling like the word meant something.

"So, is there a song you want?"

"What?" I asked confused.

"For me to cover for you. A song. Any song you want."

I let out a sharp "Ha," my laugh sounding like his.

"No, really," he said. "I'll make a video for you. Just pick a song."

There were probably thousands of girls, most of them fourteen years old or younger, who would sell their siblings to get Asher Forman to record their favorite song. After watching just a few of those videos with Bryan, I'd seen enough for a lifetime. Still, I would never say no to this.

"Beyoncé. 'If I Were a Boy,'" I said. It was the only song I could think of, fresh in my mind from Bryan's mix.

"But I *am* a boy," he said after a moment of consideration.

"Right," I said.

"Nice," he said with a nod. "I get it."

"Okay," I said, adjusting my dress as I watched him leave.

Bryan was in the backyard waiting for me when I got there.

"Where were you? It's almost ten. I couldn't find you."

He didn't look angry, just worried.

"I took a walk with Asher Forman. I had no idea we were gone that long."

"Shut your mouth," Bryan said. "Shut your lying mouth."

"I'm serious. That's what happened." I shrugged.

"Where is he now?"

"He went home. He doesn't like parties."

Bryan looked at me like I was speaking a new language, and then his eyes fell to my neck.

"Your neck is red."

I pursed my lips. I would tell Bryan about this, I decided. I couldn't get around it. There wasn't much to say, anyway, and I wouldn't have to mention the experiment.

"We can't talk about this here."

"Then we're gone," he said, grabbing my hand and pulling me through the house and out the front door. As we slammed it shut, I could hear Rita barking behind us.

Once we were down the street, I told him about the walk and the neck gnawing, and my concerns about Asher's hands on my sweaty behind.

"That must have been very stressful for you. Your behind does get *very sweaty,*" Bryan said thoughtfully, with pity.

"That was the least of it," I said, giving him a light push on the arm. "Someone has to tell him he's a weird, terrible kisser. I've basically only kissed Whit, and even I know that you're not supposed to suck on someone's neck like you're teething."

That was my one big lie of the night. Whit wasn't my only basis of comparison anymore. I had also kissed Kyle, who, compared to Asher, seemed to have magic powers. I shook my head, trying to delete the memory.

Bryan distracted me with questions about every single detail from the walk — what Asher said and how he said it, what he did with his tongue, and how I turned him down and disclosed my lack of sexual experience.

"You said 'heteronormative,'" Bryan said. "You stole my line."

"Sorry. It's a good line."

I thought the discussion was over after we got home, but Bryan wasn't done.

"Why are you so calm about this?" he said just before he went to crash in our guest room. "You're weirdly breezy, like you didn't just have neck intercourse with an internet superhero. This isn't like you."

"I'm not breezy," I promised. "Trust me, I'm not calm about anything right now. I think I'm just in shock."

It was weird to tell him the half-truth. I'd been lying to him for weeks now, making up stories about what I was doing when I was really with Ann.

"Can I ask you something?" I said, tilting my head. "Is this going to turn into an embarrassing hickey?"

"Probably." Bryan sighed. "I'll teach you how to put makeup on it in the morning."

17

I stayed up late that night, documenting everything before I forgot the details. My mom's notes had been clinical; there were quantitative data paired with small observations about my dad's reaction to her at different doses, but my work was more qualitative — and narrative.

I tried to keep the language professional, but the more I wrote, the more it felt like a diary. Whatever awkwardness I felt with Ann in person went away when I was writing, and her responses had also become more casual — and more frequent — throughout the day.

The minute I sent her a quick email to let her know that Serum Number Two had worked, she wrote back, *Tell me everything . . .* , to which I had responded, *You're not supposed to be living vicariously through this,* to which she responded, *Says you.*

By the time we were done going back and forth about my discoveries, it was three forty-five a.m. It took me another hour to relax and get to sleep. I barely got up in time to get to work by ten.

I was chugging a big iced coffee in the hallway when Yael came in.

"Thank god," I said as she passed me and marched to her workbench. I left the coffee by Tish's desk so I could follow Yael into the lab. "I was falling asleep sitting up. You have to keep me awake today. I barely slept."

"You. Outside," Yael said, pointing back to the hallway.

Yael wore a red cotton T-shirt that matched her fiery facial expression. "What's wrong?"

"Outside," she barked again, already walking out. "We need to talk."

I followed her past Tish and into the hallway, and found myself almost running to keep up with her as we traveled down the stairs and outside onto the quad. She led me to the side of Building 68b, to a shaded area, making me feel like something awful was about to happen.

"What?" I asked again in a panic. She was irate, her tiny brown curls slapping against her face as she crossed her arms in front of her chest.

"Why didn't you tell me? Did you think I wouldn't know?"

My heart pounded. She knew.

If people found out about the experiment, Ann could get kicked out of her program. I'd be in trouble before I even started MIT, if they let me start at all.

We'd stolen things. We'd misused materials.

"What exactly are you talking about?" I was barely whispering. "What do you know?"

"You hooked up with our friend. And you didn't even tell me about it!"

I exhaled. That's what she knew; she'd found out about Kyle.

"No wonder he keeps avoiding us," Yael continued. "No wonder he's been a basket case for weeks. What were you thinking?"

"He told you?"

"Yes, he told me," Yael interrupted before I could begin to explain myself. "He showed up at my apartment last night looking like a mess. We were up until two in the morning. He slept on the couch."

I backed up against the side of Building 68b and sank to the ground, my head falling back against the concrete. Yael remained standing, looking down at me like she was ten feet tall.

"I don't know what happened," I lied. "We went out. We went back to my house to watch television. And then we kissed, and I stopped it. It's been confusing for me since the breakup, I guess. It was all an accident."

It was mostly true. Kissing had never been on the agenda.

Yael kicked one of her espadrille heels into the grass and then plopped down to the ground next to me, crossing her legs.

"But come on, Maya; he's had a big crush on you since you got here. Suddenly you're single and you invite him out—without me. You bring him back to your place for a movie. You let him kiss you. And then you basically tell him you're not interested, that it was a mistake. He's just disappointed, and seeing you every day makes it hard to get over it."

I hugged my knees to my chest. A Frisbee landed a few feet away from us, and a bearded guy ran to retrieve it.

I didn't know how to respond because her version of the story didn't sound accurate.

"Kyle hasn't had a crush on me. We just started kissing. Then he said it didn't matter. He said that kind of thing happens all the time."

She glared at me like I was stupid, like I was one of the pretty girls in school—like Genevieve Moran—who were always like, "Who, me?" whenever they found out some guy liked them. I was not that girl, and Kyle had always seemed happy with our friendship. He was the one who'd been ignoring me, the one who was already running off with other people.

"If that's how he felt, I didn't know," I whispered. "I swear."

"Really, I thought you were into him, too. You guys were texting all day, even when you were sitting next to each other. All the inside jokes. If it wasn't happening in my face all day, I'd think it was cute."

"I was with Whit. I love Whit," I said, my voice horse. "Bryan texts me all day too. I didn't think anything of it."

She shook her head again. "That's different; you've known him forever."

"What am I supposed to do?" I asked, my voice frantic. "He said it didn't mean anything. He said this stuff happens all the time at college."

"What else was he supposed to say?" Yael said. Then she softened her tone. "It's not just that . . . You've been weird lately. I see you in Ann Markley's office, talking in whispers. You're with her in the middle of the night. What's up with you?"

"Nothing," I said, my head between my knees. "I swear, nothing. We just talk about my mom sometimes."

Yael nodded. I knew bringing up my mom would make it seem innocent.

"Just tell me what to do to make it better with Kyle," I said.

"Be clear about your intentions. Respect his space. You know, relationships are confusing enough without mixed signals. I don't know why every scientist I know is so smart in the lab yet so stupid when it comes to human behavior. Can you just try to be a human? Be with him or leave him alone."

I nodded and pulled myself up, following her back into the building.

For the rest of the day, I drowned myself in Dr. Araghi's tapes and kept my distance from Kyle, who spent most of the day cleaning equipment.

I felt nauseated when I watched him. It wasn't supposed to turn out like this. I was counting on knowing him next year, and not having him to talk to was making me miserable.

I wondered what Ann would say if I told her that Kyle's part of the experiment was inconclusive because he had liked me long before the serum. Then I decided I wouldn't tell her—because I couldn't risk her shutting the project down before we moved on to Whit, who was the reason I pursued the research in the first place. I was so close.

18

I've never really been in trouble—not real trouble—because I've never really broken any big rules. When I was younger, I was scolded a few times for not doing chores, but when you're a trustworthy kid with easygoing parents, it's difficult to screw up. I wasn't accustomed to deceit or the conflict that comes with it.

But I had become a person who told lies. Many of them.

I was lying every day to my dad and Bryan. I had alienated Kyle and had tarnished my relationship with Yael.

And then Tish walked in with a clipboard, and suddenly it was clear I had become the kind of person who had risked everything—my education, my career, my future.

"Ladies and gentlemen," Tish announced, Dr. Araghi standing behind her like a bodyguard, "I have a quick announcement. Yael, can you call everyone in from the other rooms?"

Yael walked back to the other end of the winding lab and gathered the rest of the scientists, including Ann, who stalked out of her makeshift office like someone had interrupted her nap. She crossed her arms over her leather jacket, annoyed.

"Sorry to bother you all. A quick announcement: Dr. Innis on Floor Two has reported some missing reagents from the first floor. It's probably just a record-keeping mistake, but with budget cuts as they are and grant money tighter than ever, we're asking all lab personnel to fill out one of these worksheets. You'll see a space for your name, lab, area of research, your lab manager, and contact information. Below that, you'll be asked to document all materials used in the past three weeks. You don't have to list equipment, just materials and reagents."

Tish walked from bench to bench, dropping a photocopied form in front of each researcher. She skipped my bench, which made me nervous until I realized that I was just an intern. She had no reason to believe I used anything in the lab.

I panicked and looked over at Ann without thinking, but she showed no signs of guilt. Her face was stony and calm, as if Tish had made an inane request that didn't warrant her time.

I had to place my hands on my thighs to remind myself not to run. My cheeks felt hot, and my stomach burned. I wished I could be as cool as Ann, who leaned against the wall and rolled her eyes.

"What specifically went missing?"

My head whipped from one side of the room to the other as I realized who asked the question. It was Yael, whose eyes were on me, and then on Ann.

"Are there chemicals missing specifically from the basement? Do they know when they were taken?" Her voice cracked.

How much had she seen that night?

Ann broke character and turned to Yael. Her face was icy; the invisible threat unspoken. Yael didn't flinch, though. She moved her eyes to Dr. Araghi, who answered, "Don't concern yourself with any of the details, folks. Just document your work, and we'll sort it all out. Nothing to worry about."

Yael looked like she might say more, but then she swallowed and nodded.

I whipped around in my seat to face the wall before anyone noticed my jumpiness.

My fingers fumbled as I turned on the tape recorder for transcription. I tried to concentrate on Dr. Araghi's voice, pretending I had nothing to worry about, but seconds later, my phone buzzed.

The text was from Ann. *Bathroom. Now,* it said.

I rose from my desk, my legs wobbling, then shuffled to the restroom in the hallway closest to our lab. Ann followed seconds later.

"This is over," she said when she found me waiting in front of the stalls. "We're done."

A florescent light flickered above us. With my back against the wall and Ann blocking the exit, I felt trapped.

"Wait," I said. "Wait, Ann. Just calm down."

"No, Maya, that's it. I told you that if there was any risk of getting caught, we'd stop. Immediately. We shouldn't have started this project to begin with. I was reckless and selfish. I missed the kind of work I did with your mom so much that I downplayed the consequences — but I've used resources, cost them money . . . I could get kicked out. I could get booted so fast and wind up teaching middle school chemistry for the rest of my life."

"Hey," I said, "my dad teaches middle school science."

"I know!" Ann said. "My aspirations are a bit higher than your dad's, Maya. I'm in a PhD program in one of the most important epigenetics labs in the world!"

She froze then and began running to each stall, looking underneath to make sure they were free of feet. Then she paced up and down the bathroom, her black boots sounding like hammers against the light blue floor tiles.

"Maybe they're not even talking about the materials we used.

Maybe it doesn't have anything to do with us, and this is all just a coincidence. How much does this experiment really require, anyway? We're talking small doses, right?"

She stopped and faced me; I could see our reflections like ghosts in the bathroom mirror.

"I'm not your mother, Maya. It's taken me a few tries to get it right. I tried not to use too many materials, but it was enough to be noticed, I guess. We can't risk doing this anymore. We'll just—we can make an assessment about the experiment based on what we already know. We've had two possibly successful trials. That's enough."

"Wait. No," I grabbed her arm as she started for the door. "Ann, the next phase is all that matters. I only did this for Whit. Subject Three is the whole point."

"Maya . . ." Ann pulled her arm away and leaned back against the bathroom door, blocking it so no one could come in. "Is he really worth it? Is anyone worth this?"

"Wait," I pleaded, not answering the question. "Just listen. We can still do this—we just have to do it right now."

Ann shook her head. "Do what now?" she asked.

"Well, they just did an inventory, right? And now they're making everyone fill out a form to say what materials they've used. Dr. Araghi isn't going to check the supplies again until everyone's filled out those sheets. If you run down today and grab what you need, no one will know. They won't recheck until after they restock. Right now they *assume* things are missing. It's the perfect time to take what we need."

"It seems like a risk, Maya . . ." Ann said.

"No. Look, Ann, if anything, they'll just think they miscounted the first time around. They know their inventory is all screwed up right now. If we get the third serum over with, we'll be done, and they'll have no reason to suspect."

"Yael already suspects —"

"What does she suspect?"

I cut her off in a voice I didn't recognize. It was low and confident, like I was a movie assassin. Like in *Hanna*. "All Yael knows is that I was at the lab late at night with you. All she knows is that we've been hanging out, talking about my mom. We can do this one more time."

"Maya, you sound obsessed. Like, Dr. Frankenstein obsessed."

"I just want to finish this. Don't you want to finish this too?"

She sighed.

"I already gave you Whit's sweatshirt. You have that information, right? All you need to do is make the serum, right?"

She'd placed her hands on her head, her elbows together covering her ears.

"Maya."

"Ann, we can do this."

She turned her back to me.

"I'll stay late tonight," she whispered. "But if I see one light on, if I see another human on my way in, I'm calling it off."

"It'll be fine, I promise."

"Go back to the lab. I don't want to see you for the rest of the day. I'll text you when . . . when the last serum is ready. And then that's it. Then we're done."

I bolted out of the bathroom, my ponytail smacking my neck as I turned the hallway corner. Just a few more days and we'd be on to the next phase of the experiment, which was the whole point in the first place.

19

I texted Ann to say that I would help her in the basement, but she said we shouldn't be seen there together again. She said that this time, if she was caught, she would say she was testing an experiment for a lecture she'd give to an undergraduate class in the fall. She'd be scolded for borrowing items from the lab without documentation, but that would be the worst of it. Hopefully.

That left me nervous and with nothing to do. Bryan had Shakespeare duty, so I went straight home after lab, surprised to find my dad's car in the driveway. At this hour, he was usually on his way to do something athletic, but he was there, sitting in a wooden chair at the dining room table we almost never used, with a stack of paperwork fanned out in front of him. There was an open pizza box in the center of the table. Two slices had already been consumed.

"We have coupons for that," I said as I dropped my backpack by the staircase and joined him at the table.

"The coupon on the fridge? I used it. We got free breadsticks. They're on the kitchen counter." He removed his reading glasses and wiped his eyes.

I was distracted by the shoes on the floor next to his feet. They were running shoes, but the kind that looked like gloves for toes. They were thin and mesh with spaces for each digit.

"Oh, no, Dad, please tell me you did not buy the toe running shoes. They are so gross-looking."

"It's minimalist footwear. It's good for my feet."

"It can't be good for anyone to have finger toes. They're so ugly."

He scowled. "Can you give me a break?"

He looked stressed, so I let it go.

"What's happening?" I dragged the pizza box toward me and grabbed a slice. My dad almost never looked stressed, and it had been months since I'd seen him use his reading glasses.

"I'm paying your college tuition."

"I thought I had a tuition grant because Mom worked there."

"It doesn't cover everything. And then there's some housing costs and paperwork. Student activity fees," he said, gesturing to the table. "I'm pretending to be one of those parents who turns everything in on time."

"Impressive," I said, my mouth full.

I looked around and began to imagine what our house would look like after I moved into the dorm. It'd be so quiet. I had chosen a school that was only about a mile from my house, so I knew I'd be home more often than the average freshman, but my dad would still be alone every night.

"You okay?" he asked, looking up.

"Nope," I said. It felt good to answer a question honestly for once.

"Is this about Whit?"

"Sort of."

The truth was that it was about Whit and Kyle, and about lying to friends and wishing I could travel back in time to the start of the summer, when everything felt normal. It was about Bryan going to college five hours away. It was about people disappearing.

"I feel ridiculous getting upset about my stupid life around you," I said after swallowing another bite.

He took off his glasses and gave me his concerned-dad face, which only made me feel worse.

"What is that supposed to mean? Your life isn't stupid, Maya."

"I had a bad breakup. It happens. You lost Mom — forever — after years of marriage. You're, like, a widower, and you're not even fifty."

"Thanks for reminding me!" my dad said, his voice bright with sarcasm.

"I'm sorry. I didn't mean it like that. It's just . . . Who cares if I had a breakup, right? It shouldn't feel this bad. It's not the end of the world."

"No," he said, "you're right. But honey, let me tell you something I learned from this one guy in the bereavement group I went to."

"You quit that group."

"I went twice. That was enough. But this man in the group — his wife had been dead for two years, and I'll never forget what he told me. He said that losing a partner to a breakup is sometimes more difficult than losing a partner to death. I'll never forget it."

"But death is death. It's fatal, forever. Breakups can't ever be worse than death."

"Hear me out," he said in his teacher voice. "We all just want to be loved, right? And your mom did love me. She loved me like crazy. When she died, it's not as though she left me by choice. If she'd kept on living, she would have stayed with me and continued to love me. But this thing with Whit — well, honey, it's about him being content to let you go. I can see how accepting that is harder than it seems.

"I think that's what the guy at the bereavement group was trying to say — that if someone leaves by choice, it's a different kind of devastation. It's about rejection. Whit rejected you."

I swallowed a big bite of crust. "Thanks, Dad. That might be the worst thing I've ever heard. Excuse me while I go run into traffic."

He shook his head and smiled. "I didn't mean to upset you. Shoot, Maya, I'm trying to validate you. I'm telling you that I get it, and that you have every right to be really sad about the whole thing."

"It's weird. I never got it, the whole heartbreak thing. It just seemed like—if someone doesn't want to be with you, then why would you want to be with them, you know? But with Whit, it's like I know something he doesn't. Like, I just want to tell him that what we had isn't easy to find. I think about how we appreciated each other, and how we'd talk for hours. How could he let go of that, right when we were finally going to be in the same place in life? It was only going to get better when I got to school."

My dad nodded and leaned over the table, pushing the pizza box closer to me.

"Thanks," I said, joining him for another slice as I thought about what he said. "Dad . . . did you ever get sick of Mom after all those years together? I know you loved her, but did you ever have a rut or ever think about leaving?"

He leaned back in his chair.

"Of course," he responded. "I got married young. She was older than I was, so she was sure, and I thought I was sure too, but I was crazy young. There were certainly times when I wondered what life would have been like had I been with more women—"

I winced. "Gross."

"No, look, just hear me out. Be a grownup for a second. You asked the question."

"Fine, fine," I said, reaching across the table to steal his glass of fizzy water.

"Your mom and I had a few ruts over the years, but I wouldn't say I was ever sick of her. In fact, it's weird; during those last few years of her life, we were like kids again. It was strange. There was this second wave of attraction that no one told me about. Or maybe it was a third wave. We were married more than twenty years. I lost count of all our waves."

"What started that last wave of attraction?" I prodded, my heart sinking as I realized that the third wave probably started when my mom began manipulating him with her experiment. "Were you just suddenly attracted to her again?"

"I'd like to think that's between me and your mom," he said, shrugging. "Let's just say we always found creative ways to get back to where we started."

He smiled, but his eyes were glassy.

"Sorry, Dad. I didn't mean to bring up all this stuff."

"No apology needed. It's nice to talk about it. I know we're close, but sometimes I wish we were closer, like you and your mom were. Talking like this is nice."

"Yeah," I said, adding, "you think you'll date again?"

We'd never talked about his romantic prospects for the future; only about the recreational activities that filled the void.

"Probably," he conceded quickly. "There's a woman I bike with. She also does some rock climbing. She's about ten years younger. I think she's waiting for me to ask, and it's all very strange."

"She'd be, like, fifteen years younger than Mom," I said without thinking.

"Weird, right?"

I nodded, feeling a little defensive on behalf of my mom, even though I knew better. "You know," I said, "I'm okay with you dating. As long as she's cool."

My dad laced his fingers together, his elbows on the table. "I know. And I'll let you know when I'm ready. I'm just not there yet."

20

There was something different about the third serum.

Whereas the first tasted like children's vitamins and the second was even more sugary, the third was a little bitter.

I'd thought about Goldilocks when Ann first handed me the small bottle. Maybe the third serum, for Whit, would be "just right." But within seconds of my dropping the liquid under my tongue, my mouth started to itch. I didn't tell Ann; I was too afraid she'd tell me to stop taking it if she suspected I might have an allergic reaction.

After taking the first dose at Ann's apartment, I'd lied and said there were no symptoms. I kept my mouth shut and rubbed my teeth against the back of my lips to quell the irritation. Then, while Ann was checking her email on her laptop on the couch, I went into the kitchen, grabbed a fork, and raked it down my tongue. Later, when I got home, I took a Benadryl and felt normal again. That became my routine at home for the next few days; I'd take an allergy pill, then the serum, and then I'd pass out from the side effects of the antihistamine as I imagined the liquid embedding itself in my system.

Now, a few days into Phase Three of the experiment, my only problem was finding any privacy to complete the routine. Two of Bryan's older brothers were in town with their wives and kids to see his last performance, so he had given up his bedroom and was staying with us every night.

I thought it'd be easy to sneak away to take the drops while he was watching television, but every time I excused myself to go into the kitchen to grab the serum from the refrigerator, he followed me to get something for himself. It was like I had a shadow.

Finally, he received a phone call from the guy who'd be his roommate at Syracuse. Bryan rolled his eyes as he said, "Hi, Paul," and then walked to the other side of the living room. "No, Paul, I didn't see your email. Yeah, I must have missed it."

Bryan already hated the guy, who was an incoming economics major from Ohio.

"What does that even mean?" Bryan had said when he received his room assignment.

"I think it means he studies economics," my dad had said.

"No, I mean the Ohio part. What is even *in* Ohio?"

"Be nice," my dad said.

"Only for you," Bryan had responded. "You make me a better person, Kirk."

Now Bryan was lying on the floor, his back against our fluffy brown area rug. "I don't see the need for two refrigerators, Paul. One is plenty. I can share if you can share."

Once I was convinced he was trapped in a long conversation about who'd be bringing what to campus, I scurried to the kitchen, reached behind the bottle of ketchup, grabbed the small vial, and ran to my bathroom upstairs, shutting the door behind me.

I ran the water, making it sound like I was washing my face and brushing my teeth before bed. Usually I wasn't so paranoid, but keeping a secret from Bryan was harder than keeping one from my dad.

I moved fast, unscrewing the top of the bottle and making sure the dropper was filled with the liquid. I took a breath as I prepared myself for the side effects; even with Benadryl in my system, there'd be a few minutes of a dull itch.

Just as I was about to squeeze the first drop under my tongue, the liquid already pearled at the tip of the dropper, the bathroom door swung open and Bryan came at me, knocking my arm so hard that that the dropper flew from my hand.

"Dammit!" I yelled, watching the dose and the tiny dropper fall to the floor. "What are you doing?"

"I knew it!" Bryan yelled, his body looming in front of the door frame.

"You knew what?" I yelled back.

He opened and shut his mouth and then eyed the dropper on the floor. "I don't know what I knew, but I knew something was up," he continued, surveying the room. "What the hell are you doing in here?"

He wore orange cotton boxers and a *Wicked* T-shirt that he'd owned since he first saw the musical at the Opera House. The shirt was old now, discolored from overwashing.

I grabbed the dropper from the floor and held it behind my back.

"What is that?" Bryan asked, looking hurt in a way that stunned me for a moment. I couldn't think of anything to say to put him at ease. I didn't even know how to describe what I was hiding. "Is it a laxative?"

"What?" I whispered, bewildered.

"Is this an eating-disorder thing? That's what this is, right?"

"What the hell are you talking about?"

"Maya, Whit never cared about your weight. He was just finished with the relationship. He's just in college now and doesn't know what he wants. He always thought you were beautiful, and I never want you to think that you are anything but perfect."

I registered what he was saying — what he assumed I was doing in the bathroom — and let my hands drop to my sides. "I'm not taking laxatives, Bryan."

Bryan eyed the dropper in my hand.

"Not a laxative!" I yelled, holding it up for his inspection.

"Then what is it?"

In that moment, I scanned my brain for possible lies.

"It's an eyedropper," I said, trying to keep my voice steady.

He placed his hands on his head, exasperated.

"You can't do this to me, Maya, okay? You can't keep secrets. You can't, like, change on me all the time. It's like, you lose your mom and it's the three of us — you, me, your dad. We were getting through it together. And then you meet Whit, and he's suddenly the center of the universe. Like, *Whit, Whit, Whit.* All the time. And I couldn't even be mad at you, because you deserved it. I wanted you to be happy. But then he dumps you, and you start behaving like someone I don't even know. You make long trips to the bathroom. You hook up with Asher Forman and act like it's no big deal — like it isn't the biggest deal in the world.

"I just don't know what the hell is going on anymore. I mean, is that a drug? Are you on drugs now? What would your mom say?"

I lowered the lid of the toilet and sat down.

"This," I said, waving the eyedropper back and forth, "*this* was my mom's idea."

Bryan cocked his head to the side. Then he closed the bathroom door behind him and lowered himself to the ground in front of it.

He stared at me, his elbows on his knees, waiting for an explanation.

"I don't have an eating disorder. I'm not on drugs," I said, pausing for a moment to figure out how I could explain the truth, because I wanted to. "I'm ingesting a pheromone-masking formula to get Whit back."

The words echoed in the tiled room.

Bryan's eyes narrowed. He tucked his hair behind his ears and crossed his legs in a way that suggested we wouldn't be leaving the bathroom for a while.

I bent over and put my head in my hands, my elbows on my black cotton pajama pants. Part of me was relieved that this was happening. It had always felt wrong, having this experience on my own, without him.

When I sat back up, I placed the eyedropper on the sink in front of me and started telling him the story from the beginning, how Cindy had told me about the research, and how I convinced Ann to continue the work.

"She did this — your mom did this — with your dad?"

"Yeah," I said. "I mean, I know he was her test subject. I don't know whether they were having marital troubles, or why she wanted to do it in the first place."

Bryan looked solemn. "If I was your mom and thought I might lose your dad, I would do science on him to make him stay too. I'd do all the science in the world on him."

"I'm well aware."

Bryan shot me a weak smile.

"So you've just been taking these drops all summer, waiting for them to kick in?"

"I've only taken these particular drops for about four days. Whit isn't the first subject . . . We sort of did some test runs first."

I told him about Kyle then, about the night we went bowling, and what I learned from Yael about his feelings for me. Bryan slapped his hand over his mouth more than once.

"I know, I know; it's horrible," I said.

"*Do* you know, Maya?"

"I never thought it would go that far!" I yelled at Bryan. "I thought Kyle was my friend. Things were platonic until I took the serum. And since then, it's just been confusing."

"Maya . . . this feels, like, gross. Unethical."

"But . . . don't we mask ourselves all the time to seem more attractive to other people? This is like . . . wearing the perfect perfume for someone. People wear perfume all the time."

Bryan scowled.

"It's not really like that," he said. "If it was like perfume, you'd just be wearing perfume."

I looked away, not wanting to see his expression.

"You know, this reminds me of *Proof*," Bryan continued.

"Proof of what?" I asked.

"The play *Proof*. You know this one. I've told you about it. It's the play about the woman whose father dies and leaves behind some big equation, and she tries to figure it all out."

"I don't remember that one. You've told me about, like, six thousand plays."

"No, you know this one. They made it into a movie."

I shook my head.

"You'd think you'd remember the one play that's about math," Bryan said, eyeing me. "The more important point is that this is not okay, Maya." He pointed to the small bottle on the sink. "I mean, are those Whit's pheromones? Like, in a tube? You took 'Essence of Kyle' and now you've moved on to 'Essence of Whit'? It's that easy?" He threw his air quotes up so high that his left hand hit the towel rack next to him.

I felt heat creep up my neck.

"Actually, there were three subjects. Kyle was the first. Whit will be the third."

Bryan was silent, his eyes closed as he processed the information. "Wait . . . who was Subject Number Two?"

Again, I couldn't think of a lie fast enough, and Bryan spoke first.

"Jesus, Maya, is it me? Are you *crazy?*"

"No! No. I would not do this to you; no way. I don't think that could even work."

"Great. I'm so glad you have such respect for our friendship and such strong 'ethics.'" The air quotes returned around the last word.

"It was Asher. I did the experiment with Asher."

"Like, Asher Forman?" Bryan shouted.

"He's the only Asher we know."

"I know, but how? How is that even possible? How would you get his DNA? You've seen him, like, three times."

"I had his coat, remember?"

"You stole that coat to . . . make a DNA potion? What kind of evil are you?"

"No, no," I cut him off. "I had the coat first and *then* decided to use it to make the potion. And stop calling it a potion! It's a serum. This isn't evil magic or anything. I just needed a subject who was a stranger — someone who wasn't attracted to me — and Asher seemed like a good fit. I had his stupid coat, so it worked. And the experiment was a success. I mean, as you know, he *participated.*"

"Maya," Bryan said, his elbows on his knees, "isn't it possible that Asher Forman would have 'participated' no matter what 'serum' you were taking? You were hanging out with him during the party. While consuming alcohol. Maybe he just wanted to sleep with you, unrelated to your weird science witchcraft."

"It's possible, but I doubt it," I said, leaning back against the top of the toilet. "He said he hadn't thought about me like that before that night. Do you really think I'm the girl he would have chosen at that party? There were so many pretty actresses there. Kimberly Katz was there."

Bryan uncrossed his legs and stretched them out on the tiles in front of him.

"Of course he might choose you. There are, like, a million guys who'd rather sleep with you than Kimberly Katz," he said.

I shook my head.

"Just tell me this," he continued. "What's the plan for later? You seduce Whit with your special pheromones and he's your boyfriend again? It's that easy?"

That was the plan, for the most part. I nodded.

"You'll just take this stuff for the rest of your life with him? Ann will keep making your Love Potion Number Nine and you'll live happily ever after?"

"No, I know that's not possible. I guess my thought was that it'd be a reminder. Like Whit just needs a reminder of the chemistry. My mom was doing this to keep couples together; that's what I'm trying to do here. Like, imagine all the breakups that wouldn't happen if people could just have little boosts of chemistry when they needed it.

"And," I continued, grasping for his approval, "maybe I also just wanted to know if this would work. It turned out Mom had this big secret — this big scientific secret that was her passion. It's felt good, you know, to be close to her. It's like I'm doing this with her. Maybe *for* her. At the very least, for Ann, who, as it turns out, is kind of cool. Or maybe not cool, but a lot like my mom when it comes to research. It's just been nice to be around her."

I said all the stuff about my mom and Ann to guilt Bryan into endorsing the project, but as soon the words were out of my mouth, I knew they were true. I did feel close to my mom when I was working on the experiment. It was like every piece of recorded data was a note we were passing back and forth in secret. At the beginning of the project, I was thinking only of Whit, but in the past week, I was also worried about the void I'd feel when the experiment concluded.

I looked up when I heard Bryan's whimper. He had started to cry a little. He dabbed his eyes with his T-shirt, leaving water marks on the *W* and *D* in *Wicked*.

"Hey," I said. "I'm sorry I didn't tell you sooner."

"I know," he said. "I think I'm crying because I'm actually happy. It sort of makes me feel good that you miss your mom. Like, what you're doing actually makes no sense to me, but you're right: she'd be into this. And I miss her a lot, you know?"

Bryan's shirt became one big wet spot.

"I know I don't talk about her much, but I don't even know how to think about her sometimes. Her being gone—I think it's too big. Like, if I start talking about what it means that she's gone, I won't be able to deal with it."

"I know," Bryan said, "but sometimes you have to think about it."

I handed him some toilet paper so he could blow his nose.

"You can't tell anyone about this, Bryan."

"Who would I tell?"

"Um, Whit, my dad, Asher . . ."

"Give me some credit," he said, wiping his eyes again and standing up. "I wouldn't even know how to explain it. Just promise me something."

"What?"

"That you'll think about what you're doing . . . and whether any of this is right . . ."

"Yeah, okay," I said with a nod.

With no secrets to keep, I rose and faced the mirror and used the eyedropper to grab another dose of the serum to put under my tongue. Bryan watched with interest as I held the liquid in my mouth, waiting to swallow.

"No. Scratch what I said. It's not *Proof.* It's *Tristan and Isolde,*" he announced like he'd had a revelation.

I shook my head, not able to speak with the liquid under my tongue.

"We read that one in class, Maya. It's the story with the love potion and the black and white sails."

I shrugged.

"Google it," he said. "But just know that no one gets what they want in the end."

21

I felt light as I walked to the lab the next morning. Confessing the experiment to Bryan had filled me with deep relief, almost like I had permission to keep going. It's not as though he'd been enthusiastic about my project or even hinted that he might approve, but he hadn't locked me in the bathroom. He hadn't ripped the serum from my hand.

I had fallen asleep without grinding my teeth for the first time in weeks. Now that I could be honest with the most important person in my life, everything was right again.

I arrived at my desk with a smile on my face, which fell the moment I noticed the note on my desk from Dr. Araghi.

Maya, it said in his familiar scribble, *please report to me as soon as you arrive.*

There was a line under the word *soon.* I stared at it as I felt a sheen of sweat cover my forehead. My jaw was tight.

I had allowed myself to believe that there was no way we could get caught at this point. I was already on Day Five of the third serum, and everything at the lab seemed back to normal.

Yael hadn't asked any more questions, and Ann and I had been careful not to be seen together in her office during this third phase of the project.

"He doesn't know," I whispered aloud to comfort myself as I wiped my forehead with my arm. "He can't know."

"Maya, honey?"

I whipped around to see Tish in the doorway. "You saw Dr. Araghi's note? He wants to see you."

I tried to read her face. Her expression was calm, but didn't she usually address me with a warmer voice and a smile?

"I'll head over there right now," I chirped, sounding guilty.

She held papers in her hand. "Will you bring these to Dr. Araghi and tell him he has to sign them before the end of the week? I've asked him twice now."

"Sure."

"I'm sick of chasing that man for paperwork. Your mother was so good about record keeping."

That must be why she sounded cold. Tish was simply annoyed that she was working as an office manager for someone who refused to acknowledge that he worked in an office.

I took the papers and marched down the hall toward Dr. Araghi's office, trying to imagine what I would do if he summoned me to tell me we'd be caught. Would I blame Ann? Would I tell him it was all me? I shuddered, suddenly imagining the emptiness and purposelessness of my life if I was kicked out of MIT before I had even started. What if other schools wouldn't let me in? What if this experiment prevented me from pursuing the thing I was born to do?

I'd been so quick to tell Ann to continue the project when we knew we were close to getting caught. I cursed my priorities.

My mom often said that the best discoveries came from the purest, most altruistic questions. Even in her secret research with Ann, my mom's desire was to help good couples stay together. Maybe she wanted to help her own marriage, but she also wanted to save other partners.

My work, however, had been all about me. My selfish question for science was "How can I get him back?" It had led me to where I was now, taking a scientific walk of shame to Dr. Araghi's office, hoping that he wouldn't bust me for theft and misconduct.

His office door was open. The walls were a freshly painted mint green. I recognized a few framed prints on the wall from my mom's old office.

"Ms. Leschinsky, please take a seat," he said after noticing me hovering in the doorway.

It was probably only the fourth or fifth time I had seen him since I'd started my work in the lab. Dr. Araghi usually left his tapes in the drawer at my bench after I'd left for the day. I had spent months with his voice — sometimes dreaming of it after hours of transcription — but there hadn't been much cause to speak to him during my internship.

"So," he said as I sat down. His owl eyes were fixed on mine, which did nothing to slow my heart rate. "You're almost done with your summer work."

"Yes, sir," I said, regretting the "sir" as soon as it was out of my mouth.

"I thought we might have a talk about your work . . . and what you've been up to this summer."

A string of expletives ran through my mind.

"Sure. Of course," I responded, my tone cheery.

He waited, as if I should speak first. He leaned forward, his hands clasped together on top of his desk. Part of me wanted to blurt out a confession and an apology, and to begin begging him not to tell MIT admissions that I had stolen, lied, and pursued an unethical experiment off the books, but I bit my tongue, literally, as I tried to figure out how many of those details he actually might know.

Before I uttered a word, he spoke.

"You've done a wonderful job this summer, Maya. You've really become a member of the team."

"Okay," I said, waiting for more, because his tone didn't match his sentiment. His eyes were concerned. Questioning. Or maybe I was projecting.

"And I must thank you for your attention to detail," he continued. "All your little symbols and footnotes — they've been quite helpful. There's really an art to this transcription. I'm going to have a difficult time finding someone else to be as thoughtful about the work."

"I've enjoyed listening," I said, feeling hopeful that this might not end terribly. "I hope all those asterisks weren't distracting. Your notes are complicated, so I tried to come up with a system for them."

"On the contrary. Those little symbols are my new shorthand. I've never had a great system for organizing my thoughts. Your mother was always better at that. Now I'll have something to tell the next grad student who transcribes my tapes."

"Glad I could help," I said.

Dr. Araghi removed a small rectangular gift box from his desk drawer. He smiled, which made his long, gray eyebrows wiggle.

"I want to talk about something more serious now."

I nodded and swallowed.

"I know how difficult this job must be for you — working in the lab that your mother called home. Tish was worried that it might be painful for you to sit so close to your mother's office, to be so close to her work. I hope it's been more inspiring than . . . distracting or upsetting for you."

I froze, not knowing how to answer. Instead of getting caught, I was getting sympathy.

"I'm okay," I said. "It's been more inspiring than anything else."

Dr. Araghi smiled.

"Well, then. I know there's only another week or two before freshmen begin moving into their dorms for the semester. You're welcome to stop your work now or whenever you're ready. Just make sure Tish knows the rest of your schedule."

"Okay."

I knew the internship would be over at the end of the summer, but August had come too soon. I had grown so used to seeing Yael and Kyle every day; I didn't like the idea of being on campus without having them as part of my routine.

Not that I had them as much anymore. Kyle was still distant. Yael had forgiven me, it seemed, but I didn't feel like she trusted me.

"Of course, if you've changed your mind and you'd like to continue the work in the fall at some point, we'd be happy to have the extra help," Dr. Araghi started.

"No — I mean, maybe. Can I see how I feel after I get a sense of my classes? I think I'd like to do more work, and the money would be great, but I should figure out how much homework I have and just get used to the schedule, you know?"

"Of course," Dr. Araghi said, and pushed the rectangular box on the desk toward me.

I picked it up and opened the lid. Inside was a shiny silver pen. It said *Massachusetts Institute of Technology* in black script on the side. My mom had about fourteen pens just like it.

"I know your generation isn't much for writing things down, but every scientist should have a good pen. You never know when inspiration will hit. Always make notes."

Dr. Araghi 's eyebrows danced as he spoke.

"Thanks," I said, thinking that my mom probably used one of these pens to make all those notes in the One Direction binder.

"Oh — and before I forget," I added, "Tish says you have to sign these papers before the end of the week." I pulled them from my bag and placed them on his desk.

He tightened his lips like an angry child and nodded.

"Thanks again, Dr. Araghi."

"Of course," he said, now scowling at his homework.

I was still clutching the pen, feeling a strange mix of sadness about the end of the job and relief over not getting caught, when I arrived back at the lab. I could hear Yael's excited shouts from the hallway.

"Of course they took you back! If they were going to kick you out of school, they would have just done it. They wouldn't have had you working in the lab. You would have been gone last semester."

Yael and Kyle were leaning over Tish's desk, their backs facing me. I stood in the door frame, not sure whether I belonged.

"Yeah, I think it's all good. Except I'll be a full year behind," Kyle said. "I'll start junior year over again."

I let out an accidental cough, and they turned around.

"Did he take the papers?" Tish asked me.

"Reluctantly, but yes."

Kyle looked down, and Yael's eyes darted between us.

"Kyle's been accepted back into his program. He met with his adviser this morning. He'll be a junior again in September." Yael squeezed his arm.

"That's so great, Kyle," I said, trying to sound casual.

"Yeah, I'm psyched," he said, walking us back into the lab. "I owe Ann Markley bigtime. My adviser said she wrote some massive letter of recommendation saying I was the best lab tech she's ever worked with, and that I was a huge help to PhD students like her. I didn't even think she knew who I was. I guess I can't make fun of her anymore. Long live her facial piercings."

"Wow," I whispered. "That was . . . thoughtful of her."

"Yeah. Anyway," Kyle continued, "I'm going to take next week off to figure out my new schedule, maybe pick up some books and stuff before I move into my place for next year. I'll wrap up here Friday."

He sounded a little sad about it.

"We should have a cake," Tish said. "Something for you and Maya. Maya, have you decided on your last day?"

I cleared my throat, my eyes fixed on Kyle's. "I'll work through early next week. Tuesday, I think."

"Tuesday," Tish mumbled, writing the information on the legal pad in front of her.

"I can't believe you guys are abandoning me," Yael whined. "Can we go to dinner Friday? Chicken skewers or something, before you both get back into your undergraduate drama and I never see you again?"

"I have plans that night. Dinner with someone," Kyle said, looking away. He might as well have shouted that he had a date.

Then I remembered that I also had somewhere to be. That night was my outing—*the* outing—with Whit. We'd emailed a few times, arranging the details. Bryan was sleeping over tonight to help me prepare. He made it clear again that he didn't support the plan but was curious to find out what would happen. Also, if I was going to attempt an evening of seduction, he wanted to choose my outfit.

"Dinner next week would work for me," I said, looking up, but Kyle already had his headphones on.

22

Whit texted about the restaurant three times before I arrived.

Are you sure sushi is okay? Because there's also a falafel place right near my apartment, he said.

I could tell he wanted me to be as comfortable as possible. This was our first time alone since the breakup, and it's not as though our run-in at Bryan's performance had gone smoothly.

I was nervous about the venue too, for different reasons. I wanted to make sure I'd be able to make good observations — that it was the kind of place where we could stay awhile.

Bryan had wanted to take me into Harvard Square to get a new outfit, but I explained that it was better for the experiment if I looked "normal." No new wardrobe or special makeup or accessories. I wound up in my most average outfit — a pair of jeans and a black T-shirt. I put my hair up in the usual ponytail, pushing all the loose frizz behind my ears, and allowed myself minimal makeup.

"Hey," I said, sliding into the booth to face him.

"Hey," he said back, prolonging the eye contact until I had to blink.

His hair was different, or, more accurately, missing. He'd basically shaved his head.

"It's easier like this," he said when he saw me staring at it, my jaw hanging low.

"I like it, I think," I said, trying to figure out whether I actually did. Now there was just an almost invisible red stubble on his skin.

"Bryan would hate it," Whit said, grinning.

"He'd despise it," I said.

"Don't tell him," he said, laughing as he rubbed the top of his scalp with his palm.

He was wearing the pink Historic Plymouth T-shirt I got for him during my trip to Aunt Cindy's more than a year ago. I smiled, noticing how tightly it fit. He had gained a little weight living in the dorms this year. The white *P* was beginning to crack under the pressure. It was cute.

We started talking like the night wasn't a big deal, slipping into our old routine, like the last few months hadn't happened. We avoided all discussion of Andrea Berger. We never referenced our breakup.

I asked him what he thought of Bryan's show, and he went on and on about how impressed he was with his performance.

"He's got that thing, you know? It's so natural for him. Really, there aren't many people who can star in a musical and then do Shakespeare. He really gets it."

"I know," I said, teeming with pride.

Then Whit mentioned Asher, and all my breath left my body at once.

"He was serviceable, but can you explain why that guy is such a big deal? I've never even heard of him, but the minute he walked onstage, these girls behind us started shrieking. One girl was actually crying. We were so confused."

I flinched at the *we.*

"He's sort of an online phenomenon," I said as a server came over and placed bowls of miso soup in front of us. "He makes viral videos, and now he's acting. The videos get about a million views apiece."

"He should find a day job," Whit said, grabbing a spoon. "I mean, the fact that the guy has the lead role in a professional production is just offensive. It's one thing to put him in the kids' cast, but in the adult production? Come on."

"He's actually in the running to star in a play in New York, off-Broadway," I said, feeling the need to defend Asher. Whit could be so judgmental.

"Good for him, I guess," Whit said, starting on his soup.

"So," I said, changing the subject, "I got my first choice for room assignments next year. A single in Simmons Hall."

"Which one was that?"

I googled the dorm on my phone and showed Whit the crazy architecture. "Remember? It's the weird-looking one — the building that looks like a big sponge."

"I've always thought that building looks more like a prison," he said, laughing. "I can't wait to see your room, though. Thank god it's a single."

My stomach dropped as I tried to process what that could mean.

I fought the urge to ask for clarification and brought up his writing instead. He told me that he'd spent the summer writing a new short film about a man who lives his whole life in a cubicle.

"It's a commentary on office culture," Whit said.

My mind wandered as he spoke. I couldn't focus.

Instead, I was thinking about what would happen next — whether I'd be able to extend the evening. This dinner hadn't given us much opportunity to get close.

He grabbed the check, refusing to let me contribute.

"You came all the way into Boston. My treat," he said, throwing down two twenties.

Outside the restaurant, the Green Line train bellowed and then squeaked to a stop in front of us.

"T or bus?" he asked.

"Bus will be faster," I said, defeated.

"I'll walk you to a stop," Whit said, running his hand across his head the way he always did. It was a strange move without the hair.

"You don't have to."

I stared at him then, my eyes darting from his forehead to his nose to his mouth. I had been so starved for the look of him, and now that we were standing face-to-face, under the bright lights of the nearby bodega, I reacquainted myself with all of his features—his crooked bottom teeth, his high cheekbones, and the small scar under his lip that he got from falling on his face during his twelfth birthday party at an ice-skating rink.

So much had happened since he'd broken up with me. I wanted to be the person I was months ago, before all this had started. I wanted to curl up with him and feel like things were simple.

"Let me walk with you," he said. "It's late. Come on."

We were mostly silent as we walked along Commonwealth Avenue toward Mass. Ave. Twice I felt my hand accidentally skim his.

I was thoughtful about my pace, moving as slowly as I could without it being weird. With Kyle, we had always been in rooms together, in close proximity, with the windows closed. There had been more variables with Asher, but we had had a long walk around the pond and had settled in that Narnia clearing, where there was nothing else to get in our way.

This walk with Whit was more difficult. The street was crowded with college kids who kept pushing their way between us. I couldn't tell whether Whit was getting anything chemical from our interaction.

"What are you thinking?"

His question startled me, and I realized we were steps away from where I could pick up the bus to get back home.

I stopped and looked up, sensing his pensiveness, and began to laugh at his question. I had asked him once, at the start of our relationship, "What are you thinking?" and he had answered with a lecture. "Never say 'What are you thinking?' Ever. It's an awful girlfriend question, and I like you because you are not the kind of girlfriend who asks that question," Whit had said.

I remember trying not to freak out because it was the first time he had called me his girlfriend.

"You just asked me the horrible girlfriend question," I said through my laughter, prompting Whit to join me. "What am *I* thinking? What are *you* thinking?"

"Wow. You're right."

"Don't worry, *I* don't mind the question," I said, grinning.

"Hey," he said, and tilted his head to his shoulder, "do you want to see my apartment before you go home? It's only a few blocks away."

He was doing my work for me. I had thought about asking to see his place, or at least meeting there before dinner, but I was afraid Andrea Berger might be sitting in his living room, waiting for his return. Or that evidence of her existence would be all over the apartment.

"Sure," I said, trying to keep my tone breezy.

I followed him to a beautiful brownstone on a less noisy side street in the neighborhood. For a moment, I wondered how he could afford this kind of apartment, but when he opened the door, I saw that it was less pristine inside. The paint on the walls in the hallway was yellowed and peeling. There were about twenty pairs of shoes in the front hallway, some blocking the door. Whit kicked them out of the way and led me to the stairs.

We were both out of breath by the time we got to his place on the fifth floor.

"The stairs are a beast, right?" he said, panting as he fiddled with his keys. "I'm hoping to get in better shape living here."

All my concerns about whether he'd notice my pheromones evaporated when we entered the apartment. It was small and hot; I could almost see the moisture in the air. Whit's apartment was basically a larger version of the warm room in our lab. I couldn't have designed it any better.

"You guys need an air-conditioning unit," I said. "My dad probably has an old one."

"No, thank you," Whit said, shaking his head. "We actually have one and kept it running throughout July and wound up with a four-hundred-dollar electric bill. I think Nate never turned the thing off when he left for the day. Now we're surviving without it for the rest of the summer."

I nodded as I walked through the place, surprised by the Dali print of melting clocks in the living room, which I figured Whit would have vetoed because it was such a stereotypical dorm-room print — the kind of art he'd say was for people who didn't know anything about art.

There were also three framed vinyl records — Fleetwood Mac, the Black Keys, Kings of Leon . . . bands I wasn't even sure he liked. Nothing in the place seemed to go together.

I found the bathroom and went in, pulling the shower curtain back like a police detective. I wondered if Andrea Berger might have left any products in the apartment, but all I saw was one industrial-size bottle of dandruff shampoo.

"My bedroom is over there," he said, pointing.

Whit's room was more his style. Only one print hung on his

yellowing wall, a framed black-and-white photograph of a wistful-looking clown that we'd found at a flea market when we first started dating. I don't know why we loved the photo so much; now it looked extra pitiful as the centerpiece of the room.

"It's really good to see you in this room," Whit said. "It's weird, but it's good. I'm happy you're here."

I whipped around to face him. He leaned against the door frame, his facial expression matching the one on the bummed-out clown.

I paused before I spoke as I considered the strangeness of being estranged. As natural as it felt to be with him, the almost two months that had passed since our breakup felt like a year. I didn't know him now. Not really.

"Being with you — and not being *with you* — it feels unnatural," I confessed. "I don't know what my place is here."

"Come sit down," he said, walking to the bed.

I joined him there and he leaned over, reaching into the drawer of his nightstand. For a second my whole body tensed as I wondered what he might be retrieving, but then I recognized the small yellow pouch that held the Bananagrams.

I couldn't keep myself from laughing. "Cool college guys do not keep Bananagrams in their nightstands. You're supposed to have condoms and drugs in there."

"The condoms come out *after* the Bananagrams," he said, smirking. "You have to work up to these things, Maya."

I flagged the comment in my head as a possible sign that things were working. Something was happening.

I looked for more specific evidence as he set up the game. His eyes were a little red, but not quite dilated. He wasn't mirroring my behavior as much as he was falling into our old routine.

We sat across from each other on the bed, like we used to at my house, more focused on winning than anything else. We played round after round, mostly silent as we raced to build words with the game pieces. It was peaceful, just fumbling for the small lettered squares, occasionally glancing up to see whether his words were better than mine.

At some point I glanced at the clock on his nightstand and saw that it was late. After eleven. If I waited much longer to go home, the buses would stop running. We'd made progress, but I'd have to do this again for more results. I would ask Ann for more time with the serum. This was the part of the experiment that counted, and I needed to get it right.

"I should go," I said as Whit finished spelling out QUIT, which seemed appropriate.

"Maya," Whit said, interrupting before I could say any more. "Can I ask you a weird favor?"

I looked up, and his eyes were glassier.

"Of course," I said, watching his shoulders collapse like he had given up on something.

He scratched his head again and looked frustrated. Watching all those familiar expressions pass over his face made me want to grab his shoulders and yell, "Don't you miss this?" But I kept my hands in my lap and watched him, trying to make sense of his changing mood.

"Listen," he said, leaning in like he was telling a secret. "Can we just lie down in bed and talk before you go? Like we used to? I sort of want to be close right now, if that's okay with you. I can't explain it." His voice cracked.

I nodded, too surprised to speak.

He began adjusting the pillows while my brain spun like a centrifuge. My plan was to start slow, just spending time with him on his terms. Maybe he'd exhibit signs that the experiment had worked;

maybe I'd have to continue to see him before results were clear. No matter what, I hadn't planned on anything physical happening with Whit. I didn't want to be part of a cheat; that would pollute our whole relationship.

I had checked Andrea Berger's Instagram account before dinner, looking for any indication that their relationship had changed, but there was nothing. Her bio quote was the same, and there were no sad messages, just rehearsal updates and a few posts of quotes from actresses and writers she liked. She and Whit still seemed to be together, at least online.

But all he wants to do is lie down, I rationalized. It wouldn't be a cheat, not if we just talked.

The mattress shifted as he turned off the light and scrambled to stretch out next to me. I could've asked him why it was necessary for it to be dark, but I didn't. Instead, I turned on my side and went horizontal, my chest tightening as I felt him move to spoon me from behind, resting one arm on my waist.

My ethics — both personal and professional — went out the window as I involuntarily pulled the arm that was on my waist in front of me so we were even closer.

He dove in, nuzzling my ear on the pillow.

"You smell so good."

"That's the word on the street," I said, my body tense all over.

He pushed his hips into my backside and kissed my neck.

"Whit," I said, my voice strained, "what are you doing?"

"Missing you," he said, kissing my ear. "Being happy that you're here."

I turned around to face him, and he kissed me. I didn't move my lips, but I didn't pull away. He shifted so he could place his head on my chest, and I stroked what was left of his hair.

I closed my eyes, and all I could see was Andrea Berger's name, like it was etched on the backs of my eyelids.

"We can't do this," I whispered. "I know it's confusing, but we just can't."

I stopped talking when I noticed that my T-shirt felt wet. I looked down to find Whit's head shaking—because he was crying.

"Whit?" I tried to unlink his arms from my back so I could shuffle down the bed to see his face, but he held me where I was and wiped his nose on my T-shirt. He was crying so hard that his shoulders shook too. I'd never seen him get teary at all, and this was a full-on sob, and it was my fault. He had asked for a simple dinner, and I had manipulated him into wanting more. Now he was confused and hating himself because he had fallen into bed with his ex-girlfriend. I should never have come back to the apartment. I should never have joined him for Bananagrams. I did feel like Dr. Frankenstein now—like I had created a monster. I was the monster.

"It's okay," I said, rubbing circles on the top of his back. "This isn't your fault."

"She won't talk to me," he said, shuddering.

"I know this is confusing."

"It is, and I can't—I can't fix it. I can't fix her. I can't fix us. It's like everything I touch is cursed." His body jerked. "She won't even text me back."

"Wait," I said, repeating his words to myself. "Who won't text you back?"

Whit looked up at me, the tears drying up, like he had just tightened the faucet.

"Andrea," he said, as if the answer should be obvious.

Without giving his response a second thought, I grabbed his

shoulders and pushed him from my body. "Andrea Berger won't text you back?"

Whit closed his eyes after I said her name, like it hurt to hear it.

"We broke up. It's over. She doesn't want anything to do with me. I've just been—" he shook his head. "I've been a little lost. It was going so well, and then she said I was moving too fast, and that she wasn't ready for a big relationship. I don't know how people dial it back. If you're into someone, why wouldn't you be all in? What's the point in playing games?"

My brain tried to catch up. He was crying about Andrea Berger. They had broken up at some point before our dinner. He had dragged me here and was now asking me for advice. Like I might want to help.

Every profanity I knew gathered at the tip of my tongue, ready to be screamed.

"You kissed me" was all I said, my voice sounding far away.

He reached for me then, but I had already bounded off the bed, my body moving faster than my brain. I placed my hand on the wall next to me and found the switch for the ceiling light. It was bright and fluorescent and made both of us squint. I spotted a spider floating in a web above the door. The paint on the walls was peeling. All of a sudden, Whit's small bedroom was the bleakest place in the world.

Still on the mattress, Whit kicked his legs in front of him to untangle himself from his brown sheets. Then he sat up and leaned his back against the wall so that his face was just under the portrait of the sad clown.

"I probably shouldn't be kissing anyone," he said, his eyes on the floor.

"You're right; you shouldn't," I responded, my voice as sharp as I could get it. "Especially not me!"

"I know this is selfish," Whit continued. "I just miss talking to you. You're my best friend, and I miss telling you things. Can't I miss telling you things?"

"You broke up with me!" I yelled. "That's what happens — you lose the friendship! You don't get to pick and choose what parts of our relationship you want at any given moment."

I reminded myself of Yael now, blunt and confident.

"You just pulled me into bed with you and kissed me because you were sad about Andrea Berger, the girl you dumped me for. Who does that?"

Somehow I felt like I was being dumped for a second time, like somehow he had blindsided me all over again.

"Now that I'm hearing it, I know this is terrible. I get that, Maya. But when I saw you at Bryan's show with your dad and Yael, you looked so happy. I thought maybe we could move past all of this and be friends. I was going to wait to reach out to you until after you started school, so you'd be busy with your new life, and hearing from me wouldn't mean so much. But you started responding to my emails, and then things got so crazy with Andrea. I'm alone with this — all this change. You have Bryan and Kyle and Yael . . ."

"You have all your fancy college friends," I said, thinking of the group I saw at the black-box theater, and all the new faces I'd seen when I visited Whit at school over the past year. "You *wanted* to be around people who were more like you, remember?"

I grabbed a pillow from the edge of the bed and attempted to hurl it toward his face, but it was a pillow, so it moved slowly. He caught it before it landed, and pulled it into his lap.

"It wasn't all or nothing, Maya. Yes, I wanted to break up and date someone else, but that doesn't mean I haven't missed you."

"What is it that you miss, Whit? Because I understand that you miss our friendship, but it also seems like you miss the kissing. You didn't pull me into bed to talk."

"I didn't expect to want to do that. I was confused—or maybe it was just habit. It's not like I suddenly stopped being attracted to you when we broke up. That never went away, Maya. I broke up with you because I was also attracted to someone else, and I really wanted to be with her. I was spending so much time with her . . . it was inevitable.

"God, Maya, I'm sorry I screwed up so horribly tonight. I just wanted you back in my life. I swear, I had no intention of kissing you. I just wanted to hang out."

"That makes sense," I mumbled as I admitted, at least to myself, that this could be my fault too. Maybe he had meant for this to be a platonic night, and it was the serum that inspired him to take it a step too far.

I'd had all these fantasies of how this reconciliation would play out, and every one of them involved Whit having some epiphany about what he left behind. Maybe that was happening now, but it didn't seem to erase his need for someone new, and it certainly didn't seem to be bringing us back together. He just looked confused.

Frustrated with both of us, I grabbed my shoes, which I had tossed by his bedroom door.

"Hey—you don't have to go," he said, tossing the pillow off his lap and getting up.

"I do, actually. The buses are going to stop running soon."

I found my bag on the floor and checked to make sure I had my cell phone and keys.

"Please stay. Call your dad and tell him you're staying over. You shouldn't be on a bus alone this late."

"I'll be fine," I said. "I can't be here with you anymore."

He stopped in the center of the room and nodded, his eyes still red around the rims.

"I can't be the person who comforts you right now," I said. "I can't believe you ever thought I could."

"I know," Whit said, sounding defeated. "I want you to feel good about me again. I don't want you to feel bad about us."

"You can't force people to feel things!" I yelled.

The irony of the statement wasn't lost on me.

Angrier at myself than at him, I about-faced and slammed the door behind me, then ran down the five flights of stairs, barely breathing until I was out on the street.

23

I'd never been so desperate to put distance between myself and another human being. In the last fifteen minutes, I'd gone from thinking that my experiment had worked and that all I'd lost had been returned, to finding out that Whit was as sad about Andrea Berger as I was about him.

I found myself sprinting to catch the bus on Mass. Ave., dodging people on the street like I was in a video game. I just wanted to get back to my side of the river, back to my room and my bedspread and my computer.

I was winded when I got to the bus stop. No one was there, which was a bad sign. I found my cell phone in my bag and saw that somehow an hour had passed. The last bus had come and gone.

I began to walk down Mass. Ave., deciding I could use some air. There was a nice warm breeze, and it felt good to be outside after being in Whit's stifling apartment.

As I walked, I thought about how I would explain the night to Ann. Better yet, I wondered whether she could explain any of this to me.

There had been so many variables, so much inconsistency and room for error in this project from start to finish.

Kyle wasn't the neutral subject we hoped for. Asher was attention-starved, insecure, and on the hunt for female validation. Whit was desperate and heartbroken and searching for familiarity. How could we have expected this project to yield legitimate results? The more I thought about it, the angrier I got with Ann, who was supposed to know more than I did. Why did she let me do any of this? What was the point?

I decided that once I got home, I'd write her a final report—with my real opinions. I'd tell her that we shouldn't have messed with people like this. I'd tell her everything we did wrong, and that we should forget this ever happened.

I'd be moving into my dorm in two weeks. I would start school and develop a whole new life. This summer would be erased. The air got cooler as I got closer to the water, and it felt cathartic, like it was getting me clean in some way, so I just kept walking. At Beacon Street, I passed a pack of guys in Red Sox shirts who were probably still celebrating after whatever had happened at Fenway Park hours ago.

Not far from them, a couple sat on a bench, yelling at each other.

"It was like I was invisible!" the woman shouted, pointing at the man.

"I was right there," he responded.

"You didn't talk to me all night!" she said.

The sound of their argument faded as I bounded forward toward the bridge.

Once I was on the walking path that would take me across the Charles River, the wind picked up and whipped my ponytail toward my face.

The scenery was appropriate, I thought as I paused to take in the view. Whit and I had walked across this bridge on our first date. At the time, I wasn't even sure it *was* a date. I remembered our awkward hug goodbye, and how he texted twenty minutes later, asking to hang out again, and I felt like I could float away.

Now he was gone, and Kyle wanted nothing to do with me. Yael didn't trust me. Bryan would leave for Syracuse in just over a week.

The longest I'd ever gone without seeing Bryan was three weeks, when I got really bad pneumonia. Now I'd have to live without him until Thanksgiving.

I pulled my phone and earbuds from my bag and decided to treat myself to a song from his playlist, keeping the volume low so I could hear the traffic around me. I was dangerously close to getting to the last song, which was Bryan's deadline for me to get over Whit.

The next track was new to me, a breakup song that made me long for something, although I didn't know what anymore.

It was about going back to a better time — taking back words and love.

But the point of the song was that you *couldn't* go back. It was weirdly upbeat, despite the lyrics, which told a story I knew too well.

By the time the track was over and I'd made it to the other side of the bridge, I was furious. I hadn't done this on my own.

I found the number of the one person who I believed would have answers — because she always acted like she did.

"Are you all right?" Ann said, bypassing hellos. She sounded like a nervous parent, which made me angrier. "I thought you'd check in hours ago."

"I'm not all right," I said, my tone serious.

"It's after midnight. Where are you? I hear cars. Are you outside?"

The fact that she was asking responsible questions pushed me over the edge. Because Ann was no grownup. No adult would have helped me make this mess.

"Ann," I said, my voice as low as it could go, "do you really think my mom would have let me do this experiment? Do you really think she would have wanted me to?"

I dodged a pack of girls in sorority T-shirts who ran past me toward the bridge.

"What?"

"This project — it was bad for me. It was a risk for you, too, but it was terrible for me. You should have kicked me out of your office that day. You should have stopped me."

Ann sighed into the phone. "What happened? Are you okay?"

"He doesn't want me," I said, forcing back tears. "He wants Andrea Berger. Even if he had wanted me tonight, all of it would have been fake."

I could hear her movement through the phone. It sounded like she was getting out of bed and stumbling around, maybe thinking she'd come find me. That wouldn't happen — I didn't want to see her.

"Why did you let me do this?" I demanded.

"You begged me to do it!" she almost shouted.

We both tried to speak then, cutting each other off, our words mingling to make a high-pitched sound.

I stopped myself, giving her a turn.

"I don't know why I did it, Maya," she said, her voice tired. "I think . . . it's just that I don't have *this* anymore. I don't have anything I care about. I don't have your mother. Ever since she died, I've been trying to finish a degree that no longer excites me. I miss being a part of something . . . different. I always liked what I studied, but she made me love what I do. She showed me possibilities, and all of a sudden, they were gone. Then you came into my office that day, and I felt that excitement again for a few minutes. I wanted that back."

She paused, and then her voice was soft.

"Listen, Maya, I do feel responsible for this. I should know better. I *did* know better after our second experiment. And I underestimated your hopes, clearly. With your mother, there was one subject, and it was so simple. We were just doing some preliminary trials so we could be more confident about pitching it as a project for real study. There wasn't all of this deception and lying. Our work was secret, but it's not as though she was trying to manipulate men in her life like you did. The whole thing felt more appropriate."

"Are you kidding me?" I screamed. "She manipulated my dad!"

I sank to the ground by a tree, now with a view of MIT's dome.

"That's the thing we haven't said out loud, right?" I continued, my voice weak now. "Because we're not supposed to say anything bad about my mom, because she was a genius and probably curing disease with all her work, right? But honestly, Ann, how would my dad feel if he knew she had been messing with him like that? I thought my mom was this pillar of scientific integrity. She was always talking about the ethics of the work. But she was experimenting on her own husband. And then I went and messed with everybody, just like her. Worse than her."

"What the hell are you talking about, Maya? Your dad loved this project."

"What?"

"Wait . . ." Ann said. "Did you think he didn't know? Didn't you see his notes in the back of the binder?"

"I gave you the binder," I said, my voice cracking as I processed what she was telling me.

"But you read it first."

Ann sounded annoyed now, and more like my mom than she ever had.

"I focused on the data and the numbers, but where it got narrative at the end . . . I didn't want to read about my parents' sex life. I didn't think . . . I mean, you never mentioned that he knew."

"You never asked! I assumed you knew. Come on, Maya. Of course your dad knew about the experiment. He gave us his own notes every week. They're in the back of the binder. That's why I was so excited to try this with you. Your dad was a great sport, but we had to take his knowledge of the experiment into consideration. His knowing about the serum meant that he wasn't an objective subject. Your take on this research presented the opportunity to eliminate that bias."

My teeth chattered in the cold. I covered my face with my hand in shame. "So I'm the unethical one. Just me. Of course she got permission."

Ann sighed and then let out a harsh laugh.

"You know, there was some part of me that really believed she would have wanted us to do this, that when you showed up in my office that day with the binder in your hand, it felt like destiny, like maybe she knew you'd eventually seek me out. But now that we've been through this, I think she just would have wanted me to protect you. I should have sent you out of my office that day. I just don't even know what I'm doing anymore. You're eighteen."

"Seventeen," I whispered.

"What?"

"I don't turn eighteen for another month. And you know, you might act like you know everything, like you're the expert, but you're *Yael's age*. You're not even close to finishing your PhD."

She was silent.

"The thing that bothers me most," I said, my voice dark, "is that the science here wasn't even good. There were so many variables. We have no idea whether any of this actually worked."

"These types of studies take years, Maya," Ann said. "Had your mother and I become more confident about our work, we would have suggested starting a long-term project on the books, and the research would have been much more specific. I just thought, when you and I decided to continue this, that maybe I'd get some ideas for carrying it forward without her. I wanted to see if we could get any short-term results, but I knew they wouldn't be conclusive."

"Well, I wish I had known," I said.

I needed to be done with the conversation. I felt lost.

"I have to go, Ann. Let's just forget about all of this. Keep the binder. I don't want it."

"Let me come get you, Maya," she said. "It's late."

"No, just — just stay away from me!"

The last comment came out before I could filter it; it sounded harsh — and final, but I was furious at both of us.

"Maya, that's not the answer here," Ann started.

I hung up before she could say anything else.

I felt terrible for a second, imagining her alone in her apartment, overcome by guilt for turning me into this mess, but that's why it was best for both of us if things went back to the way they were, with me giving her a quick nod if I saw her on campus or ignoring her altogether. We were two grieving people who made bad decisions. I needed to stay away from her.

My chest felt tight, but I exhaled through it and stood up to start walking again, too close to home to consider calling a car. I could feel blisters forming between my toes, though — my shoes weren't meant for this kind of walk — but I was only blocks away, now on the stretch of Mass. Ave. with the bars and clubs.

I passed one nightclub with a line down the street, then stopped in front of the skewer restaurant to give my feet a break. That's when I thought about where I was — so close to the smell. I was steps away from Cambridge Foods, and in that moment, it called out to me like a holy place — like the smell of chocolate in front of that building could bring me back to where I was before I created this mess. All I wanted was to be standing in front of it, feeling like I used to feel with Kyle and Yael. Warm and happy.

It looked open, which made sense. If Cambridge Foods made chocolate nougat and mint filling for the entire East Coast, it was probably a twenty-four-hour business.

I had never done a whiff walk so late. The smell was stronger at this hour than it was during our trips after work. The wave of chocolate and mint was overwhelming and made me feel even lonelier without Kyle and Yael by my side.

I sat on the curb across the street and took out my cell phone, first googling Andrea Berger's social media accounts, wondering if they'd look different.

Her last post was two hours old, just a selfie of her with a friend in front of a big cake with glowing candles. *Amy's birthday!* the caption said. Somehow, despite wishing for months that Andrea Berger would make herself disappear, I was furious that she had. Whit had left me so that he could pursue her, yet she had dropped him so easily, leaving him home alone in a hot, dirty apartment. She was out for *Amy's birthday,* like she didn't care.

I closed the page and wondered where Kyle might be. I imagined him sitting in front of his laptop at home watching whatever strange web series he was into at the moment, while occasionally messaging his brother, who was studying abroad in Australia.

I stared at my phone as if I could will Kyle to text me. I wanted to tell him about my night. I wanted to tell him about everything.

A glare bounced off the screen of my phone, bringing my attention back to the building. "Oh, my god," I said, jumping to my feet.

A light had popped on in a room at the far end of the Cambridge Foods building, closer to the end of the block. I could see a shadow moving along the wall inside. Someone was in there.

"Wonka," I whispered.

I walked toward the moving light and placed my hands on the white bricks in front of me. The window was about eight feet from street level. If I could stand on something, just to give myself a boost, I could probably see in.

I could take a picture and send it to Kyle, finally disproving — or proving — the existence of Willy Wonka in Cambridge.

Really, it was an excuse to say anything to him — to send him a message he couldn't ignore.

I looked around to see what I could grab to use as a makeshift ladder. There were no benches here. Nothing to climb. My only real option was one of the giant trash cans in the parking lot of the U-Haul place down the street. I darted down the road and wheeled one over so that it sat beneath the glowing window.

The wheels on the bottom of the can made it easy to transport but difficult to keep steady. I placed my palms on top of the lid and pressed down, testing its strength.

"What are you doing?"

I turned to see three boys watching me. They were coming up the block in a cloud of cigarette smoke. They looked around my age, maybe younger.

"Breaking and entering?" the boy in the center asked with a grin on his face.

"Not quite," I said, realizing how it looked. "I'm just trying to see inside." *To see if the building is populated by Oompa Loompas,* I thought.

"Need help?" the boy on the right asked. He wore a sleeveless shirt that framed his bulging arms, and he had a tattoo of a shamrock on his shoulder.

"Sure. Thanks."

Two of them held the trash can in place while the third laced his fingers together so I could use his hands as a step and climb to the top. His arms shook as I put one foot in his hands and lifted myself onto the flat lid of the trash can. Once I was crouched on the lid, they pushed the trash bin closer to the window.

"Stand up slowly," the first boy said. It was like they had done this before.

My arms reached out, my instincts telling me to hold on to something for balance. I wasn't more than eight or nine feet from the ground, but I felt like an acrobat. I grabbed on to the window ledge, which wasn't thick enough to give me any real support, but at least it helped me keep my body straight.

Once it felt safe to look up, my eyes went to the window, and for the first time, I had a view straight into the Cambridge Foods building.

The first thing I saw was a file cabinet. Then a small meeting table. Then I saw a man at a desk who, while small and round, was not an Oompa Loompa. He was just a guy in his fifties in an ordinary office who appeared to be checking over paperwork. He didn't look like Charlie, either. *Charlie Bucket would have aged better than this,* I thought.

I was just about to sag with disappointment when I noticed that I also had a view straight into the plant through the window to my right. I could see the giant silver machines that must make the candy filling. They stretched from the floor to the ceiling and had big silver levers that flew up and down like a kick line. There was a border of colorful paint on the ceiling that looked like it was designed in the 1970s. Big yellow and purple swirls that looked like candy clouds.

This could be Kyle's place of pure imagination.

Planting a hand farther down the brick exterior of the building, I reached back into my pocket to retrieve my phone. I turned on the camera one-handed and held up the lens, trying to get a clear view of the machines and the paint job so I could get the best shot.

"Almost done?" one of the boys yelled from below.

"Just another second," I responded.

I leaned a bit farther to my right, trying to get a wider view of the room — and that's when the ground disappeared beneath me.

First the lid folded and fell into the can, and then I fell with it, landing hard on my leg on the sidewalk.

"Holy shit, she's down," Shamrock Tattoo Guy yelled, which sent the other two running, scattering before they could be blamed for the accident. "I'm sorry," Shamrock Guy said, shaking his head and then running after them.

My legs looked like bendy straws, and two of my fingers on my left hand felt twisted and broken, having taken most of my weight when I fell to the ground. I tried moving my legs and felt a sharp pain in my ankle.

Cursing, I used my right hand to push myself up so that I was seated. I crawled to my phone, which had fallen out of my hand, and called Bryan. It went to voicemail, so I left a message, saying that I had fallen in Central Square and to call me as soon as possible.

I had to find someone to come get me, and I knew that my dad was at Cindy and Pam's for stargazing; I didn't want to worry them or make him drive an hour back to rescue me.

Then I called Kyle. It felt wrong, because he wouldn't have the option of ignoring me if I told him I was on the ground, in need of medical attention, but I didn't care anymore. I just wanted him there, and I wanted to apologize. He didn't pick up, but I left a message, figuring he was probably screening the call.

"Hey," I said, my voice trembling as pain shot through my leg. "No big deal, but I sort of fell down by the chocolate factory, and I think I sprained something. It's after midnight, and I'm alone out here. Um, if you're there, can you give me a call?"

Kyle didn't get the message fast enough, though. About two seconds after I hung up, the man who had been in the small office inside Cambridge Foods ran out the front door with a cell phone in his hand.

"Miss, what happened?" he asked, crouching to get a better look at me. "Were you mugged?"

"No, I fell," I explained. "I might have broken something."

He called 911 and then made me call my dad, saying that if his own daughter had fallen and needed medical attention, he'd want to be there, even if it meant driving more than an hour from Plymouth. Then the man rode with me to Mount Auburn Hospital, where I was diagnosed with broken ring and pinky fingers and a twisted ankle. They'd take an MRI of my knee next week just to be sure there wasn't more damage.

My dad showed up two hours later, running to my emergency-room bed looking angry but relieved. It was the first time he'd yelled at me since my mom died.

"At this moment, I am the father of a person who was brought to the hospital because she was scaling a private building," he said, his voice terse. "Who are you right now?" he asked, bewildered.

He barely spoke to me until about four thirty in the morning, when they let us go home. He mostly just leaned his head against the wall and closed his eyes.

"Next time you want to go break into a candy factory, call me first and I'll get a ladder," he said as I crawled into bed, the painkillers in my system pushing me toward sleep.

24

I woke to a double knock on my bedroom door. "Are you decent?" my dad asked.

"Yeah," I mumbled. My mouth was dry, and my fingers throbbed. I'd never broken a bone before. The athletes at my high school were always walking around with small casts and boots like it wasn't a big deal, but in reality, the pain was intense, the agony validating my instinct that I was never meant to do sports. "I need more of the pills, like, now," I whined at the door.

A minute later it opened, and Kyle entered the room with two small pills in his right hand.

"Your dad told me to bring these," he said. I grabbed for my blanket and pulled it up to my neck to cover myself, forgetting that I was fully clothed.

"What are you doing here?" I asked, trying to smooth my hair.

"You called me," he said, pulling the white chair from my desk over to the bed and sitting backwards on it. "You called me last night saying that you had fallen down in Central Square. By the time I got the message, your phone was off. And then I spent the rest of the night worrying that you were dead in the street. I called Yael at, like, three in the morning. She found Bryan, who'd already spoken to your dad."

"Oh, my god," I said, my head starting to pound.

I grabbed the pills from Kyle's hand and washed them down with a glass of water — now warm from sitting out all night — next to my bed.

"I'm so sorry, Kyle," I said. "I called you, but then this guy from Cambridge Foods brought me to the hospital. I don't even know what I did with my phone."

He smiled, and I realized how long it had been since I had seen him look anything but uncomfortable around me. I wanted to freeze his face just like that.

"It's okay. I mean . . . it's not okay—I was a wreck. When I finally got ahold of your dad, he said your phone had died, but he said to come back at noon and we'd wake you up together."

I took another sip of water and willed the pills to enter my bloodstream.

"You know, I did it for you," I said, holding up my bandaged fingers so he could see. "This is a Wonka-related injury. I was trying to get a picture. I saw what it looks like inside."

"That's what your dad said," Kyle said. "So are you going to tell me what's in there? Was it all that we dreamed of and more?"

"Sort of," I said, leaning back onto my pillow. "It was sort of what we thought it would be."

"Meaning . . ."

"Well, I counted only six Oompa Loompas, and the chocolate river was disappointingly small, but, you know, everyone has to downsize at some point."

Kyle laughed, and I closed my eyes to enjoy the sound.

"I miss you," I said, then yawned, my body aching for more rest.

"Good," he whispered. I couldn't tell if he was angry or relieved.

I had no memory of falling asleep again or seeing Kyle leave, but when I woke up hours later, I could hear Bryan downstairs in the kitchen. I forced myself out of bed, made a slow walk to the bathroom, where I brushed my teeth with one hand, and then walked slowly down the steps, a process that made me crave even more painkillers.

Bryan, who was at the counter making pasta salad with my dad, began to hoot and applaud. I took a quick bow and joined them at the table.

There would be no more transcription, no more days at the lab. The doctor said I should take it easy before starting school. My dad had called Dr. Araghi, who said that Tish would mail my last paycheck.

Yael came over later that day and sat on my bed, promising we'd still have dinners once I got to campus, even though she'd always told me she despised undergraduates.

"You don't count, little one," she said. "Lucky for you, I'll always think of you as a high school kid, so you'll never really be an undergrad."

She said she had to run to lab, but she paused at the door on her way out.

"So . . . you're never going to tell me what you were doing down there, are you?" she asked.

"Down where?"

"Down in the basement," Yael said, not making eye contact. "With Ann."

I didn't know what to say.

"I mean, part of me doesn't even want to know," she whispered.

"You know," I said, choosing my words carefully, "I'm not sure whether anything really happened down there." I found myself smiling, because it felt like the truth.

On the fourth day after the fall, I was desperate to leave the house. My broken fingers no longer looked like swollen breakfast sausages, and I could make it through the day on just a few painkillers.

Bryan had called that morning to inform me that the Junior

Barders were having a pizza party to celebrate the end of the summer and to return their costumes. They did this every year as a last goodbye for the cast.

I decided to tag along because I knew my time with Bryan was so limited; in a few days he'd be leaving to start Syracuse, and I wouldn't see him for three months.

Plus, Asher Forman might be there. It's not as though I thought we were going to keep in touch — I was well aware that someone like Asher probably made out with a lot of girls and then never saw them again — but it was new for me, and I just wanted one last look at him.

Also, I was curious to know whether he had been cast in that play in New York. I found myself rooting for him.

"I'm not sure Asher Forman will be at the final pizza party," Bryan said, reading my mind as we got off the T. "It's really just for the high school kids, anyway. I doubt he wants to deal."

But he was there, sitting at the long conference table in the Boston Shakespeare Project's offices where they stored all the sets and props during the off-season.

I looked away, not ready to make eye contact. I didn't know whether I was embarrassed, ashamed, or afraid of his reaction to my being there, but I found myself looking at everyone at the table but him, my neck itching like I could feel his phantom gnaws.

Most of the Junior Barders had already arrived and were focused on the greasy slices of pizza in front of them. Kimberly Katz, who was at the head of the table, spoke first.

"Oh, my god, Maya, what happened?" she asked, her face showing more disgust than concern.

I had forgotten about the bruises. Even though my fingers felt a little better and my knees and ankles no longer ached as I walked, I still had bruises on my arms and the scrapes across the side of my cheek. In fact, my face looked worse than it had right after the fall. There were now scabs where there had been scratches, and the original black bruises had deepened to a royal purple.

"I fell," I said, shrugging. "I was just trying to reach for something high and fell down. Just a stupid accident."

"It looks terrible," Kimberly said as she reached for the smallest slice of pizza from the open box.

I took an empty seat at the table and joined them. There was an adult sitting cross-legged at the back of the room, collecting costumes. "Reagan O'Connell?" he shouted, prompting a girl at the table to look up from her paper plate.

"Yes," she said, her voice small.

"We're missing your belt. Did you return the dress with the belt?"

"I might have left the belt in my dad's car," she replied.

"Have him drop it by tomorrow, please," the man muttered as Bryan handed him his own costume. "People, you must return these costumes with all accessories. We can't be running around buying replacement belts. We're a nonprofit here."

"Sorry, Mr. Andrews," Reagan O'Connell said, her face turning red.

I couldn't stop myself from smiling. Since middle school, it seemed that Bryan was always on the hunt, in his house or mine, for some lost cummerbund or vest that he owed to an angry director. Only in the last year had he learned to keep track of his costumes and their many little pieces.

"So," Kimberly Katz said, turning to Asher, "you didn't finish telling us the details. Where will you live?"

"They'll put me up in housing, and then I'll probably just stay down there. I'm looking for my own place. I don't see myself moving back to Los Angeles—I think I'm more of a New York person," he said. "I might try to find a recording studio, just to cut some demos once I get settled. At the end of the day, I'm still focused on the music."

"He's been cast in a play," Kimberly Katz said, turning to me to explain. "Off-Broadway. It's a big deal."

I couldn't help myself from making eye contact then. He was already looking at me, his mouth curled into a proud smile.

"You got the part. I knew it," I said without thinking.

He winked.

Kimberly Katz glared at me then, which made me smile as I grabbed for a piece of pizza.

Asher talked about the play, inviting everyone down to see the show when it opened later in the fall, and then the Barders went around the table, each one giving a short speech about what they'd be doing next year. About a half dozen of them were going off to college in a week. Bryan was the only graduate of the group who planned to major in theater. The others said they'd continue doing shows maybe as hobby. Kimberly Katz said she was going to study communications. The guy who played the clown was going to travel for a year before starting at UMass.

It might have been the painkillers or the last bit of serum filtering out of my system, but I was so proud of Bryan — so overcome by the idea that he had the courage to pursue what he loved — that I had to hold back tears. Like if he did anything besides perform, it would be dishonest. When the conversation devolved and the younger kids in the group started singing songs from musicals loud enough to make my head start hurting again, Bryan gave me the nod and we got up to leave. He hugged Kimberly Katz goodbye, and that's when I got a closer look at her. Bryan's embrace had pushed her T-shirt out of line, which revealed a massive trail of popped blood vessels along her neck. It was like a choker of hickeys, left by the only person I could think of who would want to give them. She straightened her shirt as Bryan pulled away, hiding the evidence.

I waved to the group, and Asher gave me a big smile. He winked and said, "Good luck at Princeton," which was not where I was going to school, but he looked sincere, so I just said, "Thanks."

I thought he might follow us out to say a better goodbye, but he didn't. Before I shut the door behind us, I glanced back to take one last look at him before he disappeared forever, back into the internet, where he probably belonged.

25

I kept having the same dream, that Bryan was about to die in a hospital bed just like my mom, and that I had one hour to come up with a cure to save him. I'd run into the lab and grab beakers and chemicals and would stir some sort of potion, hoping I had found a magic cure. The dream always ended the same way. I poured the contents of the beaker into Bryan's mouth and waited, staring at the monitor with the squiggly lines, hoping for signs of life. I always woke up before I found out whether my antidote had worked. It had been three nights in a row.

"I don't think it requires much interpretation," Bryan told me as we walked from my house to his so that I could say a final goodbye. "It's basically the most literal dream that's ever been dreamt."

"Sorry," I said, kicking a rock in front of me, my pace slow.

"Come on," Bryan said, pulling my hand. "We can't delay this any longer."

His parents were waiting for us, already outside by their car when we got there. It was odd to see them side by side, looking like two parents who were about to take their kid to college, because they hadn't been those people. It was like Bryan had hired some random adults to pretend to be his guardians and drive him to Syracuse.

They had packed up the car that morning and were all set to go, but Bryan told them he had to run over for one last goodbye. My dad had taken pictures of the two of us, and then Bryan had asked to take a few of me and my dad, saying he wanted a real family portrait. Then, after we left, he showed me the shots. They were all of my father, with my body just out of the frame.

"You're gross," I told him. "Delete those pictures."

"Never," he said, holding the phone to his heart. "Now, before I go, are you ready for something amazing? Because I have something to show you."

Bryan's eyes danced the way they did when he was about to tell me theater gossip that meant more to him than it did to me.

"Sure."

He began typing something into his phone, his thumbs moving rapidly as he concentrated. "I found this last night," he said. "I was waiting for the right moment."

He pulled me to his side then and placed the phone in front of us, so we could both see the video on its screen. Bryan pressed play.

There, on YouTube, was Asher Forman, alone in a white room with his guitar, singing Beyoncé's "If I Were a Boy."

"Oh, no. He did it," I whispered.

"Yes, he most certainly did."

We watched in silence then as Asher made constipated faces while singing the Beyoncé song in a strained falsetto.

"I mean, it's a good song. I made a good request," I said, turning to Bryan.

"I know," Bryan said. "Looks like he posted it this morning, and there are already three hundred thousand views."

When Asher finished the last notes, he winked into the camera. The screen went dark.

"I don't know what to say," I said, heat creeping up my face.

"Well," Bryan said, slipping his phone into his pocket and grabbing my hands, "for now you have to say goodbye."

I wanted to run into the backyard with him and hide like we did when we were kids, before his parents gave up and allowed him to start sleeping over.

"I don't know what I'm going to do," I said, squeezing his hands.

He rolled his eyes. "Don't be dramatic. You're going to pack up and go to college and make new nerd friends in your special science program. You're going to get super smart and change the world."

"I meant for the next few days. Like, what am I going to do for the rest of the week without you?"

"You could call him," Bryan said, "like, as a friend."

"I don't want to talk to Whit. It's not even a tempting thought. He emailed yesterday — I just don't have anything to say."

"I was talking about Kyle," Bryan said, giving me one of his side hugs.

I teared up then, mostly because Bryan was the only person who could read my mind, and he was about to move hundreds of miles away.

"Bryan, honey," his mom said from the driveway.

The walk had been too short. Bryan ignored her.

"You know what I think?" he said, his hands dropping as his voice cracked.

"What?" I said, letting go, my face already a wet mess.

"I think you've been spending all summer trying to match yourself to all the wrong people, and it doesn't matter, because you're already my match — without having to do anything. We fit together. No potions are necessary for you and me."

"Bryan . . ."

"Not sexually, of course, because *no thank you,* but I mean that you're my life match. Everybody else is just a bonus. You already have a soul mate."

I tipped my head into his chest, and he wrapped his arms around me.

"Don't replace me," I said, looking up as he pushed his hair behind his ear. "Text me every day."

"Deal," he said, blinking tears away. "Hey—did you ever finish the playlist?"

"There's only one song left," I confessed. "I've been avoiding it, I guess. You said that when I finished listening, I had to be over the breakup. I guess I didn't want anything to be over."

"I think you are over it, though, don't you?" he asked.

I nodded. Then he squeezed my uninjured hand and walked to the car.

"Let me know when you get there!" I yelled.

"Yes, dear!" I heard him shout as he closed the door.

26

My room looked empty, partly because Bryan had taken all his stuff. I'd grown used to his mess—the laundry bag he'd leave near my bed, or the homework he'd place in piles on the floor.

Now the only clutter was the charts I'd made for Ann. I had printed and spread out all my notes on the bed that morning, thinking that I'd bring them upstairs to the attic. Maybe someday I'd ask Ann to return the binder.

I doubted Ann expected to hear from me again, but the whole project felt unfinished because I hadn't written the final report. I was restless thinking about it.

If my mom were here, she'd ask, "What's the one-line conclusion? What did you learn?" and then she'd ask me to write it all down because "writing out every last thought is how we're able to see what's missing."

What's the one-line conclusion? I thought.

The answer was nothing and everything.

The answer was that the thing that was missing was my mother.

There used to be a person in my life who had *real* answers—the answers to every question, from what time we'd eat dinner, to whether I was allowed to stay out past curfew, to how to finish my homework, no matter what subject—but she didn't exist anymore.

I understood this. I wasn't the kind of person who could be in denial about what happened to my mom—how a disease had taken over her body, and how it had ended her life — but there was a part of me that hadn't figured out what the loss of her meant.

When someone is dead, it means they'll never again have an opinion about curfews or answers to homework. It means that if there's something you really need to tell them — like the fact that you've pursued and made a mess of their research — there's no way they'll ever know.

I walked out of my bedroom, making my way up the attic stairs, and turned on the overhead light. It was the only place where I could find her, where there were answers that she hadn't yet given me. The cardboard boxes were where I had left them, on the floor with flaps open and papers facing every which way. I was ashamed that I had left such a mess, now realizing that every single document was valuable. The papers were the only things about her that were new.

I dropped to my knees and used my better hand to sift through every document, looking for my mother's handwriting. I just wanted something — some trace of her voice, some report that might help me figure out what she'd think of my warped, weird, manipulative, unreliable chemistry lesson, a bastardization of her work. Ann had mentioned that there were other projects they intended to pursue in the future. Were they outlined in these documents? What else had she hoped to do? The first page I found was an equipment order sheet for Tish. The second seemed to be a note from Dr. Araghi about a grant. Frustrated, I fanned the papers out on the floor. I began laying them out in vertical rows like solitaire cards, trying to make sense of each sheet.

"Honey, what are you doing?"

My head snapped up at my dad, who stood at the top of the attic stairs. His wide eyes suggested I looked feral.

"I wanted to look through Mom's notes." I gestured to the papers, which I'd started to arrange in categories—personal, lesson plans, possible research, to-do lists, grants, and miscellaneous.

"You need to do this right now?" Dad asked, scratching his head. "Bryan just left, and you're barely even packed for school. Why don't you work on that?"

"Because we should have done this a year ago," I said, my voice trembling. "We just threw everything up here like it was trash, when it's actually the undiscovered research of a massively important scientist who happens to be your wife and my mother."

My dad made the bewildered face of someone whose teenage daughter had become volatile for no good reason, but I couldn't help myself.

"Don't you think it's worth spending some time to look through this box before I go to college? Or did you just plan on letting it get old and moldy up here like it's garbage?"

My dad moved quickly then, and was on his knees next to me, putting his arm around me before I could come up with a reason to stay angry.

I let my head fall to his chest and closed my eyes.

"Help me with this one, Maya. Is this because Bryan just left or because you miss your mother or because you're having some weird reaction to the Percocet?"

I snorted through laughter. "All of the above?"

I imagined the look my mom would give this scene—the two of us helpless and surrounded by her paperwork.

"It's a lot of change right now," Dad said, letting go so I could get myself together. I grabbed the corner of my T-shirt and wiped it along my face. "I know the breakup's been hard for you, and then Bryan's off to Syracuse, and you're leaving the house."

He paused for a deep breath. "If it helps, it's hard for me, too. Don't think I'm not freaking out about living alone in a week."

"You're freaking out?"

"Of course."

"But you're not the one in the attic screaming about Mom's research."

"No," he said, grinning. "You've got me beat on that. What are you looking for, anyway? Do we really need to go through Mom's work when it's eighty-five degrees outside and the heat is rising to the attic? Can't we do this when you're home for fall break?"

"Yeah," I said. "I'm sorry, Dad. I just had this weird revelation that these boxes are all we have of Mom. The only new stuff, at least. Like, there won't be any new memories, only the research up here that I haven't read."

"Maya," Dad said, looking up, "your mother is more than these boxes. That's the second thing I learned from my short stint in the bereavement group — that the dead follow us. Not literally, like a ghost or anything, but you keep thinking about the person you lost and learning things. Did you know, for instance, that your mother was reading romance novels in the hospital?"

I shook my head. "She liked sci-fi."

"Well, she also liked romance novels. The historical kind, with naked men on the covers."

I shook my head at my dad as I remembered my mom making fun of all the novels I read when I was in middle school — she called them my imaginary-boy books. "How about something literary for your brain?" she'd say. "How about Madeleine L'Engle?"

"I know what you're thinking," Dad said. "Not her style, right? But last week, I couldn't find my tablet, so I dug out hers, which I'd stashed in the closet after we got back from the hospital last year. As soon as the thing was powered up, up comes the book she was reading at the time, which was some novel called *My Tempting Highlander.*"

"Gross," I whispered.

"You have no idea. The worst part is that I stayed up until three a.m. reading it. I just wanted to know why she liked it so much. I remember that during those weeks before she died, when she was exhausted and sedentary from all that chemo, she just sat in bed and ate those mini pretzels and read books on her tablet. I had no idea that it was all romance stuff, and now she's not even here for me to tease her."

"Sorry, Dad."

"No, my point is, it's great. She's still surprising me, right? That'll happen to you, too; I'm sure of it. I've now read *Highlander* numbers one, two, and three."

"Oh."

"Come on," Dad said, wrapping his arm around my waist to help me up. "You have a job to do. That room isn't going to pack itself, and you'll have to do it one-handed."

I followed him downstairs, but when I got to my room, I decided to focus on a more pressing unfinished project.

I went to the bed and pulled the computer onto my lap and opened the file called "Experiment," which is where I'd kept my notes.

I started from the top, rewriting and making painstaking edits to the research report I planned to give to Ann, my pace slow, as I had to be careful not to harm my injured fingers.

Ann and I had been intentionally vague with our notes, using ambiguous language just in case the research was found by the wrong person, but now I got specific.

I started with an introduction that detailed my hope to test my mother's research on three subjects—one friend, one stranger, and one ex — to determine whether the infamous T-shirt study could be the basis for successful pheromone manipulation.

Then I moved on to materials and methods, leaving space where Ann could write in the formula for the serum, if she was willing.

I graphed out my doses and temperatures through the summer. I used data analysis software that my mom had bought me when I started advanced-placement classes to log every number and time. I listed every side effect.

I felt my eyes closing, and my fingers hurt — I had skipped a dose of Percocet, fearing that the medication would put me to sleep — but I continued on.

I typed my results as I understood them, noting that maybe the serum worked, but maybe it didn't.

I can see how one could use pheromone modification to improve a relationship where there is already love and commitment, I wrote, *but the chemicals, on their own, can't bring two people together. I also don't think they can serve as an antidote for a relationship that has failed.* I wrote that last part maybe more for myself than for Ann.

Maybe it wasn't all relevant, but I spared no detail. I typed up everything I noticed about Asher's weird neck obsession, and how my own libido was highest with Kyle, maybe because he kissed me like there was nowhere else in the world he wanted to be.

I wrote about how having a final night with Whit didn't bring our relationship back to where it had started. No matter how much we still loved each other, the breakup had been the end of us. He only wanted part of me. The minute I realized that, it was really over.

By the time I finished my report, my word count was over three thousand and it was past midnight. Without giving it another look, I emailed the document to Ann, then put my head down, prepared to pass out next to the laptop.

Right before I closed my eyes, though, I attached my earbuds to my phone and prepared to listen to the last track on Bryan's mix. I had some guesses about what it could be, maybe a big heartache anthem or something upbeat about going it alone.

But the last song was ours, the one we always put on repeat because Bryan sounded so good singing it, the one we considered our anthem, the one that would make me think of him forever. It was a song about having someone's back and loving them no matter what.

As I relaxed into my pillow, I turned up the volume and smiled.

I wound up waking up too early — sometime after four a.m. — thirsty and in pain. Downstairs, my dad was asleep in pajama pants and a T-shirt on the couch in front of the television, a *Nova* episode on pause. I grabbed a glass of water in the kitchen, washed down a painkiller, and then went back upstairs.

I spotted the laptop on the edge of my bed. It was as if I had written the report all in a dream.

I got under the covers and pulled the computer over to me, clicking on the file, curious to see what I had come up with and sent to Ann.

It was all there — every observation and conclusion — with so many details. I put a hand over one eye, embarrassed by some of my confessions, especially the stuff about Asher.

But what made my chest tighten with shame, or maybe confusion or excitement — something I couldn't quite name — was the stuff I had written about Kyle. There was a full paragraph in the report that read like a love letter.

It's like we were already magnets, I wrote, not-so-scientifically. *If the serum did anything, it just made the attraction stronger.*

Another paragraph concluded that Kyle was never an appropriate subject.

Kyle could never be the platonic case in this experiment, not just because he liked me, but because I probably liked him, too.

It was all the stuff I wished he knew. It was all the stuff I wished I had known before I ruined what we had.

Sometimes it takes an impulsive decision to undo another one. At four in the morning, all I wanted to do was confess everything—because there was nothing to lose. I opened a new email and attached the same report I sent to Ann. I didn't include a note, just a subject line that said *An explanation and apology.*

With shaking hands, I typed Kyle's name, hit SEND, and closed my eyes.

27

My mom would have had a very specific plan for moving day. She would have borrowed a colleague's truck and brought everything to the dorm in one trip, and she would have known there was no reason to haul over all my winter clothes this early in the year.

But my dad was in charge of the move, so we made three trips with heavy sweaters packed into old suitcases and garbage bags, and it wasn't until I was inside the dorm that I realized I had no immediate need for my calf-length winter coat, which I shoved under the wooden twin-bed frame.

It felt silly getting emotional when my dad said his goodbyes—our house was only a half-hour walk from my dorm—but for the first time, we wouldn't end our nights in the same place.

"Don't stay up all night reading Mom's sexy novels," I said, mid-hug.

"I'm not promising anything," he said, pulling back and kissing me on the forehead. "Are you sure you don't want me to stay for a while and unpack?"

"Please, no."

"Am I embarrassing you? I didn't wear my toe shoes."

"No, Dad. I just have to come up with my own system for organizing this mess. I think I'm also supposed to go outside and make friends."

"Okay," he said, his voice raspy. "Well, call me tomorrow."

He paused in the doorway, looking puzzled.

"Are college kids supposed to call their parents every day?"

"I don't know," I admitted. "It probably depends on the kid."

"Well, you don't have to. Unless you want to. Just text me when you figure out where you want to eat for your birthday. I'll make a reservation."

"Okay, Dad," I said.

"Oh, wait," he said, stopping before he left the room. "I put some mail from MIT in the front pocket of your backpack. I think it's your last paycheck from Dr. Araghi."

"Thanks."

He leaned in to give me another quick hug, waved awkwardly, and then left in a rush, dodging other parents and wandering freshmen as he headed toward the stairwell that would lead him out of the building.

I went back into the room and closed the door behind me. There were piles everywhere, all my clothes and belongings out of order. I didn't know where to begin, so I pulled my laptop from my backpack and set it up on the clean wooden desk in the corner of the room. It was a start.

Next I went into the front pocket of my backpack, looking for the check. It was in a folded envelope, but not the kind Tish usually used on payday. This one was larger and was addressed to me in another person's recognizable handwriting.

The note inside was attached to the check with a bright pink paper clip.

Maya, I read, hearing Ann's voice, *I told Tish I'd send your check, so here it is. Also, that was a really good report—probably the most interesting thing to come out of the Araghi lab in the last year.*

I know you said I could have the binder, but are you sure? There are other things in it — other projects — maybe things you'll want to take a look at, eventually. Maybe there are some things in it we could look at together. Just a thought. Let me know. — A.

I wasn't sure how to respond — but I knew I would.

The phone buzzed then; the sound of it vibrating against the wooden desk made me jump.

You forgot your toothbrush, the message said. It was my dad.

I'll buy a new one, I wrote back. *Anyway, I should keep one toothbrush at home.*

The phone buzzed again.

I'll put some extra money in your account for toiletries.

Okay, Dad, I wrote back. *It's just a toothbrush.*

The phone buzzed a third time and I yelled, "Come on, Dad!" and picked up the phone, prepared to tell him that I couldn't miss him if he never left me alone.

But it wasn't him.

Under Kyle's name was a message: *Your report doesn't explain the serum. There's just a blank space.*

I exhaled all the air I could get out of my body and wrote back as fast as I could with one hand.

I never made the formula. The person who helped me with the project is the only person who knows how to make it, so the blank space is for her. But somehow I doubt she'll ever write it down. It's probably best that she keeps it to herself.

There were no little dots on my phone, no response in progress after that. I wondered where he could be.

Kyle had told Tish and Yael that he'd be living off-campus this semester, which meant he could be anywhere. Maybe he was down the street.

"Come on," I said to the phone, like it was keeping a secret from me.

I needed to distract myself, so I walked out into the hallway and began wandering the dorm. Eventually I came to one room that was open, and I could see inside. Two girls sat on beds, facing each other, talking and laughing

One looked up at me.

"Hey," she said, her voice booming. "Come in. I'm Roxy."

"I'm Angela," the other said.

I pretended I had Bryan by my side.

"I'm Maya, from down the hall."

"Oh, cool," Roxy said. "Where are you from, Maya?"

"Down the street. I'm from Cambridge."

"That's so cool," Angela said. "You can tell us where everything is."

I nodded, pleased that I could.

Roxy said she was from Pittsburgh; Angela's family had moved from South Korea to Virginia when she was ten.

We talked for an hour, and it was easy. Roxy was an incoming music major, and Angela wanted to do research like me. We made plans for the next day, and I was a little shocked that the whole thing had been so easy.

Then I went back into my room and saw that there was another text.

I have more than a few questions, Kyle's message said. *The first: Did this actually happen?*

Yes, I responded.

He wrote back within seconds.

Did it work? You say in your report that it was inconclusive, but . . .

I paused before I wrote back. It was a loaded question.

I don't know, I answered, because I didn't. Not really. *I mean . . . do you think it worked?*

Not on me, he wrote back.

Oh.

That was it for a while. Five minutes turned to fifteen and then twenty.

I folded T-shirts and placed them in drawers, and then put up a poster of the moon that I'd taken from the wall of my bedroom.

I kept checking my phone just to make sure I hadn't missed anything, but all the new buzzes were from Bryan, who'd sent a video tour of his dorm room and demanded I make one of my own. He'd also taken some video of his roommate sleeping.

"This is Paul," Bryan narrated in a whisper as poor Paul slept. "Paul is from Ohio."

By seven thirty, the sun was setting and I was on my last garbage bag of belongings, which was filled with towels. I don't know why my dad thought I'd need so many towels, but he had packed six, as well as two kitchen dishrags, even though I didn't have a kitchen.

I couldn't help myself; I texted my dad.

Why would I need kitchen towels??

Because at some point, you will be studying late at night, and you will knock your soda all over the floor, just like you do in your bedroom at home, he wrote back.

Fair enough, I wrote back.

The second-to-last buzz of the night came in at seven fifty.

Would you like to eat some skewers? it asked.

Right now? I texted back.

It would have been cooler to wait a few minutes, or at least until he responded, but I wasn't worried about my pride, and I was too afraid he'd change his mind.

Yes, please, I wrote, then sat on the edge of the bed, just waiting.

Dots appeared and then disappeared.

"Come on," I said to the phone.

Buzz.

Finally.

Whiff walk. Meet me in a half hour, Kyle wrote back.

By the time I made it to Central Square, I probably looked as flushed as I had that night when I was with him — close to him — and on the serum. It wasn't the exercise; it was the anticipation. It was the fact that maybe he was giving me another chance at something, even if I didn't know what that something should be.

I'd changed clothes so that I looked as nice as I could. I used a little of the eyeliner Bryan had given me from his theater makeup kit before he left.

I turned the corner on Main Street and saw that Kyle was already there, in front of Cambridge Foods, looking up at the window, his hands in his pockets.

He must have seen me in his peripheral vision, because he said, without turning his head, "Right here. Where I'm standing. It's the smell pocket tonight."

I wanted to run, but with my ankle still healing, I had to take my time. When I finally got there, I faced him and lined my feet up with his so that our toes touched.

He smiled and looked down at me, and then I closed my eyes, unable to stop myself from inhaling, the air around us warm and thick and overwhelmingly sweet.

ACKNOWLEDGMENTS

I must start by thanking my agent, Katherine Flynn, who encouraged me to write a young adult novel even though I had impostor syndrome. She told me to write what I loved, so I did, and I am grateful. Thank-yous also go to: Elizabeth Bewley, who treated this book like a prize, and to everyone at Houghton Mifflin Harcourt who said they loved Maya and Bryan; Cat Onder, who was sent to me from magical literary lands and made this experience wonderful; Linda Reisman (and Jack), who saw beyond the page; Benielle Sims, who was so dedicated to this love story that she made it seem real; Bryan Barbieri for inspiring Bryan, and to Eileen Barbieri, who raised an incredible son; Gina Favata, a great friend-librarian; Sophie Charles and Fran Forman for love and friendship and meals; Rachel Raczka for creativity, encouragement, and wisdom; Janice Page for making every day better; the entire Boston Globe family, past and present; Trenni Kusnierek and Michele Steele for keeping me on text chains even when I was writing and didn't respond; Paul Bernon for bear emojis in the morning and so much more; Pete Thamel and Lauren Iacono for our trio of excellence; Allie Chisholm and her sense of humor; Mark Shanahan, Michelle McGonagle, and Beckett Shanahan for family; Kyle Hubbard for being the best high school boyfriend in the universe; Dave Goldstein, who got excited about this book; the inspiring Maya Leschinsky for letting me borrow her name; Kirk Woundy, who grew up to be a very cool dad; Julian Benbow, knower of good playlist songs; VPC officers Desaray Smith, Elizabeth McQueen, and Laura

Heffernan; Sarah Rodman, who is home, wherever she lives; Susanna Fogel, who teaches me to think big; James DiSabatino for expertise; Sarah Grafman, in general; my friend in the labyrinth of life, Sara Faith Alterman; the best teacher, Ale Checka; Danielle Kost and her family; Joanne Douglas Venable and her parents; Jenn Abelson, Paul Faircloth, and their good chemistry; all other Faircloths; Ed Ryan for a decade of Ed-ness; the wonderful Joani Geltman; Liz Arcury for reading stuff; Mark Feeney for editor/friend feedback; Jenny Johnson, who had the courage to pursue her own love story; Jordyn Young and Nola Farrell, who were excellent editors; my Syracuse family; Sera Thornton, who took me to the lab and helped me make science; Deirdre Costello (by way of Fionn Leahy) for more science; Rachel Simon for loving books with me; Julia Shanahan, an incredible writer, who's been making this story better since she was fourteen; Lamar Giles for insight; Nicole Lamy and her family; Steven Maler of the Commonwealth Shakespeare Company; Jaime Green Roberts, Andrea Detar, Kim Berger Powell, Jennifer Moran Krepp, and all high school friends who stick around; Francie Latour and her excellent kids; Liora Klepper, who read early drafts; Rachel Zarrell, who is number one; the family created by Lorraine and Marty Goldstein (Nancy, Tim, Ariela, Elana, and Sarah Knight; Brad, Julie, Sam, Nate, Shula, Jacob, and Yael Goldstein); Tina Valinsky, Shirley Craig, and the memory of my cousins Rufus and Ollie; all Love Letters readers, who tell me about their breakups and beyond; Jessica Douglas-Perez for the kind of friendship I could write a whole book about; my mom, Leslie Goldstein, for loving good stories—and good music; and my sister, Brette Goldstein, who encourages, listens, makes me laugh, and reminds me to have a good time. I am very lucky.